The Trials

Liliana Drăgnescu

Liliana Drăgnescu
For Gabriel with love
and admiration!

A catalogue record for this book is available from the British Library.

First edition

Paperback edition ISBN: 978-1-7398541-0-2

For information contact:
www.lilianadragnescu.com

Cover art and illustration: Spurga

Develomental editing: Reedsy, Fiverr

Copyediting and Proofreading: Reedsy, Fiverr

Author's Newsletter And Review

Sign up for future books updates, special offers, bonus content, and other news: www.lilianadragnescu.com

Please consider leaving a short review on if you liked, loved, or only tolerated *The Trials of March*. Reviews help new authors more than you know. Thank you for taking the time to support me and my work. Sharing your review on social media with the hashtag #TheTrialsOfMarch is appreciated and encouraged.

To my grandmothers, the storytellers.

Prologue

One colour in the void, the prettiest black. Neither good nor evil, just a sense of impending change whispering my name without pause, as if I can stand against the unrelenting seasons. The night clears, and upon revealing the surprise, I prefer the shadowed sky. The lies had somewhere to hide.

One

Awakening to the sound of nothing confuses the mind still immersed in fog, and minutes pass before realising the normal pace of March has shifted. With eyes closed, I move my toes, and fill my lungs as calm washes over me, shifting my body from confused slumber to a sensation of restored strength.

My bed feels harder than usual on my stiff back, the linen underneath me velvety to the touch. The silent dawn soon to be disturbed by the 7 a.m. alarm mysteriously lingers, just as I overthink wardrobe choices.

An uncomfortable feeling creeps in when I can't summon the memories of yesterday. My eyes open and infinite dark is their field of vision. With heavy drapes drawn and secured in place, slivers of light always enter my bedroom, and in their absence I tremble.

Panic invades my thoughts, remembering I already woke up today in my house in Wimbledon. Went to work at my company's office in Canary Wharf, had breakfast from the shop downstairs, worked some more and left soon after five thirty. During the predictable hour-long commute, an irreversible event stopped the course of my day. I am uncertain of arriving home.

Rising from the horizontal position, sudden pain radiates in my forehead when it bangs on a very low ceiling with enough impact to lay me down again. On instinct, I stretch out my arms, palms rubbing against the wall above me and the one to my right. A soft material covers them, like a tightly pulled cloth. When my fingers find something else to my left, my heart stops. My ears ring from a deafening scream, and it doesn't take long to discover my aching throat is the culprit. I crawl desperately with little movement, backing myself into a panel, inches away from what feels like a body.

"Who's there?"

Seconds slip by with no answer, no movement, no sounds except for my loud panting. My imagination already colours what my useless eyes can't see, and there is no scarier reality than a mind hijacked by fear. Controlling my breathing is harder when I shake so much.

Is this person dead? God, where am I?

Invisible spiders and other phobia-inducing creatures wander about, and I pat myself down, lightheaded, and nauseous, to find nothing touching me. Pins and needles tingle and numb parts of my body, one after the other, until I'm covered in sweat. When suffocating tentacles of despair try to split me in half, shrieking is my only response. And I shriek like the gates of hell have closed behind me and my soul hurts from the unnatural white noise my voice creates. My fingertips tear to shreds trying to rip away the padding. To break myself free.

"Can anyone hear me? Please! Please, someone!" I scream my throat hoarse, hitting the walls with trembling fists. "Hello? Please, help!" I choke on my words, hyperventilating, thrashing in place, pushing on every surface for a way out with a madness I barely control, but nothing moves. Salty tears wash down my face, and I swallow them with my broken chant: "Please, please."

No answer to my cries, as eternal as they seem, long into the perpetual night of my confinement.

My body drains of fight and my mouth pauses the expel of horrified sounds enough to oxygenate my cells. My pulse cools down, and as I finish the desperate session of shouting for help, I check every surface of my tiny room for a way out, staying clear of my lifeless neighbour.

The logical explanation my thoughts offer to a padded box occupied by a stiff person is that I am in a coffin created for two people. The realisation makes me curse, but it's not possible for someone to have buried me alive. It can't be true. Why would they do that? How is that done?

Women are subject to heinous acts even in modern times, and if I'm not dreaming, I may be the latest statistic. Physically unharmed as nothing hurts apart from my dazed head, an assessment by touch alone. I think am still wearing this morning's clothes. Black office pants, black cardigan. My *Vera* necklace is missing, and I am not wearing my shoes.

Why would they bury me alive? Are they after my organs? If I die, my organs die with me. A dead body has no value to the living beyond research and a burial where relatives mourn a pain the corpse will never feel. Are they watching using a camera concealed somewhere in the coffin? It's dark for me to see, but they might use night vision technology.

I kick and scream, this time in supplication followed by anger.

"Let me out! Please, let me out! If you hear me, please, please let me out!" I inhale hard, desperately shouting. "You bastards, let me out! Let me out right now. Let me out!" Before I suffocate to death. The cramped space still holds air, a mercy I am grateful for, but for how long? If I don't get out soon, I might reach the limit of the preserved oxygen.

Breathe slowly, don't consume as much. Make it last.

No answer, and the silence screams back at me.

Checking the coffin again, meticulously, feeling my way around the corners, trying to move the corpse, hovering over it. Because hell, I need to leave this place, no time to further freak out and fear the dead. Mask the horror with purpose and deal with it much later, when I'll require a pastime as I die.

Surprise freezes my movements when I sense fresh air filtering from the other side of the casket. A metal plate the size of a fist, wrapped in fabric with round holes. No wonder I missed it the first time, it's next to the man's left ear, which I didn't want to approach, especially the mouth. I'm aware, unwillingly feeling him up, that the person I share the space with, not the air, is a man. Was a man. Jesus Christ!

He is not breathing, and his chest is not moving. No sound coming from him, luckily, no smell either. When I touch his face again, he doesn't seem in the process of putrefaction. I try not to gag too much at the prospect. Skin feels normal, and not as cold as I was expecting. Mouth and eyes closed, long hair. Upper body seems built, fit with muscles, dressed in an open-collar shirt with buttons. I don't feel my way south of his abdomen, although I know he has pants on. They chose the coffin for his tall frame, as I have spare room when I lay down, but his naked feet almost touch the bottom.

Someone put me here knowing I will not die. At least not immediately. I'm not craving food and drink. Lack of acute hunger would mean I was not unconscious for long before waking up next to a dead man.

What did I do to deserve this? What forgotten sin led me here? Condemned without a fair trial. My faults are plenty and devoured by guilt, but my past wrongdoings are not criminal. I don't think. My most hidden complaint as an adult is directed at the missing excitement in my life, while I do nothing but contradict myself when choosing the dull routine over rising opportunities. I wanted to be part of the action, yet I stood dormant.

"A karmic way for the universe to laugh at me!" I say to no one, or perhaps addressing my companion. What's worse, talking to myself or to a dead person?

When no reply comes, I go back to reprimand my past desires. I wanted adventure in my life, and I get this terror. It could easily be the end, and I die before experiencing more. Thirty years alive on this earth and not a day longer. Gone before talking to my parents one last time. Before hugging them, close. Before telling my brother how proud I am to have been his sister, to have seen him grow into the man he has become. Before cherishing my friends as they deserved to be, truly, or completing the beautiful dreams I had, so similar to everyone in the world. Travel far and wide, build a house and a family. Discover a passion to wake up to enthusiastically every day. For all those things and more, I weep, my face crushed into my corner.

Changing from actively searching for a way out to the quiet, depressed 'I am going to die, and it's all my fault' thoughts is due to shock. Surely, I haven't wasted years waiting to seize my opportunity, thinking there are unlimited chances to grow, become a better human, laugh, and connect with people until old age claims all without fail.

"The cursed shock might motivate me to find the escape hatch," I speak again, "or paralyse me to death." Breathe in, breathe out, breathe in. "And as sure as hell, it's not my fault! I did not ask for this, I did not put myself in unnecessary danger, so whoever did this to me, I hope you burn in agony, you monster!" I scream with vengeance, but the insecurity cloud is yet to dissipate.

No answer. No matter how diligently my palms hit the padded walls in time with shaky whimpers that transform into angered shouts. The most imaginative curses I have ever produced come last.

Multiple scenarios could have ended with me locked in this coffin and might influence my plan to escape. One: someone killed the guy next to me and I saw it happening, even though I don't remember a thing. No witness, no crime. They put me here with him. If that's the case, they buried the coffin under an enormous pile of dirt. But it doesn't explain the air ventilation. For all I know, they build some coffins with one.

Two: I have more than enough air to fill my lungs. Is that a coincidence? I think not. A clear path for it to enter, most likely a tube buried underground as well. Maybe I am in a crypt. So, no matter how he died – surely not long ago since he still smells fresh – they want me alive for some purpose. Which means I can get away before they come back. I need to keep my wits about me and not succumb to another fit of horror.

Point number three is the deranged scenario. Held for experiments by a psychopath, about whom someone will make a documentary later, me being one victim, the guy to my left, the other. Or the wildest theory, this guy is a vampire, and I am his meal. It takes a few minutes for me to do it, to gather the courage, but I feel no embarrassment when I finger his teeth, especially his canines. Nothing unusual, but to even acknowledge such an idea is a true sign that I'm going crazy.

When I try to move the coffin in different directions by putting all my body weight into a push, I achieve no results. Screaming for help into the air ventilation at different time intervals, leaning over my companion also gets me nowhere. No acknowledgement, no reply. I take a few minutes' break to re-evaluate, in silence.

Then, using full force, or what I have left in me, I try to upturn the cover of the coffin with my feet and legs. I do that with my head next to the man. No luck. I change my place and try to lift it with my back, sitting in an all-fours position. No luck.

I collapse and cry quietly for a while, my body shaking with involuntary hiccups. How much longer until I pass away too? From hunger and dehydration, from despair.

"Please, please." The whisper repeats itself like a shattered mantra until it eventually dies on my lips. No answer as I sit in darkness.

Perhaps I dosed off because I wake up a second time with the fragments of a dream. Or is a memory? A strobe light, yellow and blue markings. With my nose in a hard shoulder, my palms hugging a shirt-covered bicep, I shudder at the flashback. There is no immediate, nor late, reaction to move away from Ed the Dead. It might be strange and creepy, but with him here, I don't feel so alone. As long as he stays in one piece and doesn't discompose, he presents no danger.

Why is he here? Did I kill him? He's twice my size or more. I couldn't have. Sensing my lucidity slipping, with a dry mouth and an acute thirst pang, I shout anew.

"I want out! I've had enough. I want out! Let me out!" My heart goes into overdrive, and I need my brain to prevent any further panic attacks. I timidly lied to myself that I don't have a mild case of claustrophobia. "My bladder is about to explode. Let me out for five minutes, please!" I punch the ceiling and scream with all my might. "Help! Help!"

"Stop screaming, you are hurting the both of us. For God's sake, my ears are bleeding!" says a cracked voice to my left from inside the coffin.

Finally, a reply.

Two

Seventeen Hours Earlier

For those who wish it, mornings are safe, clean, and bursting with possibilities. A factor contributing to this impression is spending my childhood summers in an old-fashioned Romanian village, where the only concern was how much time I had for friends, adventure, and grandmother's cooking. Today, it's not one of those mornings.

The forceful nudging brings me closer to the train's door. I ought to pay more attention to my surroundings if I don't want to be scarred for life by a hurried commuter before arriving to the office. A job in procurement is nothing glamorous, negotiating contracts and creating elaborate spreadsheets fill my time, but today's list of never-ending tasks distracts me, ignoring the elbowing and pushing game at my own risk.

"Vera Alexandra Nicolescu, are you listening to me?" my brother, Cristian, asks. He's cross if he's using my full name. He's been sharing his plans for when he arrives in Bucharest later this afternoon, and I missed every word. We step into the carriage, keeping close to each other in the standing only area. His unexpected visit home to our parents will prove useful, as I need the alone time to deal with the extra work coming my way this week. We don't live in the same house, but we share a neighbourhood and he's at my place most evenings. Since I moved to England half a year ago, spending time with him is tremendous fun,

especially after being apart for years when I lived in Poland. But the near future is booked with reports for quarter end.

"Summarise what you said in the last five minutes." Pushing my black jaw-length hair behind my ears I grin and pat his shoulder, shifting around his luggage as the train leaves our station.

"No, it's my own fault for wanting to say goodbye properly to my one and only sister. I could have taken an Uber to the airport and avoid the Waterloo-bound crowd, but is my thoughtfulness appreciated? Not likely. You're going to miss me, and regret will eat you alive as I won't pick up the phone when you call."

"Someone should play a violin to accompany your sorrow, but alas, no space to throw a needle in this train."

"Oh, guess who is not getting any of Mum's homemade goods when I return?" He mocks offence, the hand over his heart lifting to wipe an imaginary tear from his handsome face. "If Lina were here, you would pay attention to her, I bet."

"Why am I not surprised by you dragging my best friend into your complaint? Stop arguing with her whenever you are in the same room, by the way. You and that instigator, Astrid, causing arguments over the phone from miles away. The other night was unpleasant. Lina's dealing with her father's health and needs our support. Cut her some slack." My finger pokes his chest. "But I apologise, I'm visualising my calendar to include new projects my manager wants me to advise on soon. You'll be missed, Cristi. With or without the baked treats you better hand over."

"You are overworked as it is, and he's taking advantage of your inability to say no. Fosters & Co will not collapse if you take a holiday. You should come to Bucharest."

"In a few months, maybe. I haven't seen Mum and Dad in a while. How did you get days off approved so last minute?"

"It's called having leverage and the guts to ask what you are owed. You should try it."

"Is that so, mister consultant of the year?"

"That and I might be taking some meetings while in Romania, to expand our portfolio."

"That's more like it." Glancing outside the window to check where we are, I turn and rise on my toes to give him a hug, arms crushing his neck. "Your stop is next. Have a safe flight and stay out of trouble while home. I'm assuming you know Astrid is flying to London one of these days. But she'll probably return to Romania to reunite your dynamic duo, rather than spend time with us here. Why can't you be as friendly with Lina too? Or do you know what? Stop stealing my friends."

"Astrid and I have a lot of things in common, and Lina is a people pleaser. I would wonder if she was faking it, if I didn't see how much she loves you and the co-dependent relationship you both nourish."

"Co-dependent? That sounds like Astrid is putting words in your head."

"We have eyes." He sing-songs his reply.

"You are both jealous." I use the same tune, watching him pick up his things, kissing my cheek goodbye and descending for the platform. My hand waves him off, a big smile on my face to accompany his nod.

A flash catches the corner of my eye. The strange sensation of being watched raises the hair on the back of my neck, but when I turn to look around me, everyone's attention is focused elsewhere. Odd. Was someone taking pictures of me? And weirdly, yesterday's outing across Wimbledon Common's green field was perturbed by the same 'under the microscope' feeling. Either exhaustion is bringing paranoia to the surface, or I'm not yet accustomed to the big population in London and the extra surveillance sentiment.

On the 45th floor of the skyscraper housing the Fosters & Co offices, first half of my working day is consumed with emails and a meeting with a large attendance. The conference room at the end of the corridor close to the cafeteria is filled to the brim. High-ranking stakeholders and board members from Switzerland are visiting two of our UK offices to discuss ongoing mergers and strategies.

At the front of the room facing ten rows of occupied chairs are three executives conducting the presentation. Our London CEO, Saira Husain, a petite English woman in her fifties in charge of over 750 employees with a competence I admire. Elias Bodmer from the Zurich office, a forty-something board member with a lifetime in the company. Having worked across multiple departments in his tenure, he knows Fosters & Co from the inside out. The younger executive talking now is our finance director, Mariusz Jurkowski, whom I met when I was working in Warsaw. He transferred countries before me, and in my unverified assumption, he played a decisive role in my interviews for the position I currently occupy.

"The Black Alpine Group and the W&N mergers will be discussed in tomorrow's meeting as their transition is almost final, and to be included in the last five years view." Mariusz ends his speech, checks his watch, and smiles towards the second row where Lina and I sit with the rest of our teams. We'd bet him lunch that he wouldn't finish on time as he tends to find last-minute points to discuss. Elias Bodmer takes the microphone from Mariusz, sharing an inside joke we don't hear, before addressing us once again.

"I encourage you all to compile and use the online survey for the difficult questions you have and don't wish to ask now. I know Mariusz will," the Swiss laughs. He has a smooth voice with a slight accent, and a charcoal suit tailored to perfection. "The correct strategy, customised for each function will see us move forward, but we argue that working together as an integrated, supportive team will decide whether our ventures succeed. There is both a moral and business imperative to do more than increase profits."

In the corporate environment, manipulating data is key. I have plenty to learn from people like them, and as I scribble away in my notebook, careful to register the helpful information and filter out the obligatory corporate spiel, I envision my life attached to my desk, working late hours every day, without the quests found outside the glass walls of Canary Wharf. Perhaps my brother is right, and I should leave the Fosters & Co offices on time for once, and not bring my laptop with me, because I feel like the oldest thirty-year-old in the world.

"Do you want to grab dinner in Covent Garden later, blondie? We haven't seen each other much these past weeks," I ask Lina when the meeting is over, stretching my neck to see her bright face. The tighter-fitting dress she's wearing shouldn't complement her fair skin so well, but black, like every other shade and colour, submits to my tall friend effortlessly.

"I'm swamped and most likely sleeping here tonight. Wednesday maybe? I'll make a reservation for that Peruvian place I told you about. Or should we wait for Astrid to arrive, and I'll cook dinner for us in the meantime?" Lina bites into the apple she grabbed from the refreshment table. "Let's see how we feel tomorrow. Wasn't she supposed to attend this summit in person?"

"I thought so too, but she changed her flight ticket and ended up dialling in from Bucharest."

"Astrid and her ever-changing plans," she says as we shake our heads, heading for my desk, visible from afar because of the packages piled on top of each other next to it. Presents bought for my friends, books I have yet to take home, or start reading, pretty clothes for events I don't have the time to attend. My wallet suffers when I shop for the social life I wish to have, but I see it as a consolation and a 'one day' promise.

Too obvious for me to miss, my manager signals me over to a booth where he chats with someone in accounting, and by the looks of it, I'll be lucky if I eat lunch today. An alarming group of people like to remind me about work/life balance, but what they don't know is how much I thrive at being the expert everyone turns to in a business situation, the sentiment of solving an issue before it occurs. I've been working for Fosters & Co in three different countries, for more years that I would like to admit, and I could count on my fingers the number of times I left early. It wasn't always work that kept me in the office; the community we built over time rarely made me miss the outside world. But it's my manager who walks me out of the office in the late afternoon, convincing me to go home instead of joining the after-work drinks in honour of our guests.

Five stops on the Jubilee line later, loud rain hits the dusty windows at the Waterloo station when I tap my phone to pay for the red velvet cupcake meant to be my dinner treat, but I doubt the pretty cardboard box will arrive home untampered. Especially since my journey is prolonged by the dreadful weather. If possible, the crowd of commuters is bigger than the one this morning, more unsettled and impatient by the delayed trains as I follow the signs towards the railway.

Checking my phone for updates, contemplating calling my brother, I sidestep a mother pushing a stroller covered by protective plastic. She's all wet, head to toe, concentrating on adjusting the wheels of the pram, and I wave to the blonde baby inside, safe, and warm. Later, in the coming days, when safety is a distant memory, I will realise how precious it was.

A shove pushes me forward and I lose my balance and the view of the giggling infant, colliding with a passer-by who knocks me down.

"Miss Vera Nicolescu?" a man asks, his hand on my back restricting my movements.

"Yes?"

He puts a badge in my face that I cannot see properly as he lifts me from the ground, turns my body around, and drags me by my arm. Men in uniform box us in, moving with us as one.

"You are feeling ill, madame. Let us help you." He wipes my nose and mouth with a damp material. Am I bleeding? In seconds, we are near a side exit, a car with a blue light on top waiting for us, doors opened large.

"Hmm." I try to speak, but my lips won't open.

Before I lose consciousness, a relaxed voice says from somewhere above me. "Not to worry. We are with the Metropolitan Police."

Three

In the silence that follows his words, my voice cracks in fear, heart beating against my chest with incredible speed. As expected, learning my tomb companion is alive and speaking reduces me to a primitive state. Ignoring his advice, I shout, moving towards the coffin's other side, away from the source of my shock.

"You, you!" I gasp for air, inhale too much at once, choke on it, and cough. "You are alive! Oh my God! You are not dead! Stay there, don't come near me!"

"I won't. Please calm down. Frightening you was not my intention."

"Christ! Were you playing dead the whole time? Who does that? Did you put me in here?"

"No, of course not. How could I? I cannot move my body, and I can barely speak. I wouldn't hurt you." His voice is raspy, deep, and British.

"Why can't you move? Are you paralysed? Who are you?" I say, drawing small breaths. He takes a few seconds before he replies.

"No. I don't know. I wasn't before. They injected me with something." He inhales audibly. "My name is Hector. Yours?"

"I'm Vera," I say from near his feet, crawled into a ball. "When did you wake up? Why are we here?"

"I was always awake."

"But I checked your face, your pulse. You weren't breathing, and your eyes were closed." Again, he doesn't reply to my comments for long moments. I press trembling fingers on the coffin cover and push, wishing they had the force to break the lock.

"I blame the drug for the shallow breathing, and I kept my eyes closed to not scare you. Your state was already panic infused enough. What would you have done if I blinked when you started exploring my face? Scratch them out in a daze? And me not able to speak nor defend myself," he accuses. What did he expect? To wake up in a coffin and remain calm?

"I wouldn't have done that, but I see your point. You must admit, it's difficult to act rationally in this situation. Do you know what happened? Who did this and why?"

"Someone sick and twisted, clearly. What do you remember?" he asks and coughs. What should I tell him? What if he's the reason I find myself in this situation?

"Not much. How about you? Why was I not drugged?"

"You were. But not with what they gave me. You were unconscious when they carried your body where they held me hostage, but you could move your muscles from what I could tell." I feel my skin itch all over, thinking about how they touched me. How police officers, if my confused mind isn't playing tricks on me, manhandled me in a congested train station and shoved me in a car. Were they really with the police?

"Can you tell me what happened when they brought me in? Where were they holding you? You saw them. Did they speak with you?"

"We need out of the coffin first. You lost too much time already."

“The coffin is locked. I pushed on—”

“You need to try again.” He annunciates every word, as if it’s difficult to understand his meaning.

“Listen, sir.” I am slowly crawling back towards his head.

“Hector.”

“Someone put their hands on me while I could not defend myself. They took me, drugged, and dragged me into this box and believe me when I say I tried everything to escape. I don’t have enemies, I barely have friends here. I am not kidnapping material. Finding myself in this situation could be your fault. So, I must insist – and I’m asking nicely – that you tell me what happened when they brought me into that room. Did they say anything to justify my presence?” We’re close enough to breathe together. “Don’t make me act irrational.”

“Why are you fixating on the reason of our imprisonment and not on escaping?”

Does he think I want to waste precious seconds conversing with him? He claims he was awake the whole time, so he knows I consumed all my energy and sanity to open the coffin.

“Answer me, please, and I will gladly accept any tips on breaking out of confinement.”

“One of them had you on his shoulder when he entered the room. He removed your jacket, scarf, bag, and shoes and put you on a table next to the chair they tied me to. Then no one touched you again until they brought the coffin and put us both in.”

“Okay. Then what?”

“Then they locked the coffin, put it into a car, and drove us here. A thirty-minute drive. Or around that time. They did not bury us; I am certain of that.”

“Were they police officers?”

“Yes.”

"Did they say why they took me?" I noticed he did not answer that or mention why was he taken.

"No. They refrained from explaining themselves to me. Do you have the smallest clue why you are in this position?" Does he think I am lying?

"No, I don't." I hit the ceiling again with my back, repeatedly, hoping for a miracle push that cracks the cover. When it doesn't come, I lay down on my side, facing him, gluing my spine to my coffin wall.

"What do you remember?" He asks in the dark.

"Waterloo station. I was mid-way home from the office. The crowded escalators as I was leaving the metro and following the train signs, watching the information screens for updates. A lot of angry travellers waiting for their rides. I was moving back from the crowd, close to the exit. Some men appeared. Then—"

"Then what? Were you supposed to meet someone at Waterloo?"

"No, I recall a strange smell and nothing else. And then waking up next to you. Do you think they are outside, guarding us?"

"Not sure. I heard them all leave the room."

"Where could we be? Outside London? An abandoned building? A cemetery? People should have heard my screams."

"Perhaps."

"Why did they take you? Are you someone important?"

"Not more important than you are, I'm sure." How straightforward of him.

"You can tell me your assumptions now. Did they abduct you from home? Where do you work?"

"Escaping is important now, and the only subject we should discuss. We are losing valuable time comparing notes."

"You want my cooperation, my answers, and then when I ask you questions, you evade them. If you tell me from where they took you, we might discover something else that could help us. Track all their steps."

"Help us escape? Everything else is not relevant."

"Why?"

"Because they took me from Qatar."

"Oh." That shuts me up. Who is this guy? His accent sounds very English aristocracy, but perhaps he just studied in the UK.

"Can you move your hands, legs?" I ask in a quiet voice. Again, he takes a few seconds to consider or to plan an appropriate answer.

"No, not yet. Soon, I'm sure."

"Right. Tell me who you are and how you got me into this mess. In your incapacitated state, you'll need my assistance when we are out. If we get out."

"Charming," he says in an unaffected voice.

"Continue, please."

"Should I start with my National Insurance number or the address of my nursery?"

"How about your full name? Build the suspense from there."

"Hector Albert Worthington." A lofty inheritance is usually attached to upper-class names, which could be an abduction reason. There is a familiarity to his last name. Was he in the news? "And you are?"

"I have a feeling you already know who I am."

"Dear God! What makes you think so?"

"Oh, I don't know. Why would they kidnap me specifically, having no connection to you?"

"How would I know? Do you think they gave me a choice in the matter? Gave me multiple options, and I went with the Eastern European, unknown woman, late twenties, asks a lot of questions?"

"How do you know I am from Eastern Europe, or my age?"

"Your accent is not that strong, but I can tell. As for age, I saw you, remember? Before they put us in the coffin. In which we find ourselves still. If you finished with the 'Twenty Question Game' we can go ahead to the escaping part of the programme."

"Not by a long shot, but I want out, too. I'm Vera Nicolescu."

"I'm not sure how long it's been since they left. It may be early morning already, and we need to put some distance between us and this place, assuming they are coming back."

"What do you suggest we do? The coffin wouldn't open or move an inch in either way."

"If the casket is as sophisticated as I think, the way out could be at the tip of your fingers. Nowadays they make them high-tech by building an electronic system in the cover. For ventilation and automatic lock."

"I checked every corner. Apart from the ventilation, I distinguished nothing helpful. Would they use a coffin that opens from the inside?"

"I don't think they predicted I will move or talk in order to escape. Check the ceiling again. Try to feel for a hidden panel you can uncover."

I drag my fingertips on the surface, up and down, then left and right. Nothing. Multiple square shapes form the ceiling. I glue my palms to the fabric and execute distinct movements. Somewhere over his head, a square is shifting, like a puzzle piece that moves between others. Using my fingernails, I discover the edge that opens, and inside, three buttons and a tiny glass screen. Pressing the buttons activates a soft, red light, blinding me for a moment. I move back to my wall, eyes closed, and release a huge breath. I feel exhausted by my accomplishment.

"Good job."

"Thanks." I roll my head and look over at him once my eyes adjust. He appears to be a huge red statue, an unmoving block of muscles. The crimson hues make his hair colour and skin tone unclear. He might have dark hair like mine. Hands close to his body, palms facing the floor. His shirt could be white, black pants.

"You still can't move? Try flexing your fingers. Move your toes." I lift myself on one elbow, facing him.

"I recovered feeling in different parts, but not much. Try pressing the other buttons."

Looking at his face, I don't catch what he says. His eyes are open, looking up. They probably are of a light colour. A few strands of hair are over his high cheekbones and full lips. Should I move them aside? With the darkness gone, I lose the courage to touch him. Strong nose and jaw, tense neck, big torso. My 'figure things out by touch' skills are useless if I missed this guy's size. Even temporarily paralysed, he looks masculine and controlled. And he stares at me, hovering over him, concentrating on his face.

Working in Canary Wharf, I am used to seeing good-looking men wearing suits, arrogant, sometimes overconfident, sales and finance guys. You become immune after a while and forget their faces when you turn the street corner. Especially since they don't really give you the time of day, self-absorbed and in their own bubble. You would not forget this guy's face as quickly. Not with those intense eyes glaring at me as if I've done something wrong. Hector Albert Worthington has an intimidating appearance.

"How about you check those buttons now?" Uneasy at getting caught staring at him, I shake my head. Luckily, the red glow covers any signs of rosy cheeks.

"Hm? Oh yeah. Let me see. One lights the screen and provides a confusing ambient. The second is for ventilation. Increase–decrease. The third one is for . . ." I press the button, and nothing happens. Press it a few more times and still nothing. "The third one should open the coffin, but I do not hear a click," I say, a bit deflated.

"Stop. Can you try to lift the cover now? Nothing? Press again once and then lift." I do what he says, going on all fours and try to elevate with my back. No luck.

"Hey, you can move your neck." He turned his head towards me. I guess it's his time to better check his coffin companion. My jaw-length hair must look like a bird's nest, racoon eyes caused by make-up and crying. I opened my cardigan a while ago, exposing a tight black tank top. "Maybe we break the panel, bypass the electrical system or something."

"Do you have tools hidden on you I don't know of?" I feel my cheeks heat. *He doesn't mean in your cleavage, Vera.* He is not looking at me anymore, anyway, eyes fixed up on the panel. I sit back on my side, facing him.

"I don't. Not that you have a better idea. The button is not working, they made sure of that. I could just kick the panel." I press the buttons two at a time to activate a potential pattern.

"Stop playing or risk the chance of breaking the system altogether."

"And I thought I was the pessimist," I say, still pushing the buttons. Just then, I hear a definite snap. I look over at him, smiling my most self-righteous look.

"Slowly push the lid open. Verify our surroundings."

I have to climb over him to open the lid, because of course it opens from his side. I roll my eyes as he grunts softly. He is regaining the ability to feel then. Before pushing the cover, I close the light, to not alert every one of our presence and impending escape. Am I ready to face our kidnappers? I have no weapon to defend us. What if I open the lid and they shoot me on the spot? Trade this deceitful state of protection for uncertainty?

"What are you waiting for?"

"What if we are not alone?"

"Only one way to find out."

Shifting the coffin lid off, a heavy weight, more so when I try not to drop it, afraid of the noise that would produce, I see I have no reason to be concerned – no one is nearby. As nothing obstructs the cover, I can fully remove it. They placed the casket into a stone bed, surrounded by stone walls from all sides. That's why it did not shift when I wanted to move it. We are lucky they did not put the stone lid on, but left it on the floor, close by. I get out and arch my body for a few seconds. We are in a small room, our stone bed is one of four, two of them already occupied. The moon provides enough illumination through the two narrow windows next to the entrance. Still night, but for how long? The door is easy to open. Were they really counting on us staying drugged and inside the coffin? I have to remain vigilant, because I have a feeling, locking us in that terrifying place was a scare tactic for what is yet to come. They knocked me unconscious without interrogating me on why they think I matter enough to be in this position, and Worthington clearly knows more that he lets on, and perhaps they assume the same. As far as I know, the police don't operate like this to solve their investigations, but what if are we dealing with corrupt cops working with a criminal organisation? Is Hector a criminal?

Outside, it's freezing and windy. A sinister graveyard ambiance with crosses, trimmed grass everywhere. Marble statues of angels and saints, stone mausoleums, and crypts. A long wail, nearby and unnatural, makes me jump in the air, my nails biting into shaking hands. Another noise above my head horrifies me, that of quick flipping wings, and I lift my arms to cover my hair. Nature is giving her ominous night concert, but no people around.

Back inside, my casket mate tries to lift his head and upper body, using his arms and failing miserably. He is not completely functional; I can see the frustration on his determined face. His hair is a tad longer than shoulder length. Black in this diffused nightlight.

"We are alone. Let me help you out."

"There's some power in my arms and legs, but . . ." he says, embarrassed for some reason.

"We'll figure something out." I stand next to the stone coffin, trying to pull him out. He is bigger than me, so he needs to help. "May I touch you to, you know, get you out?"

"It did not stop you before, it's too late to ask for permission."

I put one arm around his neck and another around his back. He is halfway out, balancing on the stone wall, letting gravity bring the other leg out. I get my arms under his armpits, but he falls, unsurprisingly, confirming his drugged status, and I shoulder some of his weight.

"We need to carry you outside the graveyard, to a major street, and find someone with a phone to call an ambulance."

"No police. No ambulance," he pants, crawling outside backwards, using his elbows, dragging his feet.

"What? Why? We need to talk to someone about what happened here. Maybe we can reach . . ." I am talking fast again, aggravated at his demand.

"Vera. Listen to me, please. We will find a way. We just cannot talk to anyone yet. I do not know who to trust. A person on my team sold my location, but I can't be sure who did it. I was not taken by the same officers that brought you, but they helped to bring me back into the country. So, no police. No authorities. I have a safe house we can use to rest and think. Nobody knows about it."

"And how do you propose we arrive at your safe house? You can't crawl there, people wander the streets, even at this hour. We have no shoes, no jackets. It's the middle of March and cold as hell. No phones or money for a taxi." I could run and find help, involve the police, no matter what he says. They can't all be corrupt. But looking at his weakened form on the ground, how he twitches and how he massages his muscles to force strength into them, I feel like a monster for considering leaving him to fend for himself. Surveying the mausoleum where they had us in, then my fingertips, worn-away from the desperate attempt at escaping, my instinct screams at me to not trust anyone. But in this case, how do I find a way out of this mess?

"You can leave, but I do not recommend going alone to the authorities."

"No." Shaking my head, I swallow my hesitation. "I won't abandon you here in your condition."

"That's not what I meant but thank you." He nods, face rising to lock eyes with me, to see the sincerity writing on them. "I know trusting a complete stranger doesn't come easy, but I can keep us safe once we arrive at one of my secured locations. You were right, I'm what some deem important. My wealth and reach are significant and seen as solid justifications for a specific group of people to kidnap me, but while I don't know why you are connected to all of this, I promise to use my resources to help you." For what is worth, he looks sincere. We are both outside now, alone with the frigid wind.

"I'll check the area for something useful." Shivering and barefoot, I look ahead and take the path in front of the mausoleum.

Treading carefully around the tombs and alleys, stepping on sharp stones and spiky bushes, I pass a rather extensive building with a cupola. It's locked, but a slightly illuminated poster lets me know I am in Brompton Cemetery.

As my walk continues, paranoia builds within me. Why was nobody guarding us? My feet are blocks of ice, chills go through my body, but the sheer relief at escaping the padded box warms my core.

A screech behind me stops my progress. Whirling around, I lose my balance and fall to my knees. Left and right, nothing creeps from the shadows. London sleeps and so do the dead in this cemetery. Hugging myself against the wind, I resume my search.

Up ahead, an artificial light blinks from a security booth. The cold is at home in my bones, and I can't relax my jaw. How close should I get?

A middle-aged man wearing a uniform sits in the booth enjoying a show on his tablet. Headphones on. The entrance gates are ahead, but we can't use them without unwanted attention.

I move left towards some dark structures, hoping they are for maintenance. A tool shed, which every graveyard definitely has, would be helpful. They're also locked and from the smell, I've found the restrooms. Too late. The next one behind has a bolt that slides open. The door squeaks when I push it, and my breathing stops. The small shed has a window, and with difficulty I distinguish what's inside. Pain radiates in my shin when I stumble upon a wheel attached to something with a metallic frame. A wheelbarrow!

"You are coming with me."

I make my way back to where I left Hector. Our luck turns with the wheelbarrow and the things I found. A dirty long plastic canvas, a gardening jacket I already put on and large wellies. Plus, a rake I'll use on anyone who wants to interfere between me and a shower.

Hector is sitting on the steps of the mausoleum. His slightly relaxed stance could be a sign he also found a place to relieve himself.

"Look what I found. I tried to wear these wellies, but they are too big, and I can't walk. You can use them if the size is good. And this canvas as a blanket. I'm keeping the jacket."

"Any problems? You took your time; I thought the guard saw you." He thought I left after I said I wouldn't.

"How do you know about the cemetery having a guard?"

"I know we are in Brompton; I have family buried here. I can stand, but walking is difficult, so the wheelbarrow is fortunate. Thank you." He puts the canvas over his shoulders, and I help him with the boots when I see the task is too challenging for him. "How is the situation up front? Can we use the main entrance to leave?"

"The security guy is distracted, but it's too risky to use that exit. Maybe there is an unguarded back entrance. Where exactly is your place?"

"The safe house is close to Earl's Court Station in Nevern Square. Around twenty minutes walking distance from here. Can you help me get in the wheelbarrow?"

"We are lucky your house is so close. Imagine if it was further away, in a different neighbourhood." I give him a hand, covering him properly with the canvas. He is not that noticeable.

"It's a safe house. Not where I live. Are you sure you can push the wheelbarrow?"

"Right. Probably with brief breaks along the way. Tell me where to go. Do you have more than one safe house?"

"I wouldn't classify them as such if I talk about them in great detail, would I?"

So, he has more than one. Interesting. I'll drag him out of the cemetery to his house and then I'll leave. I'll find an open shelter that takes in the homeless and decide on my next steps. Maybe a refuge for women in difficulty. They handle things with anonymity, don't they? Brainstorm a solution after allowing my mind some rest. Magically produce someone that would help me. But if Hector's the only source at discovering the cause of my kidnapping, can I risk cutting my ties with him?

Lifting the handles, I push with difficulty. We arrive at the exit after many tedious minutes, two breaks and one near wheelbarrow upturning. The gate opens only from the inside and no one is guarding it. It locks automatically behind us.

I head down Ifield Road, a side street, with no activity. My arms are killing me, and my feet are no better without shoes. I will be useless tomorrow, not that I have any plans besides sleeping.

With a few stops, we make it to Finborough Road, where we pass two guys who pay no attention to us. London. I have the hood of the big jacket on, and Hector covers his head when he hears them coming.

You can do this, keep pushing.

Soon I can unclench the tight grip of fear around my ribcage. The adrenaline is focusing my efforts, making me more determined to continue and not feel the strain in my hands when I keep the wheelbarrow in an upright position and push.

The scary notion of returning to the coffin finds its way into my thoughts every five minutes. Unease creeps down my neck even though I escaped, and I'm fine.

I escaped.

I am fine.

For now.

Four

Minutes pass, one by one, as slowly as hours, and an eternity after leaving the mausoleum, we arrive at Nevern Square. No food or water for ages, scared out of my mind; no matter how much I try to hold it in, I am close to fainting. We abandoned the wheelbarrow a few streets behind when it was clear I couldn't push it anymore. I insisted on draining my remaining power, but Hector climbed out, used the rake as a cane and my shoulder for support, and we walked close to each other the rest of the way. My arms are useless, and my feet will need time to recover any notion of feeling. I'm battered from the inside out.

Stale air infused with cleaning chemicals meets us in the safe house, a studio on the second floor of a brick Victorian apartment building with keypad locks everywhere, and I crash on the wooden floor. Not the end of a gloomy spring night I ever imagined experiencing or having the strength to finish with breath in my body.

"Here, drink this." I open my eyes to see my companion hover over me with a bottle of water that I drain in seconds. "You can use the shower first. I left towels and something to wear close to the cabinet." He can barely move, taking every step with difficulty, dragging his feet, sickly pale skin and pronounced signs of under-eye shadows. I wonder how depleted I look in this light when I know I have no strength left to depart.

The closed shower is already running as I undress. The bathroom is small and clean, in shades of white. There's a corner toilet, which I use first, and a sink with a cabinet underneath. The scalding water of the shower relaxes my body a fraction. My normally bright olive skin looks unhealthy after the horror experience of a kidnapping I don't remember completely. Pushing an incapacitated man around London with trepidation as a guide.

That I am not giving my testimony to someone in charge of locking up bad guys means this adventure is far from finished, but I've seen plenty of movies to know Hector is right about being prudent with whom to trust. My nose stings as I sniff back a cry I can't hold in any longer because I'm bloody weak and that's what I do now. Cry. I don't even trust him completely, if at all. Why am I here then?

He revealed little information, and it's true, we didn't have time for full disclosure. But he has safe houses, for God's sake! Is he in this type of situation often? And somehow got me involved? Even if I ask him, Hector Albert Worthington is evasive.

Maybe I'll recover in an hour and leave. Finish the shower, get dressed, sit still for a moment, and then leave. I helped him, and I did not abandon a person in need of assistance, I did my best and I should leave.

How far is the nearest women's shelter? My apartment would be the first place they'd look, when they discover we've escaped. They wouldn't go to the trouble of kidnapping me to leave the job unfinished. My brother and my parents will not be worried if I'm offline for a few days, busy with work at quarter end. I don't want to call my friends and put them in peril. They are normal people, not spies with guns and trained to fight. Or with safe houses.

The towel I use to dry myself is lush and enormous. My body and hair smell clean and woodsy. I haven't used bath products designed for men in years, not since breaking up with Tomasz while still living in Poland, the only local I dated in the four years I lived in Warsaw. He would have a heart attack if locked in a coffin, alive. I supposed most people would. Tomasz would suggest the police immediately. Not much of a rule breaker, and neither am I. Funny, what held us together and made us happy for a spell also separated us. We are orderly, no bullshit people. Facts and logic. But I am a debate and act kind of gal, he prefers only debate. I wanted a more confident man, and he deserved someone to spend the nights at home with him. Moving from the Polish capital to England was always my dream, but not his. Thank God I moved to London, right?

Turning over the clothes Hector provided, his tense voice next room pauses my movement. Is he on the phone? I thought *we* don't trust anyone, but he's making calls. I snap the new Paul Smith boxers into place. Expensive. Black sweatpants from Comme des Garcons, not too big for my hips, and a grey long-sleeved shirt, Maison Margiela. This guy does lounge wear designer style. My black hair is in a short bob, but longer in the front and easy to finger brush in the mirror. Round green eyes, tired and bloodshot. The ever-present black under-eye circles no longer concealed by make-up. The clothes are big on me, but I am not exactly swimming in them. I was always a skinny girl no matter what I ate until mid-twenties, when I gained some curves and a few extra pounds. Sometimes I'm frustrated and try to lose weight, but food is too diverse and delicious to be skinny too long. After using a new toothbrush, I return to the main room.

The studio is basically a large space with a king-size bed next to the window. Long drawn curtains, keeping the early morning light out. There's an armoire matching the bed where Hector is rummaging for something. On a shelf full of weapons. How so unsurprising at this point. Oh, and a kitchenette on the opposite wall.

"The shower is free," I say in a small voice. He removed his shirt and pants while I was in the bathroom, standing before me in a white sleeveless undershirt and dark boxers. Lean muscles define his tall frame. His long hair is a blend between charcoal and mahogany and looks like he ran his fingers through it for the last ten minutes. Fair skin tone, almost translucent, the light blue eyes I noticed earlier. And I slobbered all over him in the coffin, when I thought he was Ed the Dead, and I was hugging his arm in my sleep. He looks very much alive and angry right now. "Thank you for the clothes."

"No problem. Do you need anything else?" He turns to face me fully. "There is no proper food here, apart from protein bars and other non-perishable snacks. I put them on the kitchen counter."

"Thank you." In ten seconds flat, I am on my second dried fruit bar.

"Take the bed. Get some sleep. A lot to discuss when we wake up." He leaves me in the middle of the studio for his turn in the shower before I can ask him about the call he had while I was in the bathroom. I couldn't understand what he was saying, just the name Lawrence, when he furiously half-shouted at the person on the other end.

Am I staying? Both my body and mind feel shackled with fatigue. More and more with every passing second. What if I collapse on the street and someone calls the police? The same individuals that forced my unconscious body in a deluxe casket. On a side table, the clock shows it is close to 7 a.m.

Moving towards the bed, sliding under the covers on the hard mattress, I struggle to sign off my brain and rest. All that happened yesterday and today is on a continuous loop behind my eyes. 'What ifs' drift in my head like ghosts, and I can't push them away as much as I try, without a glass of something strong. Minutes later, when Hector comes back from the restroom, dressed in a black t-shirt and shorts, I am searching through the kitchen cabinets for a drop of alcohol.

"Why aren't you sleeping? What do you need?" He pushes his hair back, wet and dripping on the towel around his neck. Five o'clock shadow on his face, lighter than his naturally defined eyebrows and hair. He moves carefully towards my agitated self. My hands are shaking from exhaustion, from the need of a hard liquor release, and his deep, commanding voice is getting on my nerves. "Vera, what are you searching for? I might be able to help you seeing as this is my house."

"Alcohol. I want some alcohol. Can you give me that?" I am not a drinker, but I need aid with the pressure building rapidly, if my shaky fingers are a sign to my physical and emotional state.

"Sure. Will whiskey work? That's all I have," he says reaching in a top shelf above the microwave. I would need a chair to get the bottle, and he just raised his hand, heels connected to the floor. Over six feet tall to my five and a half. After he pours us two generous glasses, I take mine to bed, sipping slowly. I can't say I know how to appreciate whiskey, but this one is helping my nerves. He drinks his standing, leaning back on the kitchen counter, legs crossed at the ankles, looking at me. "Are you having another panic attack?"

"It's not a panic attack, I just can't shut my mind off. I don't know about you, but I started my night buried alive next to a dead person who turned out to be someone with a wardrobe full of assault rifles. In hours, I'm expected at work where I can't go for the foreseeable future, so I will be reported missing. Some individuals, not bothering to explain why they kidnapped me, are probably looking for my whereabouts. Oh, and I am still not one hundred percent sure of your role in this story."

"At least you know I am not a vampire," he deadpans. I forgot about checking his teeth, how I hope to forget the entire time I spent in that coffin.

"The jury is still out on the paranormal activity theory. I can't explain my presence in all this." Half of my drink vanished, making me feel slightly dizzy. Blinking eyes lose focus of his frame.

"Once we rest for a few hours, things might seem clearer." It's amazing he can stand after being awake for so long and not lie down somewhere. And after being drugged like he was.

"Like how to fix this and get my life back. Even if I decide going our separate way is the best approach for me."

"You are free to leave now, but I owe you my gratitude and that's worth a restful sleep and whatever else you need." Hector Worthington is a stranger still, but we were locked in that coffin together. Both our safety is at stake.

"Aren't you going to sleep?"

"I have to make a call first."

"Another one, you mean." I'm slurring my words.

"Yes."

He comes towards the bed and my body flinches as he takes a pillow under his arm, kneels, and opens a drawer under the mattress. A fluffy blanket and a yoga mat. I release a big sigh, closing my eyes. He will stay on the floor. Turning my back on him,

I give sleep another try, and by the time he comes back from the bathroom where he takes his call, I am already unconscious. Dreaming that we never made it out of the cemetery.

❖

My feet echo on a long, dark corridor with every step I take to outrun the shadows chasing me and it never ends, no matter how fast I go. Soon, they will catch me, I know it.

My hands are bloody, but I have no wounds. Is this someone else's blood? What did I do? An unnaturally pale palm grabs my dress, yanks with incredible force, and I scream.

"No! No, no!"

"Vera, wake up! You're having a nightmare! Wake up!"

"What?" I open my eyes to realise I'm thrashing in Hector's arms. I pull in a deep breath and release it in whimpered fragments.

"You are safe. It was just a nightmare. You are okay," he says in a gentle voice. The room is almost dark, the blinds offering us the fake cover of seclusion. His warm hand swipes away the wet hair from my eyes. There's pity in his.

"I am sorry. It felt so real." He releases me when I push on his chest, embarrassed and sweating. How many times does he have to see me cry?

"No need to apologise. Here, have some water." The taste of whiskey is on my tongue when he hands me a frosty glass from the kitchen.

"Thank you." I address his abdomen while he stands next to the bed, and I drink my water, looking at his hands that turn into fists and back, like he's forcing them to hold his anger.

"Nobody knows about this studio, and the door is reinforced steel. They are not coming in. We need to rest before we take any future decisions." He lies down on his makeshift bed on the floor.

"Yes. I know."

A short visit to the bathroom later, where I see a ghost looking back at me in the mirror, I return to my pillow. Lingering icy fingers of the earlier nightmare are pushed aside by exhaustion, so I don't know if what I hear next is real or my imagination.

"After what you did, breaking us out of the coffin, carrying me here when you could have left, I'm not letting them touch you again. No matter what." Oblivion takes me under, and I am lucky nothing else follows me into my slumber.

◆

The smell of coffee and breakfast at the window table wakes me up a second time, much later. Or maybe it's lunch. Still depleted to my bones and starving, I get up and stretch like a cat, forgetting I have an audience, enjoying their food.

"Finally. We need to talk, Vera Alexandra Nicolescu." Deep, no-nonsense voice, irritating attitude.

"Well, good morning to you too, Hector Albert Worthington."

A bathroom visit is required before addressing the inquisition, so I leave him to stare after me in the big room. His tone felt accusatory on sleepy ears, and my pulse is already reacting with building dread. The locked casket, the cemetery, the horror of this specific imprisonment were extreme situations to face, and my gut says those were the first representations of the trials I will face in the coming days.

Lifting my head to wash the exhaustion from my eyes, I shudder at the recognition of his name. Worthington. As in Worthington & Neville, W&N? The company that merged with my employer Fosters & Co? Grabbing the sink with both hands, the discovery stuns the breath out of me. Is that why he sounded displeased? Is my place of work a clue in this madness, and to how we are connected?

Fuck! I hoped the lack of a connection would mean a mistake was made.

When I return, face freshly washed, morning breath gone, he's already made the bed. The clock shows an early afternoon hour. I stand in the middle of the room, watching him bite into a sandwich. He called me Alexandra when I did not give him the name I rarely share. What did he find out and from whom?

"Is there any black tea?"

One of his brows goes up, perhaps in amusement at my remark, or probably my grumpy tone. My throat is sore from screaming bloody murder in a tomb hours ago, so no sunshine attitude from me while I wait for the other shoe to drop on this brand-new Tuesday.

"I'll call room service. How do you like your eggs?" He finishes one sandwich, already starting on another. No mention of my nightmare.

"Hosts should have better manners and be more attentive to their guests." I drink a bottle of water from the fridge and analyse the choice of sandwiches at the sink. "How do you know my second name?" I sit in the empty chair, hummus and veggie wrap in hand.

"I knew more than your name by the time I went to buy breakfast, Vera Alexandra Nicolescu, born thirty years ago in Bucharest, Romania. Father, Paul, a general contractor, mother, Felicia, a carpenter. One younger brother, Cristian, living in London as well. Interestingly, you started working for Fosters & Co in Bucharest as a procurement intern. They sent you to Warsaw to be part of their buyers' team. They moved you again, this time to London with a bigger role of Regional Procurement Manager."

"You found my LinkedIn profile. How exciting. I am so impressed with your hacker skills. The agency you work for must be really paying you the big bucks. Why is working for Fosters & Co so interesting?" I add the last question despite my earlier realisation, wanting to see how he uses the information he obtained while I *slept*. Like a bloody damsel in distress. Perhaps there's no need for both of us to be confrontational, but I can't seem to stop myself when the guilt of my inadequacy darkens my judgement. He's dressed in a black sweater and jeans, black boots, hasn't shaved yet, and his hair is loose on big, strong shoulders.

Stop complementing him in your head, Vera, and pick an emotion.

"Because working for Fosters & Co is what got you kidnapped last evening and gave you the opportunity to feel me up while I couldn't move or object."

"Hardly. I thought you were dead, or I wouldn't have touched you. And I don't have a position of power at my company, I am not a shareholder to use me as money leverage. What's the connection between my kidnapping and one of the most respected companies in the world?" The absurd implication that the corporation I've dedicated my years to is in the league with corrupt cops forces me to stand and move items around in the kitchen. "Did you buy any pastries?" Dessert would make this discussion bearable.

"What? No. How did your mind jump from a life and death situation to sweets?"

"That's exactly why. If you want to give someone bad news, you bring them cake first. It eases the pain." It also adds a pound to one's behind, but let's focus on the positive.

"Are you listening to what I'm saying?" His jaw tightens with the last word.

"Eh, I drift in and out when you use that tone."

“You are more annoying than funny, if you believed otherwise.” The rough voice and the heavy weight of his gaze make me push forward with the sarcasm.

“And you are the last man in the world I could ever be prevailed upon to annoy.”

“Case in point, even if you quote Austen. Don’t think you can fool me, or yourself, with a ridiculous change of subject just because the truth is an inconvenience for you. Steering back the conversation to relevant territory, Fosters & Co is behind our kidnapping. I am not a spy, Miss Nicolescu, don’t let the guns fool you. I own a bank by the name of Severe Trust.” A twist I did not expect.

“I have my account there.”

“Indeed, you do.”

“How old are you?” I stall, allowing my brain a chance to figure out where the conversation is leading.

“And that’s important because?” He looks like he is losing his patience.

“Because Severe Trust is a two-hundred-year-old Swiss Institution, according to the pamphlet with the cute older couple by the river. You are like, what, thirty-five? How can you own a bank?” He’s building up to an accusation, I can feel it.

“Am I under interrogation? You are missing the point. The one where your employer had someone shove us into a coffin with the plan to kill us, most likely, after they got the information they wanted.”

“See, Mister Worthington, you had your time to use Google on me. To do your homework. And when I ask simple questions, you dismiss them. I want straight answers now or I am taking my chances with the police. Why is Fosters & Co allegedly trying to kill us?”

“I am running a private investigation against them and clearly got too close to evidence they don’t want exposed.”

“Do bank owners investigate big corporations? Hard to believe they were looking for a loan and the investigation was your due diligence. You have employees for that.”

“This corporation bought my sister’s company two years ago under false pretence. Before the deal was done, she discovered she was selling her life’s achievement to the wrong institution and, while I don’t have the proof yet, she threatened to reveal publicly what she found. Then Helena, my sister, died in a questionable accident with her business associate. Worthington & Neville was incorporated into the Fosters & Co brand, and I have been trying ever since to prove they killed her.” It looks like he expects me to know this information, judging by his expression.

“Wow! I’m . . . that is, I’m sorry for your loss. I know about the merger of W&N with my employer, but what makes you think they would do such a terrible crime?”

“Because of a phone call I received the night before she died. Helena was working with her solicitors on the last points of the contract, but she had doubts and kept saying ‘something doesn’t add up’. She couldn’t see the big picture anymore and if maybe she was making a mistake. I advised her to rest, the decision to sell was in her best interest. There were other willing buyers if the Fosters & Co deal felt wrong. In the morning, she signed the contract. The next afternoon she was dead.” He clears his voice and moves his eyes from me to something above my shoulder, deep pain evident on his face.

“For a period, I believed it was an accident, but wanting confirmation, I looked into the agreement. After a year of dead ends, someone contacts my team saying they have damning evidence against Fosters & Co, and they will sell it to me. For the last five months, they have given us enough information to keep our interest, but nothing we can use to go public with an accusation. We believe the informant is an employee of the company."

"We are talking about a global corporation with divisions in every industry on the market, extremely regulated, and since I have been working for them, my whole professional career, they have never led me to believe they are doing shady business." Not that I have access to acquisition meetings of that level, but they promote a corporate lifestyle, a tad robotic at times and politically correct, but not mafia dealings.

"They put you in that coffin with me because Fosters & Co thinks you are the snitch. Do you still want to defend them?"

"Sorry, what?" I'm contemplating his story, and what he says doesn't register, at first.

"Were you selling me information, Vera?" Hearing how his voice suddenly sounds like we are lifetime friends gives me shivers. He is good. "You were sending small irregularities in the beginning, peanuts, but you got greedy, careless and they caught you."

"You must be joking! I did no such thing!" I hyperventilate, only thinking about it.

"The clue to the informant is their employee number. RE313129." His eyes analyse my every reaction. "That's yours, am I right?"

"I don't know it by heart." Even I don't believe that.

"Because it's such a hard number to remember. I paid a lot of money to the owner of that number. I remember it in my sleep."

"Check my account! You are my bank, see if I received a pound of your money."

"Correct. Nothing unusual in your Severe Trust account. The bank I transferred the money to is from Poland. Polish currency."

Damn! Somebody is trying convincingly to incriminate me, and this nutter believes them. The kidnappers believe it too.

"I'm not guilty of what you accuse me of, so take a step back, cause defending myself is unnecessary. Yes, the RE number is mine. Yes, I used to live in Poland. But I'm guilty of nothing! Stop looking at me like that. I am clearly being set up! For all I know, you are full of shit."

"Debatable, but if you are not the informant, you don't object to helping me weed him or her out, do you? Until we reveal the truth about Fosters & Co, you will not be safe. Constant protection is required because they will track you everywhere you go without one."

"Who in Fosters & Co dealt with the W&N merger? What names do you have?" My brain flashes out people in the organisation who are regularly involved in new companies' acquisitions, but my information is not accurate since I've worked in the London office only for a few months and they signed the deal years ago.

"The list is as long as my arm, from lawyers to analysts and external consultants, but the responsible people for my sister's death are hard to pinpoint when the entire board approved the merger under your company's standards. Knowing or not that a silencing order was given, consequences be damned."

"But surely there's a list of suspects if you say you have been investigating them diligently? Someone to persecute if you find more evidence."

He says nothing, as if any minute now I'll admit to being the mole and that I already know more than I let on. He has a name, his story has a villain, and in his mind, I just need to confirm it.

"Once we establish a relationship of trust, I'll share everything I know. All responsible parties will answer to what they did in the end. Are you willing to help?"

"You put me in a difficult position. We don't know each other, our characters, or values, we met in the most horrible of circumstance, but believe it or not, I don't take well to injustice and being wrongly accused of profiting from one. If only with the desire to clear my name, I want to help, but it feels like I do not have a choice either way since you are not as forthcoming with the information that might pardon me from all wrongdoings," I say, irritated.

"Or it could help you manipulate the odds. There is always a choice, Vera, though I don't like your chances if you leave." He uses a cold and dispassionate tone, as if he is not talking about my life and its ruination. I should have dumped him at the graveyard, rake shoved up his ass.

"How do you propose I help? If Fosters & Co is the villain, I can't exactly visit the office to investigate suspicious activities." What should I do? I'm torn between going to the closest media outpost. Will the BBC believe my story and offer me protection? I am way over my head, no matter how tough I act.

"There are other ways to use your knowledge of the company without putting yourself at risk. Such as breaking into their network to extract what we require. Or analyse the data we already have from the mole, hoping your expertise on Fosters & Co will push us forward. We are leaving soon if you decide to join me. We can't stay in one place for too long."

When he sees my indecision, he grabs my shoulder gently, clearing his throat.

"Vera, I can help you not end up like my sister. You need to trust me on this, and not only because I owe you one for hauling me out of Brompton Cemetery, but I don't want anyone else to die. Fosters & Co considers you their enemy, and that makes you my ally. No matter what you did in the past, we'll be stronger together. They put you in a coffin. Remember that."

If I gather crucial information from him and the files he has, details the authorities can investigate, maybe associating with his cause will provide a faster conclusion to my problems. I can always separate from him and stir my efforts elsewhere.

"May I use your phone? Or a laptop?"

"That's not a clever idea. You can't call your family or friends; they don't have secure lines."

"I want to use the internet, and before you say it, I won't go on social media. I assume the phone you used is secure." Come on, deny me if you dare. Frustratingly, his habit so far is to stare me down before replying to requests or questions. Probably thinking he can intimidate me into submission. Think again, Ed. Hector.

"Okay. I will allow it, but first you tell me why." I blink at his reply. He will allow it. Breathe in. Breathe out. Mother of . . .

"Fine, I want to Google you and everything you said." I'm not taking anything at face value.

"Here it is." He passes the phone, unlocked. "I'm thirty-six, if that's why you require internet. I can answer what questions you have."

"Say no more, you fountain of clarity and straightforwardness. Let me do my own research."

First, I check how Worthington & Neville became part of Fosters & Co's umbrella. Nothing screams murder or illegalities. Then I move to Wikipedia, which has an entire page on Hector Albert Worthington. Born in May in Holland Park, London, as the second child of an English aristocrat and a Swiss banking heiress. His father, George Alexander Worthington, a real estate developer and the co-founder of said company, died ten years ago. Helena Annabella Worthington, the older sister, took over her father's side of the business before she died in a car accident.

Through his mother, Lara Satie, still alive, he inherited at the young age of twenty-four a Severe Trust bank that was gradually going under. Twelve years later, he brought the financial institution back to the glory days his great grandfather was famous for, raising its profile and still keeping it a family bank. He studied at Eton and Cambridge, and that's easy to believe. An album of photos of him climbing mountains for charity, but not a lot of gossip related to his dating life. He was in a relationship with a blonde supermodel-looking barrister just before his sister's death. Nothing in the press after that. He keeps a low profile. While I scroll the web for all news related to my coffin companion, and the circumstances of his sister's death and her company's merger with Fosters & Co, he packs a bag with clothes, money from a hidden safe, water and snacks.

Closing all my searches on his phone, I put the device in my pocket. Weeks ago, I bought a present for my Polish friend, Dorota, to help her monitor her sleeping baby, and with my never-ending working hours, I delayed the visit to the postal office. Nobody knows that I have a teddy camera on my desk among the rest of my packages. I installed it the day it was delivered to me, to check if it works, but I did not activate it then since I wanted to give Dorota that opportunity. I need time to set it up and I plan to withhold this information, because it's an unsure lead and I don't want to lose my leverage if it proves helpful. Like he mentioned, trust in our partnership is fragile still.

"Where are we going?"

"To a more secure location. We must disappear until we can unmask Fosters & Co, and we can't stay in a normal apartment building. The risk is too big, our coming and goings need to be very discreet. We also need something bigger than a studio, with a more complex layout for security, more technology to help us operate our future strategy."

"Can I borrow something else to wear? I would also need to buy some clothes that fit. And shoes. Maybe I could go to my house one night and pack a bag?" To verify if it's a compromised location or not. He directs me to the wardrobe to select another sweatshirt and pants getup.

"Not a great idea. By the time we arrive, you'll have clothes that fit delivered to the new safe house."

"How extensive is your underground operation? Are they coming to pick us up?"

He just looks at me like I'm an annoyance that asks too many questions.

"No, I prefer to keep this location to myself."

"Except I know about it now."

"Don't make me regret it."

"You wouldn't be the only one regretting things."

Taking the clothes to the bathroom for a quick rinse, I ask myself if I have to go with him, but no other options have appeared overnight. My joints ache, I need a full body massage, and therapy, after this mess ends, hopefully not with me in another coffin. But what is it with me and this bathroom that spurs my imagination towards unlikely scenarios?

I stop dressing, thinking back to what Hector said. External consultants brought in to help with the merger. If, with all his research, he didn't connect the dots, why would I? There's probably nothing to it, but I might be in deeper trouble than I thought.

My hands are impatient as I open another tab on the phone, checking the internet again for details of the agreement resulting with Helena Worthington's murder. Could it be how the mole obtained my passwords?

When I find nothing to confirm or deny the scenario, I accept that my next steps are obvious. Go with Hector wherever he keeps the stolen files and pray I don't have to lie about the information they contain. For now, I will my pulse to come back to normal, because it can't betray my alarm. After all, I could just be making ridiculous assumptions because I'm tired and still in a state of shock from last night. The ramifications are endless if I don't master my emotions until I find out what the hell is going on.

Returned from the bathroom, Hector points to a black NY cap, a jacket, and huge flip-flops next to the bed. He is ready to leave in a black jacket, his long hair hidden by a cap of his own.

"Use these until we get you some proper shoes. It's not a long walk to the car, anyway. And I want my phone back."

I put the cap over my confused head, grabbing a protein bar from the kitchen area, the flip-flops next, and face the entrance where my new partner stands. To lighten the mood, and my nerves, I offer his phone back in the same way a temple goer extends his prayers to a merciful God. He contains from showing any sign of humanity, an eye roll or at least a headshake.

"Time's a wasting, Miss Nicolescu," he deadpans.

It seems childish, but I expected an indication that our collaboration is the best way to go. A handshake and a promise to keep each other safe. But at his tone, I continue with my sarcastic approach, invading his personal space, looking him in the eyes, and raising one hand towards his neck. He goes still as a rock. At the same time I take his black Ray Bans Wayfarer from the collar of his sweater, I address him with a whisper.

"You forgot to give me underwear." I put the sunglasses on my face, turn around, open the door, and leave. After a few seconds, I hear him close behind me.

Outside, in the chilly March air of the late afternoon, Hector pulls me next to him as we walk. Spring flowers from the trees above, the only messenger of light and hope in an otherwise dreary scene. The nagging impression that everyone is looking at us falters my steps.

"Stay close, don't walk too fast or too slow, and keep your head down."

I follow him to the nearest tube, Earl's Court.

"I thought you mentioned a short walk and a car," I say while we wait to cross the street to the underground station. He puts one arm over my shoulders, bends his head to my ear.

"We need to make sure nobody is following us."

"I thought the studio was safe."

"We have no flexibility for errors. Better to be cautious."

At the entrance gate, he takes out two Oyster cards and hands me one to use as I remove the sunglasses. We follow the signs to the blue Piccadilly line and wait for a train to arrive. We do two stops towards Heathrow Airport, and at Hammersmith, he directs me to the yellow Circle line, Edgware Road direction. The train is full, Londoners on their routine travels, no free chairs to sit.

A couple in front of us are extremely affectionate towards each other. Kisses and touches. Use the handles, friend, not her ass. I love it when people are so engrossed in themselves, they are unconcerned with spectators, you do you, but it makes me uncomfortable when it happens so close to me. He can turn his head, lean in, and do the saliva sharing game with me, or Hector, if he cares to lift himself on his toes. And they have that sugary type of discussion new couples engage in. I bite my lips hard not to snort, turning my head to Hector's chest when she feeds him chocolate. Looking up at my companion, still biting my lips, I take out the protein bar from my back pocket and extend it to him, a soft snort coming out. Hector just stares at me, not appreciating the prank, but when I open the bar, to eat it with half the enthusiasm the guy next to us shows, he leans in and bites into it. He chews slowly, not breaking eye contact, and smirks.

"Disguising a serious if not extremely perilous state of affairs with humour is your way of coping with matters?"

"What gave it away?" I smirk back.

"It's not the most discreet mechanism."

"I prefer sarcasm to panicking with angst. I had enough of that last night," I say as other commuters push him into me. Lifting his arms to place his hands on the train's wall above me, with reluctance, he creates a shielding bubble around my body. I narrow my eyes at him and resume our talk. "I also made an assessment. For an unknown reason, you dislike me when I've been nothing but genuine in my reactions to our situation and willing to help your cause."

"Do we have to like each other to accomplish our goal?"

"Don't quote me on this but perhaps mutual annoyance works against the flow of a partnership."

"Is that right? Stay hidden, Mousekewitz." He taps the visor of my cap, steps slightly to the right, blocking a few travellers from sight, and shifts me to face the glass doors. My tiny smile appears on the shadowed window when I notice the resemblance, in his big clothes and hat, to the cartoon character he mentioned.

From Edgware Road, we turn back to Earl's Court and then out, walking to an inside court between buildings with several parked cars. Hector opens a grey Peugeot, an older model, and in a few minutes, we weave through heavy traffic. For me, cars with right side steering wheels are a fresh experience, especially as a front seat passenger. It's incredibly strange, and I catch myself pressing the imaginary brake more than once.

And me being confused and panicky amuses my dear driver. He doesn't even hide it that hard, full evil smirk on his face after my second 'Shit, oh God, come on, dude!' combo. The streets are not familiar, and when I ask about our direction, his answer is a glare and silence. Because communication is something Worthington failed to assimilate in school. Or in life.

◆

"If you are taking dinner requests, I would like some soup tonight." We've been driving for more than two hours in and out of London, probably to confuse any badly intentioned followers, and I am getting restless and hungry. "Are we stopping soon?" As if to protest alongside me, my stomach grumbles.

"Why don't you eat a protein bar?" he says, eyes on the road.

"If I see another protein bar, I am going to vomit all over you. I'll spare the car."

"How very considerate. Here. Take the phone and find a soup shop nearby." He slows his speed.

"I already know what my cravings demand if they have a pho restaurant in this neighbourhood. You okay with Vietnamese cuisine?"

"Yes, it's fine. If the spot is neither crowded nor deserted, and they run a fast service. We don't want anyone noticing and remembering us."

"I am dressed like a man, flip-flops included. But that's not exactly memorable in this city. And you are your delightful self, I think we are good." I focus my attention on the screen, hoping I'll not get carsick.

"Do you always satisfy your cravings as soon as they appear?" It's the first question he asks in the car that's unrelated to Fosters & Co.

"As opposed to wait for divine intervention or permission? Delayed gratification wasn't top of my list before the kidnapping, and now I can erase it permanently, without guilt."

"You might want to evaluate the decision; it helps build character."

"If my character has any deficiencies, it's not because I indulge in good food, occasionally."

"What would be the reason, then?"

"I'm cursed with human traits, like the rest of us. I mean, not you, obviously." I smirk back at him as the car in front of us stops suddenly, and he breaks with force. My body pulls forward, my seatbelt forgotten after I removed my sweatshirt, but before my face hits the dashboard, his palm connects with my chest, pushing me back.

"Sorry. The guy in front of us is an idiot. Use your belt." He looks around us with eagle eyes, warm hand still above my beating heart, as I catch my breath.

"Thank you." I hold his wrist and squeeze it in acknowledgment. Maybe he has some redeeming qualities.

Minutes after our near accident, he parks the car, and we go inside the restaurant I found somewhere in North London. The hostess seats us in the back, still half packed for this late hour. After a quick bathroom break, I place my order of noodle soup with tofu and Hector decides on beef brisket curry with veggies. With my hat back on and the diffuse light, I tilt my gaze to look at him.

He is on the phone, giving someone curt instructions and telling them we will be at the new safe house by midnight. When he sees me watching, we have a little staring contest while he listens to the person on the line. He also has the cap on, t-shirt only, sweater left in the car next to my jacket. His facial hair grew since last night when I first saw him. One corner of his mouth goes up a bit in the most discreet smile, I would miss it if I didn't focus, as if he wants to hide his amusement at our stubborn eye contact. Shaking my head at him, the sharp edges of my jaw-length hair graze my lips, and I wet them with my tongue. I don't normally hold someone's gaze for that long without talking. Who does, right? Especially when that someone is an intimidating, attractive man, but I don't want to look away first.

The food arrives to interrupt our game, and by the time he finishes his call, I moan at the taste of garlic. I love sweets, I adore them, but garlic, onions and jalapenos have a special place in my heart.

"When did they pick you up in Qatar? You never said. Did you find out who gave the kidnappers your location?" I break the silence. He scans the tables next to us discreetly, but nobody is paying attention.

"Two nights ago. I was in Doha for a business meeting with Severe Trust matters. Nothing related to my investigation of Fosters & Co. I am not sure why they brought me to London to interrogate me, but a few hours after they took me, they flew me here."

"Did they torture you?" I ask, but he did not seem injured.

"No. They interrogated me about the information I was stealing from Fosters & Co and who was helping me."

"Did you give them my RE number?" My irritation at being played is spiking against my ribs.

"Of course not, don't be ridiculous. I had your RE number because the informer wanted us to have it, presumably masking it as a mistake, not something they wanted to share. When the kidnappers saw I wasn't willing to talk, they drugged me and brought you in. The rest you know."

"No matter who the informer is, without a doubt, they meant to blame me for the data leak. And you said they first contacted you a few months ago, coincidently, when I moved to London." They didn't select me randomly. Who takes pleasure in destroying my life in such an irreversible manner, for no reason?

The relationships with my colleagues in the multiple Fosters & Co sites I worked throughout the years are pleasant, to say the least. I never stole someone else's promotion, and we kept the gossip to a minimal within a selected group of friendly co-workers. I had no amorous relationships in the office, apart from a short-lived fling that ended amicably when she changed companies and cities in Romania, ages ago. It was mainly physical attraction, my first experience with a woman, a fond memory I treasure knowing she couldn't be involved in this as she's married now with her lovely partner and living in New York.

My earlier discovery about the external consultants hasn't stopped festering my thoughts. Most often than not, Fosters & Co brings in one specific outside firm to deal with mergers of UK companies. One firm with the most competitive price to their excellent service in planning every phase of a transition and what that entails. And I'm more than associated with one of their employees. No, I don't believe they could be involved in this monstrous cover-up, but if future accusations to their names appear, fake claims like in my case, those could escalate to further kidnappings and I won't allow that.

"Can I see the discussions you had with the informer? Maybe I can recognise something."

"We can discuss this later at the house. Let's go." No dessert, then. He pays in cash, and with a hand between my shoulder blades, he leads me outside.

Silence reigns in the car and I do not mind it as I am cataloguing my past interactions with Fosters & Co employees. It's hard to believe a colleague with whom I worked daily would do this to me. It makes me too sad and sick to think about it. I forged lasting friendships from the beginning, folks like Astrid, Lina, Dorota and Youssef, who I will pester and count on when I'm grey and strolling with a cane. If I survive my current ordeal.

They would have my back in this horrid situation, especially Dorota, beating the evil out of anyone with her saviour complex. Today, as a new mother, she is fiercer. With their help, I could discover who is using my work ID in matter of hours because they are beyond resourceful. But how can I ask for assistance when it endangers their lives? And if I can't get them involved, does it mean I place all my hope in Worthington's trustworthiness? If he disappoints, I'll play detective independently, until I'm out of murky waters.

He drives for another hour to St Albans. We enter a forest-like area and finally stop next to an iron gate fit with security cameras, which opens when Hector presses a scanner display on a stone post. He continues on a driveway with trees on both sides until a subtly illuminated manor comes into view. Parking next to another car, we climb out as a fair-haired man in a dark suit waits for us at the house entrance. After a head nod sign towards Hector, he directs his gaze to me. A shiver goes down my spine at his intensity. Hostility might be a better word.

"So, this is RE313129, our little lying mole," he says in a hardened, nasal tone.

Did I fully understand the implications of choosing Hector Worthington as an ally before arriving at an unfamiliar location where I'm outnumbered, inadequate in surviving skills and terrified of tight spaces? Was it my decision at all?

Five

Seven Years Earlier - Bucharest, Romania

If I keep my eyes on the notebook, they won't call on me to answer. Why does it feel like I'm the most inexperienced person in the room? Four rooms, if I take into consideration the people from the three other locations connected by video conference. Day three of my one month training period at Fosters & Co and the impostor syndrome crams my space in the office chair I occupy.

After being accepted into the programme, I spent the two weeks before it started studying the materials shared by HR and devoured the information I could find online about the company and what my new role in procurement would entitle. I still feel unprepared when dealing with the corporate lingo, the systems we need to use, and the big personalities of my trainers and new colleagues.

Curious faces peer through the half-covered glass wall of our conference room whenever they pass on their way to the restroom. No matter my nervousness, I'm excited to work in such a modern building in the peripheral business area of Bucharest, even if it takes me a while to arrive in the morning. The open space desks were filled with a young to middle-aged crowd when we were introduced on Monday, everyone buzzing with energy, busy schedules, and a more capable than me attitude.

"Before lunch we decided to divide you in groups of five, from all sites, and spend the rest of the day going through the exercises in the manual. As I told you at the beginning, we'll have a short test at the end of the week to assess the materials we've studied so far, with the final test deciding in which department to place you when this month is over," the curvy redhead conducting the training today explains and then puts a laptop in front of me. "Vera will be the leader of group one and she'll have to present the results in the afternoon." So much for my strategy. My cheeks burn from being put on the spot. "Who wants to join her? We'll keep these groups until the end of your training." Nobody speaks for a charged minute and a different kind of embarrassment pushes to the surface of my skin. Because of the difference in time zones, we have a couple of classes with only our local members, but the rest of them include the broader audience, all taught in English.

"I do." A raised hand identifies Lina, the woman on the screen volunteering to end my suffering, her name tag underlined in red next to her as she smiles at the camera from Berlin.

"Count me in." Youssef from Tunis waves from his part of the world.

"Same here, if you'll have me," Dorota from Warsaw adds.

"Great team so far. We need another person from Bucharest, as we are the largest group. Astrid, what do you think?" the trainer asks the girl on my left, younger than me by a year, if I remember correctly the details she shared, but she definitely dropped the reluctant attitude of youth a long time ago.

"Can I be the leader of the next team? I score well as a manager."

"The leaders were already decided." And you are not amongst them, the Fosters & Co veteran seems to imply with her raised eyebrow. Why was I selected when this eager lady wants to rule us all?

"Then I guess it's fine." Her eyes roll halfway to the ceiling, but then she reconsiders and gives me a practised smile, mouth closed on tightly pressed lips. Oh goody, a rival.

A few hours later I am alone in a tiny huddle room discussing over video the merits of a PowerPoint presentation with Youssef and Lina. Dorota's laptop was about to die so she disconnected from the meeting to search for a charger, and Astrid left to grab a coffee thirty minutes ago and has yet to return. I spy her back leaning against a man's desk, confirming she already has some friends in the company, as she mentioned at lunch. We solved most our exercises and raced to create the best excel macros, bonding as a team and sharing bits of our outside life with each other.

"Did you know there will be an EMEA town-hall in Berlin in six months' time? Maybe you'll come and meet face to face. I'll show you around the city," Lina offers, pushing dyed dark hair from her eyes, the blonde eyebrows betraying her natural colour. She's been very engaging with all of us, kindly sharing her computer expertise and teaching us shortcuts for the systems used in the organisation.

"Do you think they'll bring us along since we are the newcomers?" Youssef scratches his beard. He wears a striped shirt over a lean body, if I correctly interpret his figure in the video.

"We won't be by then, and I've heard Fosters & Co spares no expense for these events." I debate if I should say more, talks about the mentioned town-hall are keeping the Bucharest office in a state of anticipation.

"Have you guys travelled outside your respective countries?"

"No." Youssef shakes his head. "Wait, I've been to Egypt when I was younger with my family, but nowhere else since then."

"Not yet for me, even though I was close to do it once in high school," I reply, thinking of flirty jokes and hours spent online, chatting away the night.

"What happened?"

"Nothing important. Teenage drama. You?" I change the subject before memories best left in the past resurface.

"I spent a few months with Erasmus in—"

The glass door opens with a bang and Astrid enters with two mugs, placing them on the table, then some candy bars from her pockets, pushing half of them towards me.

"Guess what they usually ask in the weekly tests?" She takes her seat next to me and nods her chin at our colleagues on the screen, Dorota appearing once again as well. My fingers do a fast job of the chocolate wrappers, as I give the petite woman a side glance and an amused expression.

From that day, our group of five develops a friendship beyond the long working hours and the shared projects we have in Fosters & Co. We see each other at company functions across Europe where we extend our stay to explore our own adventures with weekends of drinking, dancing and sometimes, love.

By the time I move to Poland, where Dorota works, followed by Youssef's move from Tunisia to the Polish capital, we are inseparable. Together we visit Lina in Berlin and vice versa until she moves to London, paving the way for my second relocation. Astrid remains in Bucharest, and after experiencing working for other companies, she returns to Fosters & Co. In her new role, she travels often to London and other European cities, joining me and Lina for dinner at least twice a month. We cheer and encourage individual successes, we praise, or fight, instigate and add to the group's drama, and even if life separates us occasionally, we return to each other.

Six

The darkened sky in St Albans, similar to the one I got accustomed to in Wimbledon, is several shades more intense than in Central London. The flickering stars on the busy canvas usually create a calm setting for a dreamless night, or a pleasant one at best. Tonight, their blinking alludes to caution.

"This was a mistake. I should leave." My reluctance is palpable, when normally I challenge myself to disarm people with an attitude, but did I come here to defend myself?

"Tonight, it's just us three, but in a few days, we'll have a team to support us with security and other needs. Get inside, please." Hector stops my retreating steps with a hand grabbing my wrist.

"Let go of me!" I pry his fingers from my skin, and he lifts his palms in an apologetic mode.

"We are miles away from public transport and it's the middle of the night. We have reports showing the men that took us combing the streets of London for both of us. They only need one camera to catch sight of you to be in their hands within the hour," he says, turning his phone towards me. A drone footage of Brompton Cemetery in daylight plays on the small screen.

The recording was taken from afar, but men in uniforms were visibly scouting the mausoleum area. Others in plain clothes are monitoring the alleys.

"It continues for a while, but let me show you how it ends, and where." He forwards the video to the last twenty seconds until a brick house from the seventies appears on view. There's a magnolia tree in front of the second-floor windows where a man walks into a room. My bedroom in Wimbledon. In my chest, the heart takes flight as my eyes try not to blink, so focused on what's happening inside my house that they miss a figure appearing from below with an arm extended, firing a silent bullet into the drone. End of transmission.

My feet are glued to the spot, and I don't move for what feels like forever. Dazed and unseeing, I only enter the house when Hector's fingers press on my lower back. In my peripheral view, he hugs the new guy, and they whisper among themselves, clearly happy to see each other, while my home is no longer the sanctuary it was before yesterday. The entry hall leads directly to an open living room area, decorated in a modern way, not the heavy wood style I was expecting, but I still feel out of place. No restroom in sight, and I am too tired to investigate without permission.

"Could you direct me to the bathroom, please? Perhaps we dive into your strategy regarding Fosters & Co afterwards. Let me review the files you obtained." I try to shake my mental fog away, hoping the documents won't show me the worst possible outcome. And if they do, I will assume responsibility for everything and take the truth to my grave.

"Miss Nicolescu, my name is Lawrence Neville. Welcome to The Hyde. While I appreciate your initiative spirit, you'll have to address my claims before we share any pertinent information with you. This way if you don't mind."

A nod is my reply, even though I have a few choice words for him and his claims. Everyone is tense and still reeling after yesterday's events, friction is normal. That doesn't mean I can't be civil, or so I tell myself in the marble lavatory. When I re-emerge minutes later, the two men watch over a tablet, tense discussion stopping at my presence. Demanding transparency after midnight is asking for trouble.

"Your bedroom is ready if you'll allow two urgent questions requiring your assistance," says Neville. "An action plan needs to be set in motion right away, and depending on your answers, we'll find out the precise direction to move forward." He has a more affected air than Hector, and I assumed that was impossible.

Walking towards a blue velvet sofa by the living room window, I change course when Neville indicates a different spot for our discussion. An office? Down a flight of stairs, we arrive in a grey, tight corridor. My shoulders tighten and clammy hands brush my sweatshirt-covered stomach. I turn around, expecting to see both of them. Something feels wrong.

"Where is Hector? Why . . ." Neville blocks the way and I struggle for appropriate words to convey my bewilderment.

"He will join us in a few minutes after he finishes the call with his mother. Lovely woman, have you met her?"

"Can't say I've had the pleasure."

"Lucky." Neville stops us in front of a black metal door, last in a row of three. He opens it with a palm scan and shows me inside. Once I step in, I curse my naïvety. I should have trusted my instincts.

"What is this? Why am I here?" I'm in a medium-sized interrogation chamber with two chairs, a big mirror on a wall. Probably a two-way glass device. The door closes behind Lawrence. Who has this kind of safe house?

"Hector, what is happening?" I direct my fury at the glass. Is he there? My voice betrays the rising panic. "You used that video to get me inside, to bloody interrogate me?"

"Take a sit, Vera. Let's not complicate things." The guy set to ruin my night is already lounging in a chair.

"You know what, you can call me Miss Nicolescu. And spare me. Let me out of here. I wanted to help, but I refuse this kind of treatment. It's unacceptable!" This can't be happening. "Does Hector know what you are doing?"

"Of course. I found an interesting piece of evidence while waiting for you to arrive at The Hyde. Upon relaying the information to Hector, we both agreed it is best if you and I talk. Alone."

"You don't say. Care to eliminate the suspense and share with the class your findings? Who are you, Hector's lackey?"

"Hardly. My father was the business associate they killed with Helena. Worthington is not the only interested party in the Fosters & Co investigation."

"Sorry for your loss, and I mean it, but that doesn't give you the right to lock me in this room and treat me like a criminal. What did you discover?" My posture stiffens at the timbre of my own words.

"Calm down, no hysterics necessary. We are just talking. If you cooperate, we'll be upstairs in no time."

"I'd prefer a battle of wits, but sadly, you appear unarmed." I'm this close to hitting him with one of my flip-flops, repeatedly, over his condescending mouth.

"Expressive vocabulary on you East Europeans." He shakes his head at me, smirking, and all I can do is grind my teeth. He wants to push my buttons.

"I'm letting that slide, on account of your grief, but if you don't get to the point soon, I'll not be responsible for my actions."

"Very well. The informer used a Polish bank account to receive money from us. The account is connected to you. A previous investigation revealed they associated the setup to a company in Warsaw. Company that appears to be in your name. Not only that, but someone also transferred money from the Polish account to one in Romania, linked to your relatives."

"That's ridiculous! If you are not lying, not trying to make me admit something I did not do, even if everything leads so obviously to me, it doesn't mean I committed the crime! For crying out loud, a bloody imposter is setting me up and you are buying into it! Didn't Hector tell you?"

"We might have considered the use of your employee number a trick to disguise his or her identity, but the money trail usually shows the incriminating party. And the money ends with you."

"I wouldn't be that stupid! To set up a Polish account. To incriminate myself like that. Aren't there a decent number of banks in the Caribbean to pick from?"

"I don't know, Miss Nicolescu. Maybe you didn't think you would get caught. You certainly don't seem the type to predict the consequences of your actions. I am truly surprised you accepted to come with Hector here, in my house, or anywhere. What did you expect? That we would take your word for it and keep you safe after all signs implicate you?" The nasal quality of his voice flattens my lips together. Is he calling me stupid, on top of everything? I turn around and launch for the mirror, hitting it with my fists.

"I thought I could trust you, that we could help each other!" I address the jerk I helped carry from a coffin. He's watching, no doubt. I honestly believed someone who witnessed the horrific panic I woke up to in that box wouldn't treat me like this. That he would have more compassion.

"There is no need for dramatics. You will find it in your best interest to confess. To give us the rest of the classified information you have on Fosters & Co. How were you stealing from your company? What exactly did you do to give yourself away? Because of your incompetence, the only person I have to call family nearly died."

"Neville, pretty please, listen to me! I did *not* do it!" I stand next to him, invading his space. I do not care that he is bigger than me. Or that he called me incompetent. I am beyond insults.

"How did you discover we were investigating Fosters & Co to begin with?" He rears back, remaining calm and seated, like this is a counselling session.

"They set me up. I have no clue how that blasted company has my name and why they transferred money to my family." How can I convince them it's not me? "For argument's sake, who received the payment, which member of my family?" I walk in circles around the room. The breathing techniques are not working their magic. All my fatigue evaporates, and I want to smash things.

"Your grandmother, Greta Nicolescu, received the equivalent of tens of thousands of pounds."

"Well, I wouldn't hold my breath for a thank you note from her. Since she's been dead for almost two years! Can a dead person have a bank account?" I sigh heavily, hands in my hair. "This is a setup, Neville. And a poorly executed one. Don't you see?" I turn again to the mirror and address it. "I thought you possessed a working brain and decency, but money can't perform miracles, can they?" Is he there? How can he allow this?

Hours of continued questioning conducted by Neville follow at a slow pace. Hector, the dear bastard, remains out of sight, conveniently, because I would claw his eyes out. My palms twitch badly to slap my interrogator after he makes other insulting comments. But I keep my cool, some of it, and refrain from physical confrontation.

They are holding me against my will, so violent actions aren't totally uncalled for, but where would that lead me? If a man becomes aggressive, it's his right to defend his honour, if a woman reacts identically, she is unreasonable. He would block my attack, as he is stronger than me. Probably as tall as Hector, with dark blonde short hair, pasty complexion. Not unhandsome, but very unlikeable. Him and his typical pinkie ring, the poster figure for snobbery. I know I'm judging, but give me a break.

I have nothing to tell them. My past is clean, or decent enough after living for thirty years. My present is a loop of madness, but I'm fighting for my future, knowing I'm not the mole. And Neville mentioned nothing about the consultants either, and now would be the perfect time to use that kind of manipulation.

To annoy him, I summarise the story of the best high fantasy book I read years ago, my obsession as a teen, from which I still remember all the major scenes. He just stares at me, not taken with the change of subject and my storytelling skills.

I scream at him, at the walls, until I lose my voice. I plead, I insult, I use reason. Nothing helps. What I don't do is cry.

At one point, right when I want to stop speaking altogether, he stands and leaves the room, locking it. Probably to consult with the other jailer. Minutes later, the light in the small space increases in brightness and suddenly I am in a tanning booth. So predictable that I look towards the two-way glass.

"If I knew soup would be my last meal, I would have poured it on your head, you deceitful asshole." My pulse tries to regulate itself, but fear, disappointment, and rage win.

Nobody comes for me in long, anxious minutes. No energy left in my body to scream anymore. I remove the flip-flops and sit on them in the corner next to the mirror to hide from prying eyes. They probably have a camera somewhere too. The light is maddening, but I am so tired, I shut down. They want to isolate me until I break. A freaking glass of water is all it takes to crack if guilty, because I'm a terrible spy, but being the oblivious victim comes with no advantages.

Thinking they could resort to different techniques to force my cooperation is daunting. Even though they are businessmen, supposedly not hardened felons, are they willing to sink lower and torture me further? Look where I am, I should not underestimate them. Or trust Hector's treacherous words ever again.

Would I use similar methods if the roles were reversed? Probably not. But maybe it's a mistake to hesitate between empathy and ruthlessness when your life is at risk. I can't believe I'm in this situation, and so soon after the coffin. I'm completely alone in this mess, and it scares me. We weren't the best of friends, but it stings that Hector agreed to such treatment.

Laying down, I turn to face the wall, pull my feet inside the sweatpants, and with my eyes closed I try to clear my mind with meditation. A long while later, sleep invades my awareness, but not before noticing the lights dim considerably.

My entire body shivers on the cold concrete floor, and my bladder is full, despite waking up incredibly thirsty. I stand and address the mirror, hoping one of my wardens is awake.

"Can I use the toilet? I don't think we want to embarrass ourselves with me eliminating waste all over your lovely interrogation room." Nothing. "Hello?" My voice sounds like I swallowed a bucket of nails as I knock on the glass.

The door cracks open and Hector's frame appears, bed hair and tired eyes. Poor him, did I disturb his sleep? We stare in silence for a tense moment.

I hate the sight of him.

"I am not selling corporate information, to anyone. I do not know how to prove it or to tell you why they used me, my name, and details. You are wasting your time. Is that clear?" When he says nothing, I push on. "Now, I'll use my bathroom privileges, then I am free to leave this basement, this house, and your hospitality altogether. Any objections?"

"Where would you go? Do you have more options to choose from than you had yesterday morning?" he says from his spot next to the door. Voice deep and rough, he didn't shave since his kidnapping. Wearing sleep shorts and a t-shirt, all black, like his soul.

"Removing myself from your presence is my first step. The others are for me to know and none of your business."

"I never intended to . . . Lawrence has my support, but he—"

"Spare me the explanation, and the good cop, bad cop routine. Locking me up all night did us no good. But it convinced me to proceed with caution, relying on my own strength. I did not put myself in this shitstorm, but I will manage it, no help needed."

"You don't have money. They are looking for you. You cannot blame me, or Lawrence, for not trusting you with all the incriminating evidence we uncovered."

"Don't worry about me. As for blame, I view you with indifference bordering on disgust." I don't need to listen to further nonsense. He seemed like a reasonable person before, condescending but logical. Had valid points regarding our situation and future steps, but we are not a team. He gave the other jackass free rein, and God knows what they have planned next. If yesterday I thought working closely as partners was my only choice to avoid capture or murder, the cold floor I slept on and the bolt on the door showed me I'm better off alone.

Moving towards the door, he barely steps back for me to exit. Using last night's route, I arrive in the living room as Neville descends from upstairs. Morning sunshine is visible through the windows, and it surprises me somehow that the natural order of things is progressing as usual when I'm stuck in this nightmare.

"Allow me to ask a few more questions before we release her." He addresses Hector, who stands behind me, like my opinion doesn't matter.

"Why, do you want to hear another book synopsis?" I turn to have them both in front of me. "I want to leave." While my body requires warmth, if I am to face the cold wearing flip-flops, I can't spend another minute here.

"Let me show you upstairs to the guest room. You can take a shower and change into warm clothes."

"I rather not."

"Vera, please." Hector's tone says this is not up for debate. They can keep me here no matter if I use the bathroom or not. He waves his hand to take the lead, but I'm not falling for dirty tricks twice, like turning my back in their presence. We stare at each other before he shows me the way to a pastel-coloured bedroom.

"New clothes in the wardrobe and other accessories. Breakfast in the kitchen downstairs when you are ready." He retreats, leaving the door open.

Closing it and turning the lock once, I skip to the bathroom before it's too late. Checking on the barred windows, the realisation that the front door is the only way out of the house comes as no surprise. I drink a small bottle of water and crawl onto the king-size bed, needing a minute to process my situation. One minute transforms into ten of staring at the ceiling. No helpful ideas materialise from tin air, no genius plan on where to travel, how to survive.

I move to the shower, bigger than the one at the first safe house and more luxurious, and while I wash my hair and body with quality feminine products, I decide what to do. On one hand, I can't jeopardise the safety of my friends, from or outside work. That did not change. And I'm hesitant about who to trust at the office apart from my friends, half of them still in Poland. It seems impossible someone from the new London group I eat lunch with daily would be the mastermind behind the informer. But what if, right? Contact my family? Out of the question. The authorities? Trust that the justice system will help me? I prefer to keep that as a last resort. Very last resort.

A fair assumption would be that all my associates are under surveillance. And with social media, a normal hacker could figure out how to check my private accounts, my conversations, and interactions. Going to ask for help from strangers is just crazy.

Or maybe my options are not that limited. A dignified face jumps to the front of the line, crowded with half processed ideas. This could work if I ever depart the Creep Manor.

My pride screams to take nothing from the downstairs duo, but after finishing the shower, I search for clean clothes, because I can't walk the streets naked or in the dusty, sweaty outfit I had on before my bath. Opening the wardrobe, I find several new items for women. They prepared this room for me before the interrogation treatment switched their plans. Perhaps they intended to lock me up all along and present this offer when I snapped under their questioning. To show me how grateful I should be to have them in my corner.

A set of matching underwear later, black high waisted jeans, a skin-tight white t-shirt that I tuck into my new pants and over it a black wool cardigan, I return to the bathroom wearing Chelsea boots and dry my short locks. The reflection in the mirror shows a tired face, dark circles under green eyes. Nose bigger than I would have liked, a family heirloom. Lips quivering, the bottom one curvier than the one on top.

Don't cry, don't cry. Stay focused. Pick an emotion and stick with it.

I fill the sack backpack the boots came in with a few clothing items, since they bought them for me. I have nothing and I need clothes no matter where I choose to go. Scanning the room, I grab a coat, the backpack, and go downstairs. I'll skip breakfast and just leave.

My plan derails when I find Hector in the living room, wearing his version of black jeans and sweater. Again, with the long, glowering minutes.

"You are really leaving. I wish you would reconsider. There is no limit to what they'll do to you if caught."

"How would you know?"

"Was the coffin not convincing enough?"

"What, are you afraid I'll tell them where to find you?" I tap my forehead with conviction. "My brain will find ways to stay alive and hidden. I'll solve this mess without apprehension." Or at least I can try. I move for the front door, but he blocks me.

"Please have some breakfast and while you eat, I will tell you ways to contact me if you get in trouble and need help. I won't stay at The Hyde forever. No harm in having backup, even if that backup is me." He doesn't move, so I guess they include a meal with the room rate.

"Where's the kitchen?" He walks in the opposite direction from the basement, and I follow him.

Lawrence is sitting at a sturdy wood table. The room has a vintage countryside vibe combined with new appliances. Brick, wood, metal, and large windows. French doors that lead to a rose garden. I take a seat as far away as possible from the blonde man watching his tablet intensely while sipping a hot drink.

"Earl Grey, right?" Hector puts a cup in front of me, a little milk jar next to it, and a small plate with sugar cubes.

"Yes. Thank you. Milk, no sugar." Not removing my coat and backpack, I grab a piece of toast and spread crushed avocado on it, a poached egg, a pinch of sea salt.

"Why are you leaving us, Miss Nicolescu? Not a wise decision if you ask me."

"Nobody asked you, Pinkie," I say with my mouth half full, inhaling the toast, not eating it. I'm so hungry.

"Let me guess, you are the type to hold a grudge after a little confrontation. A misunderstanding. But the name-calling is a surprise."

"I wouldn't call it a misunderstanding when it breaks the rules of the Geneva Convention."

"That's applicable during war."

"Aren't we in one?" I finish my tea. "Can I have a copy of the files the mole sold you? Or a glance at them."

"That's laughable," Larry says, giving me his snidest glare.

"Neville, please behave," Hector intervenes. "We owe Vera an apology. Last evening was unpleasant, but unavoidable."

"It's not like you believe me now. Not completely." I lock eyes with both of them. Silence on all fronts. "That's what I thought. Well, this was lovely. Let's do it again. I'll call you." A quick scratching noise comes from my chair when I stand and Hector hands me a paper card with an HW scribbled on it. "I won't need it," I say shaking my head.

"Please. It's a number to an automatic conference call assistant that my company uses. Memorise it now, the card stays here. Upon calling, the robot aide will ask questions only you know the answers to."

"And you. Why not just give me your phone number?"

"Yes, and me. Because I will change my phones regularly. The conference system will pinpoint your location, no matter from where you are calling. I will find you if needed." The intent in his pale blue eyes and the grim set of his mouth, coupled with a rushed hand passed through his long hair, confuse me. I repeat the numbers a few times in my head.

"Okay, got it." He takes the paper back as Lawrence ignores us, working on his screen again.

"Let me walk you out." We leave the kitchen and head towards the entryway in silence. "Here. This is something you'll need." He presents me with an open envelope with cash, and for a second, I disassociate as I look at the money, then my bloodshot eyes lift to his blue gaze. I already took the clothes, ate his food.

"So, you can ease your conscience? How did you calculate how much to give me? No, thank you. Suffer in silence whenever you remember what a shitty human being you are."

"You accepting this money for shelter won't make *me* less of one." He leans over and shoves the envelope inside my coat's pocket. "Throw it away or donate it. I am sorry things worked out this way. Truly. Good luck." If I didn't know better, I would say he means it.

This is it; I'm really leaving. Without knowing what the files from the informer look like, what they present on the people that killed Helena and her associate. I'll obtain them somehow. Nervousness and disbelief obstruct my throat when I try to swallow. Exhaling slowly, I prepare myself for the challenges ahead.

Will I ever see Hector Worthington again? And do I want to?

When he opens the door for my first steps into the cold, we hear Lawrence shout our names from the back of the house. At the property gate, the one we passed last night, the screech of tires announces the arrival of several cars that smash into the iron bars, trying to force their way in. A police car and others. Hector drags me inside and slams the door.

The expectation today will turn out differently crashes down on me like a spring heavy rain.

They've found us.

Seven

Three Years Earlier - Bucharest, Romania

The bottoms of my flat sandals will soon attach themselves to the hot, melting asphalt but I'm pushing my luck, continuing with our walking visit until Astrid, without fail, will protest for a third time to demand a break. She's sweating heavily, and she's not the only one. I pass her my paper fan, but she returns the cheap item in seconds with an eye-roll. Slightly shorter than me, with long black hair and brown eyes, her high ponytail sticks to the fair skin of her neck. Her delicate nose wrinkles with displeasure, moisture glistering the tip.

I'm visiting my family for a couple of weeks, before returning to Warsaw to lead an important project at work. My schedule looks hectic in the upcoming months, as we prepare for the busy third quarter, and I'm glad I flew to Bucharest to enjoy this overwhelming weather. Lina joined us for the weekend from London, her brand-new home since she left Berlin. We are showing her the worthy sights of our capital, but between us and the giant burning sun, there's a little misunderstanding regarding the essential and what can be scrapped from the tour. Thank God we are all wearing airy dresses.

"Please, push me into the river or give me a cocktail. Let's even pick another air-conditioned museum." What did I say? But she's right, we can't face the heat anymore. We did the gargantuan Palace of the

Parliament, the Old Town, the Romanian Athenaeum, Cismigiu Park, and the National Museum of Art. Strolling along the Dambovita river, the afternoon temperatures are not relenting.

"I second that with all my heart." Lina pushes her sunglasses on the top of her head to wipe her face with a napkin. She's taller than us, and as always, we use her height to block the punishing disk in the sky. And because she's amazing, she lets us with a grin, a headshake, and a cheesy blue-eyed wink. We have a similar hairstyle, but where my hair is dark, Lina has the most incredible natural light blonde hair. She dyed it a few times since I met her, but she brought back her original shade. Who knows what she'll do next?

"Can you wait for the beer garden behind those buildings? It has great shade with outside fans and indoor seating." My dry lips blow a soft breeze between my chest and the sticky dress. I let go of the material and grab their wrists to drag them after me.

"Mercy! Your coldest gin and tonic for the table, and I'll pay you a fortune!" Astrid shouts in Romanian once we enter the safety of the establishment I selected.

"And enough water to bathe myself in," Lina says in English. Funny enough, while Lina is from Germany, one of her grandmothers was Romanian, so she understands the basics.

"I'll be over there, writing my obituary." I point towards the free table in the corner.

The service moves fast, our tips will reward its efficiency, and we soon recover in our seats, chewing ice cubes from our respective glasses.

"How's Tomasz?" Lina asks about my Polish boyfriend. She knows we had a disagreement about summer plans before I left Warsaw.

"He's okay, visiting his parents in Lodz. He filled my phone with pictures of books from their library and the flowers his mother planted in the back garden."

"Boring," Astrid comments.

"Hey! That's my lover you are talking about." I didn't share the same details with her.

"You know what I mean. Does he deserve the 'lover' moniker?"

"Of course. I don't keep him for conversation alone. Even though we can talk for hours."

"But does he make your blood boil with passion? That's what you want, don't lie to me," Astrid insists.

"Who has time for that?" Lina says with a snort, and I high five her. "Men twisting your passion around are not good long term. You want stability. Passion is for summer flings that should end when you send them out of your bed the next day. Don't linger. Break it off, shake hands, walk away. Just like the doctor ordered." Lina finishes her speech, and we slap the table, laughing. We know she's joking in part, but she follows this philosophy more often than not. I've never seen her broken-hearted even after ending commitments with men she fancied more than she let on. And it's surprising because she puts so much dedication into her friendships. With guys, she prefers the uncomplicated.

"Brutal, Haas. I respect your vibe; however, long relationships also need spice. And everything nice. Vera's fella is a sensible guy, sure, but he lacks the trill and the challenge she needs to be happy for more than a semester." Astrid's hands fly below her face as she gesticulates her point. She calls Lina by her family name when they disagree.

"Shall we talk about other lacking relationships and leave mine alone?" I sip my drink and wave the server over to bring the food menu. I'm buying my ladies dinner and dessert for putting up with the itinerary I chose.

"So, you admit you are missing excitement?" our sudden passion crusader says, victorious.

"You are not completely misguided but I'm content now."

"Content. Wow, settle down, lady, or you'll burst at the seams."

"Before she does that, can we congratulate her on the award she received at work?" Lina shifts the conversation in a different direction, and I'm grateful for her fast thinking.

"Well, well! Congrats, Nicolescu! Financial award or the standard recognition of a pat on the back?" She clinks our glasses together and asks for a high five.

"Both. A bonus and a framed paper diploma signed by Bodmer himself all the way from Switzerland."

"He's the only guy not pushing one-hundred-years-old in the leadership team, right? Since you're mingling with board members, you can buy us a round." Astrid suggests, and both women cheer.

"I'm sure they don't know I exist, but we'll drink in their name."

Eight

"Fuck."

Eloquently put.

"It's them? The kidnappers?"

"Yes! Let's go this way. Quick!" Hector takes my arm and runs for the kitchen, half dragging me out of my daze. Lawrence is opening a hidden safe next to the fridge and grabs a set of keys and a little bag. Hector is already shoving a door to a stairway going down, and we run. My heart is pumping faster, and my hands are trembling on the railing, but my feet are steady, thank God. I hear them both behind me. In the basement, Lawrence opens the door furthest from the interrogation room. Inside, lights flash in and out for a few seconds, illuminating two vehicles. A sleek sports car with two seats and an SUV type. The men go for the smaller one.

"Why aren't we taking the bigger car?" I ask.

"This one is armoured and faster. Get in the boot to look like I'm driving alone," Lawrence proposes, and Hector is fast to accept. He opens the boot and tries to push me in, but I cannot move, I just stare at the cramped space. My brain would not give my body the command to get inside. It resembles the coffin I woke up in West Brompton, same suffocating aura.

"Vera, we are losing time. Get in." I hear him like I'm in a tunnel. When he sees that I'm not moving, he turns to me, hands on my shoulders, and looks at my terrified face. "Hey, hey, hey. Look at me. I'm coming with you. You will not be alone in there. Lawrence will open the door once we are somewhere safe." At the mention of that name, my eyes go big. "He will open the door, Vera. He is my friend; I have complete trust in him. I know you have no reasons to believe me, but I promise you, I want to get us to safety and then you are free to do whatever you want." He shakes me a bit, and I nod.

"Okay, yes, okay. Go in first." I'm shocked, not stupid. He looks at me, climbs in, helps me after and drags the door close. With the next breath, the car drives away. The space is indeed small. I have my back to him, and he is so close, we are embracing. Lawrence takes us outside in seconds and drives like a maniac. I feel the slight and then the big trepidations of a gravel road.

"The property has another gate?"

"An exit road crossing the forest, not marked on maps, bringing us faster to London."

"That's where we are going? To another safe house? Just as safe? How did they find us?"

"I don't know." His coffee and mint breath on my neck sends shivers over the sensitive skin.

"You said that he is your friend, but what if Neville sold you out? Was he aware of your location in Doha?"

"He was. Lawrence is my oldest friend, he is not working with Fosters & Co. He wants to bury them as much as I do, if not more."

"Why? You both lost important people the day your sister and his father died."

He doesn't reply with words first, and I interpret the sounds he makes as crammed with indecision at how much to share.

"Because he feels responsible for it. He was the one convincing them, Helena, and Neville senior, to sell the company to Fosters & Co. He will regret that for the rest of his life." After a few moments of silence, he says, "Keep that to yourself. I just told you so you can relax around him. He is not a bad guy."

"Debatable." I get it, but we won't be friends anytime soon. "Do you think they are chasing us?" The road noise is so loud I cannot distinguish anything. We are in a race car, or that's how Lawrence is treating it. He doesn't want to get caught, so I guess that's one point in his favour.

"I can hear another close by. Probably the rest are still catching up, but he will lose them, don't worry." My entire body is tense, adrenaline bumping in my veins.

"It seemed too simple, thinking back. We escaped the cemetery without issues. Walked to Nevern Square with no interference. Why?"

"They trusted the seal of the coffin. They were morons, and we got lucky."

"What if their aim was capturing Neville? Were they after him as well?"

"Most likely. We are both investigating Fosters & Co, but not publicly. We shouldn't have been on their radar. The informer switched and sold our location, or that was the intention all along, provoking and eliminating us."

"This is madness. I'm not the informer, believe me."

"So you say," comes his reply at the back of my neck. I try to turn to look at him, even though it's dark inside the boot, but the car makes an abrupt turn that has me screaming. Then three shots, one after the other, pierce the gravel noise.

"Oh God, they are shooting at us!" A storm brews in my stomach. Gagging shakes my form, and I cover my mouth with a clammy palm.

"What's the matter? Are you sick?"

"Yes." An *awful* time to have motion sickness kick in.

"Don't move, I'm going to hug you, okay? Put my arms around you." He turns, enveloping me in an effective and protective clasp, bringing me closer to him. "Breathe, in and out. In and out. Slowly." In doing what he says, the vortex slows its spinning. My head is dizzy, but the embrace grounds me. "Let me know if you want me to release you."

"Hmm."

"I think we lost them." He takes his arm from around me, the one I'm ashamed to say I was cradling, and finds his phone. "Good driving, mate. Where are we? Yes, we are coping. Vera is a bit shaken up. Let me put you on speakerphone."

"I apologise for my driving, Miss Nicolescu." His cheery tone contradicts the remark.

"That's okay. I only puked once," I lie. "Are we safe?"

"Yes. Man, that was a fun ride. We had three cars on our tail at one point and one got pretty close. The arseholes tried to take us down with massive guns but failed."

"Your friend is enjoying this too much." I say to Hector upon hearing the laugh in Neville's reply.

"I lost them a while back. We should change cars anyway and find alternative means to arrive at the next house. I will pull over in half hour somewhere quiet."

"Thanks, Neville. See you soon."

The phone conversation ends, and Hector returns the device to his front pocket as his hand brushes against my round behind. I should put some distance between us, not that we have the space. But I don't. The cuddling is affecting me, I must be mental, or dizzier than I thought. An hour ago, I hated him for his betrayal and called him names.

"Motions sickness and bullets mix well together. Still a step lower than waking up in a coffin," I remark, and he laughs in the dark, the exhale caressing my hair.

"Are you still nauseous?"

"Rather not say."

"My sister got violently ill a handful of times when we drove with our grandparents in the Swiss mountains as kids. She was turning a shade of green, my teen brain associated with frogs. My grandmother massaged her wrists like this. May I?" He places his fingers on the inside of my left wrist at my confirmation nod, starting under the crease and applying pressure for long seconds.

"Were you sick too?"

"No. I was singing with my grandfather to distract her attention."

"Did that work?"

"The acupressure did." He switches wrists and my stomach calms. A relieved sigh blows past my dry lips. While his fingers work their magic, melting my entire body, his other arm shifts, pulling me closer.

Closer yet, at my shiver and moan. He exhales in my hair.

"I'm sorry it's so cold. We'll be out soon." The embrace changes, like it's his job to keep me warm. The sudden shift of energy between us should put me on guard. I ought to remember last night, not melt at his attentive tone and protective attitude. Am I so starved of touch that I would take comfort from Hector Worthington? When I said I was sick, I wasn't expecting him to do something about it. The independent streak I've built over the years, the one encouraging me to explore living in different countries, fixing my own problems, relying on internal strength to see me through highs and lows, warms at the alien feeling of support. Different from the one offered by friends and family.

Unconsciously, I arch my back into him when I feel his hard presence behind me, his breath on my skin, one arm under my neck and one around under my breasts. Legs entwined. His hand moves to my belly. In an immediate reaction, my body pushes into him once more. *What the hell, Vera?* His heat surrounds me, even with my coat on. Perhaps the chill is forcing me to behave so out of character.

"Do you feel better?" Does he have to whisper in my ear? I feel something and I curse myself for it. God, this escalated quickly!

"Yeah," I whisper back. The fine hair on my neck is all up. The hand on my belly moves to my front and then retreats to my hip. Gripping it. Stroking my ribs.

My coat is open, so the only thing separating my skin from his hand is the delicate t-shirt. Am I imagining things? I'm usually bad at reading signals from men and women, if they are not 'in your face' obvious. Hector, if I have to guess, is part of the category of men usually attracted to gorgeous, posh women. Like his ex, the blonde legal professional. I'm not as perfect, yet I don't consider myself plain or uninteresting, just on the normal side of the spectrum. But my ass definitely feels his interest poking. Maybe adrenaline and the tight space we occupy are to blame for our confusing embrace.

"You are coming with us to the new safe house. Before the morning scare, I wanted you to be on your own for a period. That's not possible anymore when we barely escaped, with cameras on the property and a fast car at our disposal. Imagine what would have happened if you were alone."

And just like that, he pours freezing water on my overheated self. The bastard is using my body's reaction to his closeness to lure me into staying with them. To trust him again. I refrain from reacting with a gag and a shove, even though I'm brushing my pride from the dirt slap she just took.

'Hmm' is the only sound I offer, buttoning my coat up and removing his hand from me. Miraculously, some space exists at the front, my body shivers, now that we are not touching anymore, not as completely as before. *Subtle, Vera. Say something.*

"Where do you think we are? Where in London is the new place?" My voice still holds some arousal, or so I imagine. I'll break my own fingers before trapping myself in his disillusioned cage. He doesn't reply right away, clears his throat first.

"Hampstead Heath. That's where we are going. Lawrence will probably stop next to an underground station so we can get there using public transportation. Make sure nobody is following us." Okay, I can work with that. I need to evaluate next steps, not how I was rubbing against him like he didn't keep me confined last night.

"I understand." My breathing exercises are useless when I know I won't be comfortable in tight, dark places ever again, especially in a fume polluted car.

"Vera, I want you to know that I will help you no matter what, if you are honest with me. We can find solutions if we show our cards openly and work together. My goal was to bring justice to my sister's memory. Add survival to the list now, and permanent damage to Fosters & Co. My problem is not with the informer; they did what they considered appropriate, and it's not in my interest to pursue them for retribution if they switched on me. Fosters & Co is the fish I want to gut, and that's where I focus all my power, energy, and anger. But I cannot help them much if they continue to work against me and Lawrence. They might end up being collateral damage." That's a nicely disguised threat if I ever heard one.

"I'm tired of this repetition, so do what you must, and I will follow my path. Can you please remove your hand from my ass now?" It was not on my ass per se, more on my hip again, trying to move me to face him, caressing me. I do not wait for him to act; I do it myself. Enough with the touching.

"Sorry. And I hope you know what you are doing." You and me both, I think to myself. The car stops for more than traffic, and Lawrence opens the boot with a big smile.

"Time to rise and shine, my love birds. You can continue your canoodling tonight." As if to show he sees my cheeks redden at his remark, Lawrence's smile transforms into a wolfish grin. I should puke on his shoes, but alas, my stomach has a mind of its own. Refusing his offered hand, and mumbling for him to move, I retrieve my backpack once Hector climbs out. Avoiding his eyes, I take in our surroundings, a hidden street peppered with blooming trees, a few cars, no people.

"Willesden Green Station is relatively close to Hampstead, but I suggest the Jubilee line to Waterloo Station. We transfer to the Northern Line and return. Then we rent a room, or several" – he smirks again – "at the Fenton House, closer to the park and wait for night's coverage to reach the safe house. I gather you are coming with us now, Miss Nicolescu."

"No."

"Yes, she does."

"I don't want to; I can tell you that. Do I have a choice?" I ask, making eye contact with them both, lingering on Hector. Red cheeks no more, I hope.

"None," Lawrence announces at the same time that Hector answers with, "No. It's for your own good."

"Imagine how many questions I have now, Miss Nicolescu. We can make things extremely uncomfortable if you don't follow us."

"Great."

"Threats are unnecessary, Neville. She knows we are on the same team and her best chance at survival." We'll see about that, but before my legs follow my mind's command to run, he takes my arm.

Flanked by Lawrence on my left and Hector on my right, we walk to the underground station. They had jackets in the car, and I am grateful for my coat, as the wind is in big shape today. No cover for my hair, it whips furiously at my eyes. Hector wears his in a low bun, and when he gives me a quizzical glance, one eyebrow raised, I look ahead, hands in my pockets.

At the station, Lawrence offers Oyster cards from his man purse. He plies the card from my hand once we take our seats. Zero level of trust. I don't foresee my relationship with them changing in this matter. The metro car fills in after every station and I watch people move around us while the men discuss quietly over me the merits of a potential relocation of their covert operation to Scotland.

Three ladies occupy the seats across, heavy makeup, clothes far too revealing for the cold March we've been having, but more power to them. They are loud and having fun, alcohol induced fun. Their jokes are crude but have a waking up effect on me. I snort and bite my lips to avoid joining in on the laughs.

My companions direct their attention to them, long enough for a head-to-toe glance, before resuming their discussion above my head. The ladies notice the looks and one by one, they act in discreet ways, or so they think, to win the men's attention.

I don't particularly like Hector and Neville, because I know their shining personalities, but they are attractive men. Add the expensive clothes and watches, they look like a good catch. On the outside. I'm surprised, yet indifferent, the women seem to overlook me sitting between them. For all they know, one of them could be my boyfriend, we sit that close. When the guys ignore them, the ladies turn jealous and angry gazes at me. So, they see me! Have at them girls, they *really* are charming; I try to communicate with amused eyes.

At Bond Street Station, many people descend and the seats next to Lawrence and Hector become available. Not for long. In a remarkable move, two ladies snatch them. I would never have the courage. The bold ladies, one blonde, one brunette, also laugh at the one that missed her chance to obtain a seat. Another brunette.

"You snooze you lose," they tell her.

"Indeed," I say. More laughs. The guys stop their discussion and throw them and me irritated looks.

"You don't mind, right, love?" the blonde close to Hector asks as she leans in. She doesn't really care for my answer, already licking her lips, gaze fixed on him, but I still tell her cheerfully, my hands in surrender mode.

"Not at all, by all means." I nod towards him.

At the next station, Westminster, when the train is ready to close its doors and continue the journey, I take advantage of the men turning to the dynamic duet, probably to tell them something patronising like they don't engage in conversation with people they meet on the tube, I run for the door.

Heart beating like a hummingbird's wings, I make it in the very last second. I turn to peek at the already moving train. Lawrence looks pissed, still in his seat, showing me the cash envelope that dropped from my pocket. Hector stands close to the door I just used, face determined, maybe a bit disappointed, most likely thinking I really am the Fosters & Co snitch. Screw you, buddy.

I smirk and wave. And show him the finger.

Nine

The chances of Hector Albert Worthington and Lawrence Neville coming after me, their presumed informer, are ones I don't want to bet against. Dashing on the automatic stairs at the Westminster Station to reach the outside touristic crowd usually found in this area, I keep my cool in front of the exit gates. Searching for a TfL employee to beg for mercy, I approach a young woman, shorter, with a good-natured face. Her tag name says Mahira, and while dishonesty makes me queasy, my life is not my own anymore, and until I steal it back, I need to get used to manipulating facts to my advantage.

"Hi."

"Hello, madam."

"Sorry to bother you. Could you help me? I got on at Canary Wharf and, I don't know how, but I lost my monthly pass. I just renewed it a few days ago. What should I do?" What I say is true, I lost my actual card, stolen by my kidnappers. Recently paid. With the corner of my eye, I spy a tall guy approaching and my heart jumps in my ribcage before realising he's a regular commuter.

"Did you register the card when you bought it?" She brings my attention back to her.

"Yes."

"You need to call this number and get it cancelled. I can help you out of the gates." Ding! Ding! Ding! She hands me a flyer and uses her pass to open the slide doors. I thank her and run for the last stairs, bumping into several travellers.

The city equipped the centre stations with multiple exists and I choose the one leading me to my planned destination. A crazy idea formed while I was showering, thinking I was leaving The Hyde by myself. There might be someone that could help me, someone nobody is aware I met my first month in London, when I went to one of my favourite spots in the city. Room 43, Beyond Impressionism: Seurat, Gauguin, Van Gogh at the National Gallery.

As usual, idling crowds on the sidewalks, taking pictures of the Big Ben, the London Eye, and the other attractions of the City of Westminster. I turn left on Victoria Embankment, parallel with the Thames, another left for Whitehall, the road leading to the Gallery. London is a trill.

I love visiting museums no matter the collections they present because I get to admire thousands of years old artefacts, unique objects, where an artist focused all their attention to recreate a piece of themselves for others to see, and judge. The duality of vulnerability and strength one can experience in a museum inspires me, so it is a known fact among my family, friends, and social media that I go to museums. When I had time in the last months, I visited plenty of exhibition halls and art galleries, if someone is looking for me, they might watch the places I frequented recently. But I am not actually visiting the Gallery, the person I wish to meet, crossing my fingers for the slim chance, should be sipping tea in the Waterstones across the street from Trafalgar Square. Their weekly ritual is to explore the National Gallery and after spending a few hours in the presence of greatness, their words when we first met, they drink tea and buy a good book at the Grand Building store, sometimes moving to Bronte restaurant next door. I joined them there a few times for a snack. I hope this is one of those days.

When was I taken?

I stop in the middle of the sidewalk until someone pushes me aside, next to a newsstand. The papers declare it's Wednesday, March 15th. Was it just Monday when my life spun upside-down? It feels that it happened ages ago. What are people at work thinking? One of them should feel very guilty about my absence. Did my manager call my brother? Was I declared missing? Sensitive questions disrupt my current objective, and I need a minute to focus on handling one urgency at a time.

Inside Waterstones, I look for Margaret. She has grey hair, is around my height, slim, born and raised in London, always nicely dressed, like a Yves Saint Laurent-wearing granny, without the grandchildren. She was a curator, retiring only to take care of her sick husband, who unfortunately died of lung cancer. Margaret is a powerful woman, with vast knowledge in art history and plenty of gossip about artists. She has the best stories.

When I cannot find her on the second floor of the bookstore, I'm disheartened. It was a long shot. I close my eyes and will my brain to come up with another idea. It's around 1 p.m., as per the clock downstairs, I should check the restaurant.

If she's not there, what other options do I have? Do I have any? What's wrong with me? I should have thought of multiple plans before I escaped.

You are completely alone! You have to rely on others to survive, because you have nothing! My self-doubt mocks me. *You should have never left Hector's side. You'll die without his help,* she says, delivering another blow.

How can I second guess myself so easily?

Because if you walk a step in the wrong direction, you're done for! My vision blurs out of frustration, and I hold a cry in.

I'm ashamed of my thoughts and what they say about me. How they paralyse my limbs.

You should be . . .

Shut up! Shut up!

"Vera? Darling, how are you? Just in time to join me for a late lunch." My eyes turn hopeful as they clear, and I see Margaret coming from the bathroom. The surprise is so big, I run and envelop her in a tight hug.

"I'm so happy to see you. So, so happy," I say as she pats my back, then cups my face and looks at me.

"How about you tell me why over a glass of Pinot Grigio, hm?"

"I have no money, and someone is looking for me. I did nothing wrong, I promise, but I have nowhere else to go. I need your advice and help, but it's safer if they don't see you in public with me."

"Nonsense, darling, we'll eat at Bronte, a secluded table, if you prefer, and you can tell me all about it." God, I love her.

"If you are sure."

"Of course. If you say you did nothing wrong, I believe you. I know you are a kind person, Vera. Now come."

They seat us at a corner table within seconds of entering the restaurant. Margaret requests water and the bottle of white wine she mentioned. After placing our food order and downing a glass of Grigio, I tell her everything. How I woke up in a coffin on Monday night. About Ed the not so Dead. How I had to carry him to the safe house, the connection with Fosters & Co. Hector's story, the informer theory, my interrogation. What happened this morning until I met her in the bookstore. I leave out the game of twister I played with Hector in the car's boot. By the time I wrap up, Margaret finishes her food.

"So, I couldn't stay with them, not after locking me up. He doesn't believe me, anyway. I can't call my brother or the authorities. I don't trust the police. I thought of you because nobody knows of our connection. I'm sorry if you think I shouldn't have bothered you, and I'll completely understand if you want to leave. I'll pay you back for lunch, somehow."

"Stop that. I'm seventy-seven, Vera. I survived breast cancer. Twice. I don't scare easily. I was five when the Second World War ended. Yes, you are in quite the pickle, and that Worthington boy makes it a pretty pickle. With that face of his."

"You can say that again. Wait! How do you know how he looks? Do you know Hector?" My eyes enlarge as the plate in front of me.

"Not personally, no. Francis, my husband, knew his grandfather, the Swiss banker. We saw the family at social functions. His mother is a troublesome person. Hector was always very polite, always, despite the environment she must have created for him and his poor sister growing up." Margaret takes my hand, greasy from the burger, and gives it a squeeze. "I'll help. It's not like I have a terribly exciting calendar."

"Oh, thank you! Thank you!" I sigh, feeling the pressure on my shoulders lifting. "What do you suggest I do?"

"First, let's get you out of the public's eye. Let me send for a car." She takes her phone out of her elegant bag and sends a message, then she pays the bill. "Finish your burger."

◆

Margaret's place is in Dulwich Village, South London. She has a well maintained two-storey town house on a little hill.

"You have a lovely home." I am amazed at the diversified art in her living room, but I shouldn't be considering her past profession.

"Thank you. I'll put for tea. Come, I have a cosy sofa in the kitchen."

At the back of the house where the big cooking area is located, she hands me a hot cup of Earl Grey. With cookie crumbs all over my pants, I lean my head on the pillow cushion, exhausted. I try to pay attention to the polite conversation Margaret is engaging me in, to put me at ease I'm sure, but my eyelids are so heavy, and this sofa is that comfortable that sleep takes me for a dreamless ride.

I wake up a few hours later, for it is dark outside, startled, still in the kitchen. A blanket over me. My host, nowhere in sight. I find her finishing a phone call.

"Hi dear, feeling better? You went out like a light."

"Sorry for that. I did not realise I was so tired."

"Don't apologise. You experienced a challenging situation without comparison, and you felt safe here, which I am glad, and your wearied body took advantage. I'm happy you came to me, and I can help, at least with a place to hide and regroup. Even thou, I can do more than that." She winks. "Let's prepare dinner, pasta if that is fine with you, and I'll tell you how I spent my time while you were napping."

"Pasta sounds perfect. Margaret, I don't know what you did, but I cannot ask you to put yourself in a more dangerous position than the one I already forced you into by coming here. Maybe I should go."

"Where? These unknown crooks are most likely running surveillance to capture you. Involving your friends is a bad idea. But nobody knows we know each other. Since Francis died, what I do is no one's business and do not worry about putting me in danger, I took care of that," she assures me when we arrive in the kitchen.

While cooking, Margaret mentions that her late husband was a diplomat and some of his activities were not exactly official or by the books. He was not a spy, as I excitedly assumed, but in his line of work it was convenient to build a wide network of associates.

"My husband made friends and kept them. He was loyal and guided everyone in need. He was also a shrewd manipulator." Her eyes sparkle with a distant memory. "Francis ensured if I require help, someone is available to assist. Revealing no details, I placed a call to a good friend of ours, very trustworthy. He worked with Francis in some capacity."

"Also a diplomat?"

"I wouldn't call him that, his job description is not important for now. I asked if he could guide me with a little issue, explaining I needed discretion and protection, so he sent an associate of his, who is waiting in a car outside, making sure we are safe and taking note if anything suspicious happens in the neighbourhood."

"Wow! That's unbelievable! If you trust your friend."

"Implicitly. And he sent only the best. You share what you are comfortable with if we invite him in. He handles next steps, if you know what you want, or he can help us brainstorm what is most recommended for this type of complications."

"I don't know what to say. Thank you so much for what you are doing for me."

"Nonsense."

"No, really, you saved my life. You will be forever in my prayers to all the deities out there. As for next steps, I have to leave London. They might expect me to do that, thinking I am still with Hector, which works to my advantage, if I hide in Romania. He wouldn't go there, right? I wouldn't bother my family, I don't want them exposed, but there are so many places I could use as a hideout. However, if I run, how will I uncover who framed me? Fosters & Co will still look for me, they wouldn't exactly clear my name and apologise for the kidnapping."

"Reveal the scammer and share that information with the Worthington boy. He will believe you then and apply that evidence to his own investigation, eventually exposing the whole production to the public."

"Definitely not. I do not trust him not to use me for his own purposes. He bloody locked me up. Regardless, fleeing the scene as I did, I'm clearly the impostor in his view. And I am not giving him the satisfaction of knowing I need him."

"But you do. He has high stakes in this, the safe houses, the money, the connections. What Francis' friend could do for you will have limits, I'm afraid. What purpose will serve Hector to harm you if you can prove you had nothing to do with this corporate espionage?"

"I hear you, but my priority is to lie low and figure out who thought it was a perfect idea to blame me for the information leak, and my gut feeling rejects any Hector Worthington associations." And my pride.

"Think about it, dear. I will let you retire to the guest room and if you are ready with a decision in the morning, we can talk further and introduce you to our protection detail. Please feel welcome to stay in my house as long as you need."

"Thank you. Margaret, I appreciate everything you have done for me." A lengthy hug later, she leads me to a quiet bedroom with garden views.

After a quick assessment, I congratulate myself for adding pyjamas to the few items I borrowed from The Hyde. I cannot possibly ask more from Margaret; she's been plenty helpful, and I need to adapt my resources for the next stage of my life on the run. Whatever that stage is.

Dragging the covers forcefully from the bed, I get in and curse this nightmare. Where should I go? As much guidance as Margaret and the guy outside will give me, I decide my fate. It's my life expectancy at stake. I can't just blindly follow what others choose no matter how much I want someone to fix this for me. I need to use logic and find the ideal strategy.

This approach sounds awfully business oriented, but what if I analyse everything like a difficult project? Determinate where I am, a big scary mess, almost zero people to trust. I would identify what is important: staying alive, not putting others in danger by associating with them, clearing my name. Define what to achieve, locate the impostor. Accountable parties, Fosters & Co for kidnapping me, for killing Helena and all the other horrible actions they might have done. Hector and that slime Lawrence, they know what they did. The one using my name.

Hiding in London or the UK from the extensive list of folks looking for me will prove problematic fast; I have limited knowledge on how to resolve issues in this country.

Is Poland an optimal location to achieve what I need and not die? I still don't speak the language. Then where, Romania? Could I infiltrate the Fosters & Co building easier from Bucharest, taking advantage of the weak spots in security I discovered during my employment there?

Uncovering the mole is another sticking point. I am decent enough with a computer but nowhere near hacker level to break into the network at work and see how they used my access. I need a cyber genius on my team. Even in Romania, where would I find one that could help me? My mind flies to someone outside my home country, though we *met* while I was a high school happy-face girl, living with my parents. I haven't thought of him in ages, his cunning mind and stellar smile, his custom-made chocolate gifts sent from afar, and I couldn't presume he would help. Our young and fragile tie broke long ago with hurt feelings and harsh confessions. I doubt he remembers me even if his letters, the written evidence of our *unique time together* and his old contact details can be found in discarded journals on the shelves of my bedroom in Bucharest. Should I dare ask of him actions I condemned with a passion in the past? Romania reveals itself as an ideal candidate for my next step if it wasn't for the risk I would bring to my parents.

Whenever I face a tough decision at my job or in my personal life, Youssef works the list with me. We are so similar in our anxieties and how to fix them, the girls joke that we share the same brain and therapist. Where Lina is impulsive, Dorota overconfident, Astrid disorderly, he and I are worriers, analysing and discussing things over meticulously. He was the one teaching me that is perfectly fine as an adult to not accept cruelty disguised as honesty from friends and family. I won't bring the burden to his doorstep in Warsaw. Youssef would say to not allow fear to become my enemy, but to use it as a friend that keeps me safe.

Pros and cons float in my head like paper planes until the early morning hours, when the notion of a working plan forms behind my eyelids. Imaginary dots connect places on the blurry map of Europe as I create options and solutions to my problems from sheer determination and love for my family, whom I wish to see again in this lifetime. Either way, slumber takes me and with it come dreams of waking up in coffins and tight places, buried alive in muddy ground.

But nobody sleeps next to me this time to prevent darkness from shoving dirt down my throat.

Ten

Sitting at the living room table with Drew, if that's his name, the security expert sent by Margaret's friend, is how I start my Thursday. Despite the bad dreams and the weight of a million questions, I wake up empowered for battle. They don't consider me a force to reckon with, but I will not be a sitting duck, I will fight with everything I have to stay alive and return to normality. Or a normality where mysterious individuals are not wishing my demise.

Sharing little details, I tell Drew that I need a new ID. He doesn't want to know my name or my nationality, and I am fine with that. He might suspect something anyway, he looks like a guy who knows his stuff, late forties maybe, really built, taller than me but not by much. Attractive in that not attractive way, rough, scruffy face. Magnetic silver eyes that miss nothing.

"With your skin tone you could be from several Mediterranean countries, I will make sure we get you a European ID so you can move around easily. My colleague will bring a wig, some glasses, contacts to change your eye colour then photograph you for the document."

"Thank you. I will pay you back soon."

"Don't worry, I am not doing much. Here's some free advice. Buy your tickets, for wherever you go, at the counter, not online. Wear a hat when you are in public, keep your head down, or in a book, avoid looking at cameras," he says to my nodding self. "Don't stay in a location because it's comfortable and leave nothing behind." Honestly, I have no valuable possessions, but I keep that to myself, not wanting to state the obvious.

Half an hour later, he takes my picture in front of a light grey background. I opt to wear a long black wig, no contacts, make up by Margaret to highlight my cheekbones, slim my nose a bit, and my jaw. A brush, eyeliner, and I look like a stylish version of a distant self.

By nightfall, Drew comes back with a French passport. Ama Monteil is my new name, and it matches the face in the picture. Luckily, I speak the language well in case anyone asks, thanks to the Romanian education system for equipping me with as many languages as they could before I left the school benches.

"They now have Ama entering London five days ago at London St. Pancras. When she leaves, she'll have no problems exiting the country," he says as parting words. "Good luck, Ama. Do a little search where you can travel freely with this French passport. I can't forge visas in such a short time," he mentions, shakes my hand and leaves.

I help my lovely host with dinner and tell her I'll be out of her hair come morning.

"Love, stay a few more days, if you feel inclined, but I understand the urgency and the necessity to cover some ground in sorting this out." For her safety, and mine, I reveal little to her of what my future holds.

What I find using her laptop later that night is that a French citizen with a passport can travel to one hundred and eighty-six countries and territories, visa free or with one on arrival. That's highly convenient. I also search news sites for mentions of missing persons, without typing my name or what I am looking for, and come empty-handed. My name is not in the press, as expected, and I have mixed feelings about it. Relieved my family is still in the dark, but knowing nobody cares to report me missing is not the best feeling in the world.

My first attempt at setting up the teddy camera I have at the office fails when the website I'm supposed to use doesn't load. Hours into my struggle, I grunt my exasperation and consider the sign the universe wants to deliver, but I'm not that great at reading between the lines.

I'm sipping my tea the next morning, bright and early, in a formfitting black dress, knitted and long, courtesy of Margaret, while she is applying the same makeup as yesterday. A more pronounced cat-eye look. Other loans from her are the short heel, knee-length black boots and the navy coat hanging by the door. She convinced me to borrow them as part of my disguise, and pack all I had from The Hyde in a leather carry-on bag, as I'm attempting to avoid recognition by multiple people now. Long black wig on, cashmere grey hat, I resemble what Cleopatra in a beret would look like. Probably not, but it puts a smile on my face to think about it.

As if she didn't do enough for me already, my friend handed me an envelope with cash yesterday. One I hope to not drop, and I am beyond grateful for her kindness, guilty that I put her in this position when she refuses to hear my apologies and repeated thanks.

"Return immediately if you feel stuck anywhere and you need a place to regroup. I mean it." She kisses my cheeks in her driveway a while later. "Don't cry, you will ruin your face." I can barely contain it as it is, but her words are resurfacing my tears. The lifesaving kindness this woman did for me, I cannot express with words no matter how much I try.

"I'm forever in your gratitude, Margaret. Stay safe as well, and I'm glad you will have security on you. Drew seems confident but prudent to remain in his position for a few more days." I give her another hug and take my leave, passing by the nondescriptive security car, from where the above-mentioned man is scanning the neighbourhood.

The sky is cloudy, but luckily there is no wind. At the nearest shop, I buy an Oyster card to use for public transport because the money Margaret gave me, and I'm planning to pay her back, is a little over a thousand pounds, and I need to spend wisely.

Riding only buses to Ebbsfleet International, two hours and a half later, I arrive there feeling disoriented from trying to act normal and thinking that everyone is looking at me with an ulterior motive. Wanting to avoid major London train stations and airports, I chose Ebbsfleet because the Eurostar stops here prior to leaving the UK for Europe. Ama Monteil's passport might be safe, but I'll take all the precautions necessary before starting my journey as a reluctant lawbreaker using counterfeit documents.

After staking the station, I buy an early afternoon ticket to Brussels. I'm nervous when I hand over my passport to the teller, hoping my voice does not betray my uneasiness. Since most people would travel to Paris from London by train, I hope my kidnappers and the wonder boys at The Hyde will not look for me in a Brussels-bound vehicle. Technically, they are not at that mansion in St. Albans, but wherever the road took them, I hope it's far away from me.

While I wait for the train, images of Hector and Lawrence cross my mind for more than a second, since we parted ways. I immediately regret it and try to erase Lawrence's face from behind my eyelids. I refute that particular annoyance, but the look on Hector's unshaven face when I ran is haunting me. His eyes were accusatory, and the set lines of his mouth found me guilty of everything. Running away was the proof he needed. Why does it bother me so much?

I shake myself internally, as to not mess up my wig. I don't need to feel bad, lest I forget what he did when we arrived at The Hyde. Or did not do. The manipulation in the car's boot I ought to delete from my mind if I want my dignity to remain intact. A moment of weakness which he tried to exploit. The unscrupulous bastard doesn't deserve my consideration or any of my thoughts.

With his resources, I would be safer. Maybe. His team would help deal with the risky conditions, but at what cost? Was it guaranteed that he would ever believe me when I say I'm not the snitch? If that blonde weasel he calls friend had his way, I would still freeze in an interrogation room. No, thank you, I'm fine on my own, and look at that, I survived. Nobody chased me down for two straight days. I cross my fingers while I think this, not to jinx myself.

All thanks to Margaret, don't delude yourself into thinking you've got this figured it out on your own strength.

Shut up!

Aboard the train somewhere in the middle, I take my aisle seat, facing forward. I bought a magazine earlier to keep me busy, especially from poisonous thoughts, and to cover my face if needed. When we leave, I open the salad I bought at M&S and start eating.

Was it not suspiciously easy to reach this point, crossing the channel to the continent, since I left Hector? It bothers me, the nagging feeling that I am still under surveillance, that they, everyone with ill intentions, want me to think I'm safe when I'm actually anything but. I might as well embrace this sentiment if it keeps me vigilant. Pray to Cleopatra, because God left me a while back, it will not drive me crazy instead.

I spend the two-hour ride to Brussels, Belgium, with my coat covering my feet, magazine in hand, hat pulled as down as I could over my forehead. I don't even use the restroom to avoid notice from the other passengers. The middle-aged man sitting next to me is working on his laptop on a spreadsheet. This takes me back to my normal Friday routine at the office. Free company breakfast first thing, replying to the never-ending chain of emails, and by this time, I would have had my bimonthly review with my manager. What is he thinking of my disappearance, and is he involved in this mess, or is he worried? I don't take sick days or even holidays without discussing it with him beforehand. Am I stupid for feeling like I'm skipping school and worrying about it? I always had a problem with defying authority. Weirdly, it still applies in this case. I'm lucky I'm not skipping life altogether in that coffin, dead by now.

With a lot to worry about in my head, but little real action happening on the train, we arrive at ten minutes after four in the afternoon in Brussels-South. The busiest station in Belgium as they announce it on the train. And it is indeed. People of all nationalities travelling their own way to their final destination, be that their home, a holiday, a business trip, or a run for your life in an itchy wig extravaganza. Pack accordingly.

My language skills don't extend to Flemish, but French and English will suffice. I buy euros, a sandwich for the road ahead, and board an internal train to the airport. The sun was missing in London, but it's fully present in the Belgian sky. Pity I can't visit the old town, alas, no sightseeing for this fugitive. Thinking of the beer I'll buy at the airport while I decide where to fly is comfort enough. I won't spend my money on hotels yet, the plan is to travel until I hit my designated marks. Last-minute train and plane tickets are, with fortune on my side, cheaper, or if the trouble continues, awfully expensive.

How do you feel about your luck this week?

Not great.

Boisterous laughter from the mixed group seated close by interrupts my overcrowded mind from going over the plan I made at Margaret's house. The one riddled with question marks and inconsistencies but still giving me the confidence to cross several borders into countries I've either never been before or where my resources are limited. A rough idea is better than letting others dictate my movements.

"Cheers!" The ladies sitting in front of me start an avalanche of well wishes from their diverse entourage. The accessories pinned and proudly displayed on celebratory outfits give away the nature of their travel. Bachelorettes and bachelors from the same wedding party going to Prague, of all places, on their last hurrah. I kindly refuse the canned cocktail they offer, but I express my congratulations to the happy couple.

"You have sad eyes, and nobody may be depressed on flying Fridays. Aren't you excited for your new destination?" Before I answer the petite brunette woman with huge dimples to my left, she gives me a side hug and continues talking. "My name is Farah and I'm in charge of smiles and keeping the bride in good spirits. These are Angie and Patrizia."

"Hi." Angie salutes with a grin while fixing her side braid. Her natural sandy hair might be longer than my wig. Patrizia nods before accepting a long kiss from the guy collecting empty drink containers from everyone and disposing of them at the back of the train coach.

"I'm Ama. My destination might not be ready for me or vice versa."

"Then come with us. We had one cancellation in our group, unfortunately. There's plenty of space and Lars and Juliet won't mind." Farah points in the general direction of the bride and groom to be. Her direct approach reminds me so much of Astrid, I have to smile at her suggestion.

"That's an attractive offer." I divert the conversation from me to inquiring about their itinerary in Prague. Is meeting the bridal party a 'go ahead' signal to my mission? Could success be on the horizon, or a dead end disguised in coincidence?

Farah and Angie share details of the fun activities they have booked and plenty of anecdotes from their time at school, where they all met. Appreciating the inclusion sentiment, I smile alongside the blend of cultures and opinions, my body relaxing with tiny laughter outbursts. Their friendship and light teasing envelop me in warmth and a bittersweet exhale passes my lips when I think of my own beautifully knitted life companionships.

But with the BRU airport now in sight, my pulse spikes. With all those cameras, security, and passport control, I'll need to be extra careful and act like a regular traveller. I was afraid to include flying in my exit strategy, but they can't check all European airports, right? The necessity to arrive at a potential new home base faster rather than never forces me to fly as well. Unfortunately, I think they will look into every Romanian border control point for all women entering the country. That's what I would do.

Finishing with the final train ride of the day, I use the cover of the large group to enter the Departures area. The happy couple chuckles with their friends, lovesick puppy faces, and I wave goodbye, sighing at the cliché of a drunk bride and groom, not in judgment but envious of their position when my current struggles might kill me before meeting someone to gaze with equal adoration into my eyes.

Thanks to their welcomed ruckus, nobody is paying attention to me while I scan the upcoming flights. The board is full of possibilities and pressure. Two flights to Romania, one to my hometown of Bucharest and one for Bacau, a city in the North-East part of the country I never visited. Ideally, the second option is promising, as no links exist with that location. Other flights to Zurich, Munich, London (no thanks), Alicante, Bergamo, Prague with the party people, Lyon, Vienna, and the list continues. Decisions, decisions.

Half an hour later, I go with my gut and purchase my selection. Moving towards security, I don't check-in my bag; I put my coat on the tray, another one for the rest of my belongings.

Here goes nothing.

"Stop!"

"Moi?" I say in French, pointing to myself.

"Oui Madame, vous devez retirer votre chapeau avant de passer!" Ah, I still have the hat on! My pulse is racing, my fingers are numb.

"Oui, désolé! Juste un moment!" I nearly pull my wig off when I remove the damn hat.

"S'il vous plaît, Madame! Avez-vous des liquides dans le sac?"

"Seulement de petits cosmétiques."

I take out the small makeup purse Margaret gave me to look like a different person and show it to the guy. After a careful inspection, I move on to the body scanner. Everything goes faster from here, and in mere minutes I am in the duty-free area, running for the nearest bathroom. Closing myself into a stall, I release a broken breath, unsure if I want to puke or hide forever. Probably both, but I promised myself a beer.

Using the 'when in Belgium' excuse to calm my nerves, I end up buying two framboise Lambic bottles, one of my favourite types of beer, not that easy to find elsewhere. Hanging around the food court, waiting for my flight to board, I notice a couple of men staring at me, and not because they find me alluring. Maybe I should hold off the alcohol, keep my wits sharp. One big guy with muscles everywhere sits at the opposite table, pretending to read a newspaper, and the other one is by the improvised bar on my left. The second guy is shorter and leaner, but still capable of snapping my neck in two. He has that look about him. He scans the area and returns his attention to me several times. Are they familiar or am I too fearful?

Creepy isn't strong enough of a word to describe the way their attention makes me feel. I want to leave for my gate, but I'm scared they will come after me and it will prove I'm not paranoid and my enemies caught up with me. Remembering little from my kidnapping is a blessing, or a repressed episode I will pay decent money in therapy to deal with, but now I don't know whom to be wary of. Even if I learnt my villains' faces, they might have sent other guys. The person at Fosters & Co responsible for my undoing because it's hard to believe the entire company wants me dead, has the money to employ all the criminals in the world. I know they have money; I help them strategise their savings quarterly and I do an excellent job at that.

I bought a disposable phone from the duty-free area before coming to the restaurant, but I don't want to call Hector for him to describe our kidnappers. He's in a different country altogether, I ran from them for a reason, and these guys could be just perverts. I would give away my position for nothing. Lawrence would rejoice and laugh at my stupidity. I stand, gathering my things, and stroll towards the gate sector.

Goosebumps raise on my neck as I feel my body eyed from different directions. Before turning the corner, heartbeat in my throat, I glance back to empty chairs.

The mystery men left.

I run.

At the Blue Air counter for the gate to Bacau, Romania, the flight attendant is announcing a fifteen-minute delay for boarding, which should start in ten minutes, making me even more nervous when I take a seat next to some of my compatriots.

"Hai, frate! Mereu avem întârziere!" One guy wearing a red jacket is complaining about always facing delays. Should I strike a conversation with him and his buddy? It might come handy to befriend my fellow countrymen, if the creeps from earlier appear. I move closer to them.

"Bună! Vă întoarceţi acasă din vacanţă sau acasă este vacanţa?" I find the nerve to ask if they are returning from their holiday or going home for a holiday. A lot of Romanians work abroad, and it feels like the expats are part of a big group of acquaintances. Not regarded as a component of the country they left behind, no matter the visits back, nor fully members of the society they currently live in. The inbetweeners. I've assimilated London as my home even before I moved there completely, my adoration for the city knows no boundaries, but I've yet to deserve the Londoner title, and thanks to Fosters & Co I might never receive it.

"Mergem acasă pe weekend. Tu?" The one next to me confirms they are going home for the weekend and before I get the chance to reply if that's the case for me, the restaurant thugs take a sit in front of us and give me definite menacing looks.

Fuck!

I look around in panic. When did they catch up with me? Have I had a tail since London? Beads of sweat accumulate underneath the heavy wig, sliding down my spine, frozen in terror, not for my own fate, but Margaret's. Please let her be safe.

What do I do?

The loudspeakers announce the final call for the gate next to ours and people shout and run towards the flight attendant desk with passports in hand, trying to avoid travellers queuing for the flight to Romania.

I foolishly thought it will be easy to go home and find help from friendships built to last who don't expect constant messaging and social media interactions to love and appreciate each other. It was home, and it was giving me hope.

"Eşti bine drăguţă? Te-ai făcut roşie deodată." I turn to my new Romanian friend who asks if I'm good as I turned red suddenly and I realise I need to move to Plan B.

"Vezi tipii din faţa? M-au încolţit la baie mai devreme şi acum au venit aici. Nu ştiu ce să fac!" I lean close to say the guys in front of us cornered me in the bathroom and now I don't know what to do.

Voice quivering, eyes filling with tears, I stand.

The goons follow.

Red jacket guy does the same and I make a run for it, bag across my chest, passport and ticket clenched in my fist.

A commotion forms behind me as the Romanian guys block the way of my supposed attackers, other men getting involved when the shoving starts, and I throw myself at the gate to Prague. The gate next to us, where they have been calling Ama Monteil's name for the last few minutes. Two attendants are waiting, and I show them my passport, apologise, smile, brush off the tears I let fall on purpose. They check my papers, look at the scandal happening close by, then back to me.

"Hurry, the captain is ready to leave," says the blonde flight attendant with a Petra name tag fastened to her shirt after she scans me in.

"Thanks. Merci beaucoup!"

They let me pass and I run down the corridor, the attendant fast on my heels. I hear the big metal door closing after us as we take the stairs down to the waiting bus filled with people ready to board their flight to the Czech Republic. The bus moves for the plane, and I'm surrounded by the bridesmaids I shared jokes with earlier in the afternoon on the train to the airport.

"Hell yes, you are coming with us after all!"

"Excellent decision, lady!"

"We'll have so much fun!"

"You will forget about your lying boyfriend in no time!"

They speak all at once and I thank them again for the invite to spend the next few nights at the villa they rented in central Prague. The city where my old computer genius friend used to reside. The guy that broke my heart from a distance with his online stalking tendencies. My memories of him being an expert at hiding and evading various authorities don't help my cause. What chances do I have at finding him if he still lives in the shadows?

As the bus stops, we rush into the plane, take our seats and in minutes we are in the air. I guess I'll be doing some sightseeing after all. Limited money aside, it's always good to have a backup.

I can only hope nobody waits for me when we land.

Eleven

One Year Earlier - Warsaw, Poland

"Can you all hear me? Youssef, babe, wear a shirt. The girls want to turn the video on," Dorota mutters over the line. Her laptop camera's blocked by the usual yellow post-it. It always takes us five minutes to synchronise the video, the sound, the snacks. Our monthly group calls are unruly but satisfying. I'm working from my apartment today so I can lounge on the sofa and sip my tea, waiting for my friends to settle in their places, scattered around Europe.

"Youssef, don't! Stay as you are. Let us see you in your splendour," Lina shouts and whistles like a cartoon villain. She's in a meeting room in our company's office in London, dancing in her chair.

"Keep it off, keep it off!" Astrid applauds from her kitchen in Bucharest. Then she returns to chopping vegetable for her famous hangover soup. Meaning she has plans for the upcoming weekend.

Youssef and Dorota's camera opens, revealing both of them clothed.

"Boooo!" I yell.

"You are such a disappointment," Astrid deadpans.

"But I paid for skin on skin," Lina cackles.

"Oh, shut up and find your own entertainment. My man retired from the public eye. Now, first order of business. Astrid, why in the hell did you return to Fosters & Co?"

"The pay, obviously. The new role is more flexible, and I travel a lot. Which is fine after the mind-numbing job I just left."

"Congrats on the salary, Richie Rich." Lina smiles.

"You are one to talk," I add.

"The rent in London asphyxiates my wallet in silence every month," she cries.

"But who has Thames views? Your apartment is spectacular," Youssef says to her.

"Nicolescu, are we talking about your interviews, or we don't want to jinx them?" Lina questions.

"Have we finished interrogating Astrid?"

"Yes, you have. I'm back at the mine and it's fine. The projects moving my way excite me. I'll get to visit Haas in London and you guys in Warsaw soon."

"Great! We are happy for you. Especially if you buy us drinks when you visit. For my part, I had an interview with the office in Paris. It went well. Interesting role. Salary could be better. Then," – I slap my thighs for a drumroll effect – "I had an informal chat with the London hub. I'm waiting for numbers. I have a feeling they really want me. The hiring manager hinted at pulling all the strings to convince me."

"Of course, they do. You raise productivity everywhere you go." Lina grins, thumps up for all to see.

"If they unroll the red carpet for you, go with London. But a worthy mention, the hiring manager is an unscrupulous bastard. I worked with him on a project, and he gave me a bad impression only from emails and video calls." Youssef pushes a hand through his tight black curls. He shared those thoughts with me before, but my instincts didn't flash any alarm bells when I talked with the guy.

"She'll be fine. She knows how to deal with these people. Vera, go to London. You always dreamed about living there," Astrid says with

conviction, pointing the sharp knife she's currently using from her side of the screen.

"Why do you have to leave? Don't you like Warsaw? And having me close?" Dorota asks, her freckles and pleading green eyes take over their chat box when she leans forward.

"You know I do. And I'll come back often. Not that I accepted the job yet. But London . . . I have a feeling that city will change my life."

Twelve

The limit to how much a person can drink, walk, and laugh in a weekend and remain reasonably sane is one my Belgium friends are on a mission to test. It's only lunchtime on Saturday, the day after we arrived in Prague for Lars and Juliet's stag and hen party. There are seventeen of us breaking those boundaries, myself included. While they live in Brussels, some are from The Netherlands, Spain, Italy, Nigeria, and Egypt. We are strolling the streets of the old town, singing, and telling stories in different languages. Activities helping my undercover mission of retrieving clues about my old acquaintance.

Spring reigns at last, the sun followed us here, illuminating the front windows of the stores we pass. From the hundreds of shops at our disposal, one has to be the chocolate boutique my friend's grandfather owns. If it even exists anymore. The challenge ahead and the passing hours will not discourage me because the company I keep this weekend fills me with support and hope.

When we got to their rented accommodation late last night, they gave me a bunk bed in a room with Angie and Farah, which I gladly accepted. The villa has several floors with a hipster ambiance, old furnishings, and fittings with minimal contemporary furniture.

During our flight, when I met everyone, the guys and gals took me in like an established group member. I think I'm older than all of them by a few years, but officially, Ama, my new persona, is similar in age at twenty-seven. They went to university together and remained friends throughout busy lives, careers, and now their first wedding of the gang.

They are so happy for the opportunity to spend the weekend together; they started partying yesterday, and even though I was tired, I ended up celebrating with them. Not because it was rude to retire early when they accepted me with open arms, and refused my compensation offer, but I did not want to be alone. I wanted to surround myself with good-natured people who tease one another and tell anecdotes of past adventures as they laugh hysterically. It's what I used to do with my friends, who I pretended were mingling within the villa with the younger crowd, Lina mixing cocktails and Astrid saying everything needs more alcohol.

We woke up early and had a big breakfast with mimosas, as one does on a holiday, and started a visiting tour of the Old Town Square with its famous astronomical clock, one of the oldest in the world still operating. Then we saw The Church of our Lady Before Tyn, a gothic structure with two signature towers, Kinsky Palace with its delicate pink and white stucco façade.

Now we stopped on Charles Bridge to enjoy the views, take pictures, and decide where to go for beers, fries, and schnitzel. I'm quickly becoming a master at not appearing in their photos, offering to act as the photographer. I'm still wearing my long black wig and a hint of smoky eyes with red lipstick, but I decide against the full dramatic makeup I had yesterday, with all the shading and highlighting. The fake parts would have been visible after spending some time together with everyone. However, they have been drinking since Brussels, so I'm not entirely sure how focused everyone is on such details.

"I saw a restaurant on our way to the bridge, quite close, if we want to eat now. And I'm way too thirsty to wait for another one."

"Let's continue over the bridge. That restaurant was packed. We want one outside with extra sitting."

"Our only chance to get enough tables." The group continues discussing. They are rather good at fast decisions and compromises, but now they are hungry and demand their Pilsner. They walk ahead while I follow close by, hinting at making a phone call.

"I will catch up with you guys in a minute," I say to Marc, the cute Belgian guy keeping me company since breakfast. He's one of the few single men of the group, tall and lean, with curly auburn hair and smart clothes. He is also four years younger than real me, the 'on the run' woman with an evil entity after her. And with a coffin buddy convinced I'm the informer who screwed his investigation. So, I am not truly replying to Marc's flirting. He is not over the top pushy, knowing from the girls I'm suffering after my terrible boyfriend. But I appreciate the interest.

"Okay with you to stop at a bar first, Ama?" he asks, walking backwards to face me and advance with our crew. "I'm afraid if we don't find a restaurant soon enough, they will give up in favour of a quick beer. Nothing to do about it." He shrugs, grins, and wow, his face melts hearts when he does that. Pity.

"I'm fine with whatever. I had a big breakfast." I wave to show that I need a minute, giving him a genuine smile, not to offend him.

I have been using the phone bought yesterday at the airport to hourly check the international news for my disappearance. Typing no words that would trigger alarms set by those looking for me. And that's difficult. I am very much afraid Ama Monteil's cover was exposed in Brussels on Friday night, but nobody stopped me upon landing here. I did not use my passport for accommodation, but a different ID is necessary, safety wise, or travel without one, if that's possible.

Again, nothing online about me, and it's been five nights since I've gone missing. Not one mention. Or I couldn't find anything without typing Vera Nicolescu in the search engine. I'm thinking Fosters & Co are purposely hiding the fact that I've disappeared. I want to ring my brother so badly, to tell him and my parents that I'm alive and kicking if they heard I'm in trouble. I wonder if they called my old cell by now. We don't allow longer periods without speaking, but it's common to have a week or two without contact. I don't know which is worse, them not knowing about this disaster or worrying endlessly for my sake. Since I am still alive, I prefer to keep them in blissful ignorance about the whole situation.

Next, I send a prayer upstairs and downstairs as I reload the teddy cam website. With all that has happened since London, I forgot about it. The office is empty on Saturdays, but if it works, I'll activate it and check again Monday. Maybe people will talk about me next to it. I can access it remotely on a website using the unique code found on the box easy enough to remember even following my near-death experiences.

After a few minutes of rebooting the camera's system, it goes live. I can see part of my work surface, keyboard, my chair, the wall behind it, lined with boxes, the corner connecting to the floor to ceiling window by my desk. The audio is working, but it is not picking up any noise. The perfect thing about this camera is that it auto-starts when movement is detected close by, recording what it sees and transmitting everything to my fake email. Buying this gift for Dorota might have been the best decision I took this year, if it pays out.

I wonder what my friends are doing. Before my kidnapping work kept me away from our group chat to where even with Lina, the only one living in London with me, I've seen little of in March. She took some time off to handle family business, and it makes me mad I cannot be there for her when she calls. Instead, I have to bloody take a corporation down and avoid getting murdered in the process. She and Astrid have been my closest friends since I started at Fosters & Co all those years ago, when Dorota and Youssef married, and we had to give them space to enjoy their new chapter. It was at her guidance that I applied for the role in London. She's always pushing me to be braver and more outspoken. We balance each other. Lina motivates me when I am living too much in my head, and I am there when she needs grounding. She's the tall to my short, the fair to my dark – we work. The silly laughs we have, the internal jokes, the t-shirts we print with ridiculous pictures and comments nobody would understand. Thinking of her motivates me to push forward to reach the day we'll be reunited, Dorota, Youssef, and Astrid by our side.

Returning to the main reason I bought two tickets at BRU airport, one for Bacau and one for Prague, besides trying to create a diversion, I refresh the searching pages I opened this morning. Meeting the bachelorettes on the train and learning their destination, I immediately remembered the person I always think of when someone mentions Prague. Years later, my first real friendship with a boy is fresh in my memory. First time falling in love with someone from another country. When that happened at seventeen, I believed myself so cool to talk with a person my age in a different language, to come from school and find his letters in the post and wanting to reply. Young love, heartache, and eventually heartbreak. We connected on the web when internet cafes were popular and mIRC was the programme to use for communication with other cool kids out there. Back then nobody was using actual names and details online. I was obsessed with *Lord of the Rings*, so my nickname was hobBit321 and his was ThL8HackER. Classy, we were not.

Last time we spoke was over the phone. While I was still in Romania, he called me one night when he was sad and drunk and twenty-two. It was his birthday, and he was celebrating with his army mates and wanted to hear my voice. I was cold and short with him, the whole discussion only forty-five seconds, after two years of no communication, no less. Past anger from our breakup resurfaced, and I wanted to hurt him, too. How dare he call me and ruin my summer? Now, eight years since that discussion, I'm trying to contact him.

Debating the fairness of reaching out is pointless because I am out of options. He was, as his nickname suggested, fantastic with a computer. Some of his immoral activities were the reason we broke up, coincidently, and he owes me in a way. If he thinks as I do once I track him down, I'll be pleasantly surprised. I don't have a phone number, an email address, or his social media accounts. I don't remember the address I used when I was sending him handwritten letters, he could live somewhere else by now. And the chocolate shop had a Czech name that hides behind my memories.

Tiny fact to consider, if one would care for such things, we didn't actually meet in person, ever. I know how he looks. Pictures were exchanged. Or more how he used to look. Blonde, sunburned from all the time he spent swimming at the public pool, brown eyes full of mischief. Lips that teenage, and new adult, Vera, dreamed of kissing. An eternity later, I might end up seeing him after all.

I return to my group while I brainstorm another idea. They settled for a beer garden, and Marc is waiting for me with a glass of golden goodness I can't refuse.

"Today we continue with our touristic activities and later do a pub crawl, but we should keep our energy for tomorrow night," Gemma says to the general audience as she removes her fashionable oversized cardigan, her strong but feminine arms on display. Her smooth dark skin admired not only by her boyfriend. She's kind of the leader of the bunch, organising flights, accommodation and visiting list; I like her a lot. She's a woman with a plan and amazing black curly hair.

"I can't wait for the show Sunday night! So many DJs, so little time. I'm still annoyed we couldn't find tickets for tonight too." That's Jonah, repeating himself for the hundred time in the last hours. The reason they came to Prague for Lars and Juliet's weekend was also to attend the Transmissions Music Festival. The group's majority loves electronic music and festivals, and the rest don't mind the partying and drinking programme.

"We also have the spa reservations tomorrow to spoil our lazy asses. And the newlyweds to be! To Lars and Juliet!" says Farah, my roommate, starting a chain reaction of cheers.

"To Lars and Juliet!"

"Here, here!"

"Shots, shots, shots!" Anton and Gio run for the bar. They designated themselves as the Alcohol Committee for the trip. It's safe to say we'll be here for a while. I can't bring myself to care, right now, that I am not hiding, running, or an official missing poster. These guys are 'living young and wild and free' and I crave the freedom and security. Especially since at night I'm always in that damned coffin.

Sealed in with no air.

Alone.

Throat bleeding from the endless screams.

Several hours later, I am nowhere near my objective of finding my past crush. He doesn't have online accounts in his name for social or professional purposes. And Google gives me nothing that could lead me to him. I've tried online forums for things he was interested in, a long shot, but when desperate. In the real world, the confectionery shops blend together without a distinguishing element as I pass them.

We find our way to Prague Castle, rather inebriated, after a short shopping spree sponsored by Marc, who bought everyone *I Heart Beer* baseball hats. Well-received, as it covers my face better than the beret I was using. I am wearing black again, high-waisted jeans and a chunky sweater. I haven't consumed the same amount of happy juice as my posse, so I'm left to help them navigate the 9th century medieval castle grounds. This place is amazing and has everything. Churches, palaces, halls, towers, gardens in its 70,000 square metres. The architecture alone is magnificent and represents virtually every style of the last millennium, a Gothic and Romanesque love blend.

"Do you need a hand with that? Looks heavy," I ask Angie, my other roommate, who is caring two bags of souvenirs and Czech sweets.

"I know, don't laugh. I had to buy everything today or else I would have forgotten. I have a big family I spoil by always bringing them something from my travels," she says.

"Same."

"Then the colleagues at work are expecting their treats. You know the office environment; we jump like vultures on anyone coming back from a holiday." She is searching for something in one bag. "And Ama, come on, check this box of chocolates. How good it looks. Just the illustration on the cover deserves the price I paid, and I bet the candy's amazing too."

"Can I have a look, please?" I reach for the box. There is something familiar about the painted picture she mentions. I have seen something similar and not today. Traditional Czech folk art with flowers in beautiful colours on a white background, but the pigment is melting away, creating a psychedelic finish. "Where did you buy it from?"

"This one shop across the street from where we ate breakfast. I came in late to join you guys, remember? I couldn't decide between all those amazing boxes," she tells me as I hear a click in my mind. You are a saviour, Angie!

"Thanks a million, doll! I have to get one!" I say, returning the box and calculating the best route towards the exit, the streets below, and the madness in my heart.

"What? Now?"

"Yes! Sorry, dealing with other stuff, too! I'll see you guys later at the villa, okay?"

Could it be just a coincidence? Is my brain creating impossible links out of desperation?

Not waiting for her to reply, I fly like the wind to find a store where the boy I've been thinking of all day used to spend his weekends, every holiday, helping his grandfather sell chocolates.

Thirteen

A self-declared prophet, my dentist, told me sweets will be my ruination someday, but the opposite happening is beyond my wildest dreams. I am trying to process my thoughts and carefully run the streets of Prague. There are people everywhere this early evening, all focused on stopping my quest.

It couldn't be just a fluke. Normally, if I see that image, I wouldn't react to it, but today was a flash retrospect of many memories. I received a wooden version of the box Angie showed me years ago for my birthday. Three days later, when my teenage soul got demolished, I destroyed the box, and I put it out of my mind. There were still chocolates when I trashed it, so distraught I was. I never envisioned looking upon that design again, so similar to the product packaging on sale in this country, but for a twist making it unique. A computer-generated twist by boy genius extraordinaire, artist on top of delinquent hacker.

"Hey!" the guy I bump into shouts. Is every person in this town and their mother out tonight? I try to offer apologies, but he's already gone.

Never mind, Vera, keep running!

How much longer will they hold the shop open? Another half hour by foot to my destination, and I can't take a cab with an unknown address; I visualise the street we had the mimosas, but I don't remember any names. It's close to our accommodation, and traffic complicates matters.

Stopping for a minute to catch my breath, it's incredible how out of shape I've been lately. I lean on a building door when I can't feel my legs anymore. Fosters & Co couldn't have picked a worse period to start this avalanche of crap by kidnapping me on Monday. Hector wouldn't even break a sweat, I bet.

Since London, I've been keeping him on the back of my mind, but this impromptu exercise brought him front and centre by remembering the morning chase to the car at The Hyde and the following compromising ride. I'm overwhelmed by recollections of his touch, his breath, and his smell. My sensors have assimilated that much of him so fast without realising. Although I was in his presence at urgent, impactful moments just days ago, it makes sense to recall these details. But one man at a time in my head, please and thank you, and the one who I want to focus my energy on is blonde and Czech.

Resuming my sprint, trying to use my nose for air intake, not my mouth, I feel like I did those five sessions of yoga last December for nothing. Money well spent, they said. I'm happy my sarcasm is making an appearance if it prevents me from keeling over.

Push a little more, Vera, then find a ditch and name it after you.

My surroundings look familiar. I hope I'm not running in circles while avoiding all the moving obstacles. When I want to turn and retrace the streets behind me, I spot my point of reference, the restaurant, meaning the shop I'm searching for like a madwoman, is on this sidewalk. Slowing down, I check with big eyes, sweaty forehead, and chest pounding, all the commercial spaces I'm passing and when it's visible, lights still on, full of customers, I nearly collapse.

The prints are there. This is the correct shop. I should have figured they would be open late, until the tourists retreat to their hotels, but I'm taking no chances. My pulse comes back to normal in the duration it takes for the medium-sized shop to clear a bit. From the outside it looks like an old-world establishment, antiquities boutique with confectionery items. The name is in Czech and has the word chocolate in it. Warm and inviting, I don't understand why I hesitate to open the door. If the store has no connection to the man I'm looking for, come Monday when my new friends leave, I am left on the street. Enough money to spend on either food and a few nights at a cheap hotel or continue my travel to God knows where.

The shop assistant is an older man, not a grandfather though, too young to have an adult nephew. The problem is, my boy hacker only had his grandfather left alive, nobody else. No other family. The remaining clientele is leaving. Clearly, it's now or never. Still pushing my spleen in, I enter.

"Good evening."

"Hello." Why is my voice so small and timid?

"We are about to close; you are the lucky last customer. Feel free to peruse our products while I dim the lights and change the door sign." He smiles and I glance around the shelves filled with beautiful bonbons. I need to make a purchase and find the courage to ask my questions.

"Everything looks so lovely."

"Thank you. I suggest the pralines with walnuts." He returns to the register, waiting patiently.

How to phrase my query distracts me, how much to share with a stranger. Usually, I pay more attention when one talks of pralines.

Letting my hand decide the items, I pick a little bag of marzipan stars and another with berry glaze hearts and put them on the counter. He scans and wraps them as I fish for coins in my pockets.

"Many thanks."

"Anything else?"

"I'm wondering if this shop belongs to my friend's grandfather. Are you the owner, if you don't mind me asking?"

"Yes, I'm the owner."

"Oh," I say deflated.

"Well, part owner. I presume if we are speaking of the same person, your friend is my associate. Unfortunately, his grandfather passed away a couple of years ago. What is his name? Your friend?"

I hope we don't mean the same person, and Aleš still has his family.

"I'm sorry to hear that. Aleš Hemský is my friend, we knew each other when we were younger."

"Should I tell him you stopped by, miss . . . ?" He's hesitant to share more.

"Are we talking about the same man? Is he coming to the shop tomorrow?" I can't give him my name.

"No. I'm the only one dealing with the shop every day."

"Can I have his phone number, please? We haven't been in contact for years, but I'm visiting Prague until Monday and I wouldn't mind reconnecting."

"My associate is not in Prague at the moment, but I will let him know you enquired after him if you share your name." Why is he so secretive? I'm the one with the good reason.

"I must be going. Thank you for your help." My spirit is in pieces. He evidently doesn't want to share any pertinent information, and neither do I. Can't have my name searched on Google these days. I turn towards the exit and take my leave.

"Wait! Your chocolate."

"Oh, yes, I paid for them," I murmur, barely audible.

"Where can I tell him to find you, if he comes in time, and he's inclined to meet?" He sees my blurry eyes. Thank you, Jesus! Where should I say?

"The castle? The Prague Castle? I'll be there all Monday."

"That's a big place. Can you be more specific?"

"I'm sure we'll find each other if we look long enough." Listen, mister, I want to trust you, but my life is on the line. Should I risk it and give him my Belgian phone number?

"St Vitus Cathedral is the site to take in at sunset. My recommendation."

"I will not keep you longer. Thank you, again. Have a pleasant evening." I'm outside and gone in seconds.

That was draining, and I don't know what I accomplished. I'm inclined to say the expedition was a success, but until I have a direct conversation with Aleš, my search is not over.

With no destination in mind, I wander the streets of this beautiful city, deep in thought, until late evening when the effort of being outside all day walking takes its toll. My head itches with the desperate want to throw away the wig.

Ending up at the accommodation my friends are renting, nobody answers my knock, so I punch the code designed for these situations when there are not enough keys to share among everyone. Some friend I am, lying about nearly everything, starting with my name. I climb the stairs to my room, one step at a time, removing my sweater and the dreaded wig.

"You cut your hair! It looks so nice, brava!" I turn in a panic to see Patrizia and Gio in the doorway of their bedroom, wearing only sheets. I guess I wouldn't have bothered answering the door either, if otherwise occupied.

"Yes, spur-of-the-moment thing." I hide the fake hair between the items I am holding.

"So that's where you disappeared. Marc was looking for you," smirks Gio. "He will be pleased with the change." Right.

"Yeah, cause that's why she did it, idiota," mumbles Patrizia when she pulls him back into their bedroom with a small wave my way. Until they fly home, the wig stays in my luggage. Can't say I'm too upset about it.

A quick shower later, I force my brain to shut down, but unfortunately wide-awake eyes continue to stare at the ceiling for hours. By the time all of our household returns, loud drunk whispers in the corridors, one guided meditation ruined, I still have no clue what to do from Monday. The plan to meet Aleš is uncertain.

What is Hector planning at this moment? I bet his strategy could kick my strategy's ass.

Sunday starts as yesterday, crazy breakfast with the group and a solo walk to the chocolate shop only to find it closed. Odd since the schedule indicates the store should operate normally even today. Is this related to my visit? I pray bad luck doesn't claim other victims.

Crossing several streets to catch up with my friends, we arrive at the spa centre together. They invited me as well, all expenses included, since I'm replacing the girl who could not make it to Prague. As Farah mentioned on the airport train in Brussels, she cancelled because of an awful toothache the day of the flight and I get her bed, spa appointments, and tonight's festival ticket. I would call myself fortunate if only nights ago I wasn't busting out of Brompton Cemetery pushing a wheelbarrow. Having Margaret and the Belgium gang in my corner is a godsend.

"The new hair really works for you, Ama!" Marc mentions at the restaurant later and I am so relaxed, I give him a big smile. The manicure and pedicure deal, along with the facial and the body massage, worked wonders on my mood. My current status is fugitive with not enough answers to the many problems I've been having, but my fingers and toes nail polish matches and that's a start.

"Thank you! It was time for a change." I've been saying this phrase so often today, I almost believe my jaw-length hair is a recent addition to my look, not something I've been rocking my entire adult life.

We are having an early dinner before getting ready for the big party, and since tonight is the last night I'm to spend with this amazing group, I intend to enjoy it. Still in disguise in public, a hat, some sunglasses, hidden in plain sight around a bunch of tourists, this whole weekend recharged my batteries and helped release the shock I've accumulated from the moment I've been on high alert. I used little of Margaret's money since landing in Prague, and while I feel like a freeloader, desperate times overwhelm the embarrassment.

A few hours later, wearing my borrowed knee-high black boots and unbuttoned navy coat, I make my way to the festival arena, arm in arm with Farah and Marc. Underneath, I'm wearing a white oversized t-shirt dress. A party look that's neither tight nor too large, showing decent amount of leg but not something to draw attention. I refused Farah's offer to try one of her sparkly short dresses because as amazing as they looked, being that much on display in my current position would not be wise. I let her do my make-up of light smoky eyes and perfectly painted red lips.

We check in our coats and do a restroom stop after the half hour spent in line to enter. People from all continents come to this event. The streets were packed, and the crowd's energy excites everyone in our group.

The arena is alive, the amplifiers boom a second pulse in my veins. Three warehouse spaces, each presenting different artists playing trance music, a genre of electronic dance music. I recognise some DJs playing tonight, but it's been a while since my festival attending days back in Romania with my crew of after-hours chasers, and the scene has changed significantly. I ultimately realise, after mingling two hours with the sweaty masses, it's still about the music, the dance and the illegal drugs; I'm just older now, saying things like 'these kids are nuts' or asking to borrow an extra pair of earplugs.

Switching between stages, we stop at the multiple bars scattered around the room to do the customary group shots. Tequila or Jägermeister. The guys are drinking both, because why not, but I stop after my fourth shot of liquid fire of the night. Bottles of water and a gin and tonic keep me buzzing. For now.

Some of my housemates partake in the funny little pills I experimented with in my early twenties, and while I have nothing against people doing their thing, I don't care for a repeat. I've got enough adrenaline pumping in my vein these days as it is. The music is too loud to talk to each other properly, but you don't need words to move your body to this insane collective rhythm. People added fluorescent paint to their clothes and faces. They pass around glow sticks from all directions. We jump and sing to the few lyrics electronic music has, laughing with anyone joining in on the fun.

Our group diminishes as some stay in the back where the air is fresher and more breathable, a break from the crazy atmosphere, and some decide to go all the way to the front, where the volume is insane and the frenzy unavoidable. I'm dragged by Farah to join the adventurers, and I put little effort into fighting her.

"Come on, lazy, we need to shake those waffles off! I'm having seconds tomorrow!" The alcohol is strong in this one as she shouts in my amused face, and I've been pushing her to finish bottles of water to minimal success.

We navigate the crowd and form a small dancing circle in the heart of it all. Patrizia to my left, Juliet close by, Farah and Angie to my right. Lars, Gio and Marc are getting us more drinks at the central bar, mere meters away. Marc has been dancing with me, holding my hand, and while I am enjoying it as a touchy-feely person, who holds hands at a rave? I also don't want to give him the wrong idea. So, when two guys bump into me and Farah, getting us to turn around to their apologetic faces, we twirl with them.

I lift my hands in the air and let my body move in time with the music filling every cell of my body. The strobe lights above change from purple to black light and back to purple, then green and white in seconds and further elevate my pulse. The latest tequila shots we did not ten minutes ago are chasing away my inhibitions and troubles. I don't mind my dress riding up on my thighs while I'm blending with the slightly erotic dance of the sweaty, wonderful mess of partygoers. I am not sober anymore, but I'm still in control of my senses. Most of them. We move and touch and exist as one, and all my worries melt away. Sex is wonderful, but have you ever hugged a complete stranger on the dance floor because a record made the whole room fall in love?

Sensing a hard body push his front to my back, I close my eyes as big hands grip my waist with confidence. Leaning my head on the stranger's shoulder, or chest, he feels so tall, my arms move to his neck when his breathing intensifies on the sensitive skin of my cheek, my jaw. I entangle my fingers in his short hair when he bites my ear and speaks.

"You look better with the wig off, but I am happy you kept the smoky eyes and red lips, Vera!"

Fourteen

Often, people can't control their responses to the unexpected timbre of a familiar voice, and at present, I'm no different when I choose to run without so much as a glance back to confirm the speaker's identity. I am too quick for him to grab hold of me, and I take advantage of the large corridor formed by bodyguards assisting the skilled performers to their dancing stages. Consumed by the electrified mob ahead, I zig zag around like on an obstacles course.

My heart races before I'm even analysing the excitement filled pleasure I felt at his touch and at the sound of his gruff words. Is he chasing me? I change direction in the sea of people still enjoying their night. Or is it morning already? How did he know I was at this event in Prague to begin with, and how the bloody hell was he able to find me in this crowd?

Pushing across dozens of wired-up people near a bathroom exit, the opening notes of a beloved song play on the loudspeakers, and the entire pack of wild dancers go savage, screaming and shoving. Losing my balance would end with me trampled to death by the mosh pit. An elbow, or some other body part, hits my back hard, catapulting me forward to a group of dancing men. They put their arms around my shoulders to get me to twirl with them. My protests are ignored, my throat hurts from shouting when an arm circles my waist and lifts me, effectively removing any connection with the clammy embrace I was in.

"Back off or I'll fucking make you," the authoritative voice holding me tight says when the guys attempt a second hug. In a flash, he carries me away and drops me in front of a black wall.

Strong naked arms cage me in on both sides, and I have yet to turn around. People are still going crazy near us, and I know the reason he brought me here, and not continued towards an exit. It's impossible to move in any direction without getting a black eye. They push him into me, his chest to my back.

Powerful hands flex on the wall from the force of his restraint, and my eyes close at their sight. We are both breathing fast from the chase, and his hasty exhale cools the top of my head. My heart is threatening to break through bone and flesh in its forceful beat, no doubt from the run, the loud music. Not from the heat and the closeness of the man behind me. The song reaches its peak as I turn, brushing his front, pressing my spine to the vibrating wall.

He is watching my face when my eyes open, and I tremble in the intensity of his gaze. My heaving chest gets his attention, and I blink repeatedly. He's dressed in all black again. His hair is short now, probably his version of a permanent disguise. Without thinking, my legs part to accommodate his body when the moving masses press him into me. He peruses the exposed skin of my thighs as my dress rides up and up. Raising his stare, the blue nearly overcome by the black of his dilated pupils, he moves his lips a fraction to the right and up in a barely perceived smirk. The infuriating wolfish sign makes me bare my own clenched fangs, but instead of intimidating him, his fingers dare to brush the sticky hair from my face. They mock me further when they cup my cheek, his thumb smudging my lipstick with intent, while the others press into the skin of my neck in a possessive grasp. Rebelling against his hold, I lift my chin to confront him, even though I doubt he can hear me.

"Hector, you have some nerve—" I swallow the rest of my lecture when he leans in to press burning lips to my red ones.

Well, hello!

His tongue demands entry, eager teeth bite into my bottom lip, and my head hits the wall once. Before a second time happens, his hand fists my hair, angling my head how he wants it. My lips part to kiss him in return, the tip of my tongue tentatively licking his, and the hand in my hair tightens.

It's my turn to punish his bottom lip and to moan into his mouth. He tastes of mint and whiskey, and I forget where we are. My hands go to his neck, to link behind his head, to pull on the short locks at his nape. His other hand goes to my hip, moving down to where my dress meets slick skin, further down to lift my leg onto his body, pressing his jean-clad pelvis into me. All the while kissing me with powerful strokes of tongue and lips. The foot still standing on the ground goes on tiptoes, impatient to match him. To get to him faster. At a better angle.

The wolf is back to bite my already swollen mouth, my jaw, my ear, my neck, licking and piercing to the rhythm of his moving hips. With his hand on my leg, the dress is at midriff level on one side, and I feel the force of his arousal directly through my high-waisted thong. He grabs my naked ass cheek and squeezes with a grunt, his fingers pushing into my heated flesh, making me wetter with every passing second.

Greed for more of his skin replaces my common sense, giving my hands-free rein to drag his t-shirt up so they can tremble on his muscular abdomen. He shivers at the touch, breaking our kiss to glance at my nails on his skin.

You could drown in this power.

Desperate want of his strength and command on my willing body weakens my balance and I would slide down the wall if not for his flawless mastery at keeping me where his body wishes mine to remain.

As an afterthought, I notice the mad army of dancers around us has calmed down a bit. Hector continues to lick my collarbone, oblivious to all but me. The crowd sways with the music at a short distance, but a few smirking onlookers are appreciating the show we offer, and my tequila-induced brain wakes up.

Shoving at Hector's chest, not moving him an inch, I hold his face to speak in his ear. He misinterprets my actions and takes my mouth again with a bite. Removing my leg from around him to rearrange my dress, I refuse to give him my lips a second time.

"Why are we stopping, Vera?" he rasps in my face.

"Hector, they are watching us! People are looking at us!" This message penetrates his aroused state, and he lets me push him away, but not too far. He sobers up in front of me, becoming alert. He takes my hand, pulling me towards the nearest exit and I remember my friends, why I am here, in the Czech Republic, my abduction a week ago, The Hyde and my interrogation.

"Stop! Hey, let go of my hand! Hector, let go of me!" I try to remove my fingers from his. He continues our stride to the door, mostly dragging me.

"You loved holding hands all night with your teenage crush, so is it me you don't like to hold hands with?" What? Was he spying on me for long before he made his appearance known?

"He is not a teenager and I need my friends to tell them I am—"

"You want to drag them into this? The entire town is swarming with Fosters & Co assassins, and you want to go back to your fucking party and your Belgian?"

"He's not my . . . wait, I can't go outside like this! I need my coat!" I say as we arrive near the arena's exit.

"Fuck your coat!"

"Stop cursing, you jackass!"

"Can I go back to kissing?" he says casually, turning to glance at me, sweaty from top to bottom, sore lips, and crazy hair from the activities we reluctantly finished minutes ago. He seems to agree we need to cover me, whatever one looks like after a dance off and a hardcore petting session against a wall. With his arm around my shoulders, God forbid I move alone one step, we join the small queue by the Wardrobe sign.

"How did you find me?"

"Tonight, in here? Or do you mean how I found Ama Monteil's itinerary from London to Brussels to Prague?" he deadpans, speaking not directly at me, but to the room he scans for threats. Okay then! Another identity I can't use anymore.

"Are the kidnappers really in Prague, or are you using them to manipulate me into coming with you? Which, for your information, I did not agree to. We parted ways for a reason."

"We did not part ways. You fled in a very dangerous move and in a critical moment."

"I'm not apologising for doing what I thought was right for me. You let that creep torture me with his presence and stupid questions. And may I remind you I spent the night on a concrete floor? Kindly remove your hands before I break them in half." I am getting worked up again, embarrassed that I let him kiss me and worst of all, that I kissed him back after what he did in London, with a ravenous and all-consuming passion. After checking to see how serious I am about my threat, he gives me some breathing space.

"We did not find you. Fosters & Co had surveillance on Eurostar and its destinations. In airports as well. The commotion you caused in Brussels appeared on our radar, and it wasn't awfully hard to obtain the Prague flight manifest once we knew where our running damsel was off to. Pretty standard stuff for people with money and motivation."

"Can you be more obnoxious?" The attendant hands me my coat. "You don't have one?"

"It's in the car. Thank your new friends for posting their itinerary all over social media this weekend, that's how I found you here. Not to spoil your mood, in case you still wish to disco, I wasn't the only one wasting hours searching for you inside the arena. At least a handful of confirmed steroid-pumping mercenaries were ready to snatch you. You are lucky I was the most determined amongst your pursuers. Let's go, your chariot awaits."

Steroid-pumping mercenaries? The creeps chasing me at the airport?

People are mingling outside of the arena, some leaving, others just arriving. Taxis block the cold streets. The wind hits me in the face as I listen to Hector give orders to someone over the phone.

"What do you mean, you are not here anymore? Who made you move? We are at the main entrance, but we'll walk towards the underground station. Come pick us up on the way there!"

"Great escape plan. Is Dumber the runaway driver?"

A hand placed on my back directs me down the road. We walk a few minutes in silence and I think it's pointless to mention I need to pick up my things from the accommodation I shared with my friends. What would they think of my vanishing act? Did they see me run from Hector or did the dance floor chaos offer the perfect cover for my disappearance? We stroll at a faster pace now. The station is minutes away.

"Why have you come for me, Hector? Do you still think I sold you the information from Fosters & Co?"

"That's not important at the moment. They've come for you, and we need to keep you safe. Running away did not help your cause in convincing me of your innocence. Quite the opposite. But I'm not letting them control the narrative anymore. We need to work together."

My stride falters, but I recover quickly. His declaration pierces the soft bubble my heart created, thinking he cared for me as a person, not wanting to see me hurt because I matter. Not because I'm a cog in this fucked up conspiracy and getting to me before Fosters & Co is a win against them. Silly me.

Someone separates us from behind, pushing me to the side, and interrupting my thoughts. A group of enthusiastic Czech-speaking men, having difficulty keeping themselves upright, try to catch Hector's attention and I stumble a step.

"Vera! Vera! Over here, to your left! Quick!" Turning, I see a tall person next to an open car door. Is that Lawrence? The side street he's on is dark. When I look at Hector, arguing with the noisy drunks, the mysterious man must have raced towards me because a second later he pulls my arm, dragging me towards the idling car. Before I shout and yank myself free, he covers my mouth with a gloved hand, and his head appears in front of me. He is a stranger, yet his features are familiar in a way that stops my breathing.

"I'm rescuing you, pretty hobbit! You can kick my ass later, deal?" I nod at his smiling, perfect face because Aleš Hemský has found me!

When I open the passenger door, Hector shouts my name. He's held by two men who aren't so drunk anymore.

"Vera, don't! Vera!"

I refuse to look at him when we speed past their group.

Fifteen

Six Months Earlier - London, England

The madness on Oxford Street assaults my already irritated mood once I step out of the underground station. Travelling like sardines is not what I signed up for. Luckily, the chilly Friday evening is bound to improve in minutes. My favourite people wait for me with a drink at the trendy rooftop that I have difficulty finding courtesy of the Central London human maze in front of me.

Leaving Poland was harder than I thought, from an emotional perspective, but my new city is slowly seducing me in the fortnight I've been here with a gentle fall transition mostly spent between sunny park days, museums, and cosy eateries. Adjusting to eight million individuals and a longer commute to every destination is a separate process.

"Did you have a great first week at work? Was everyone nice?" Lina kisses my cheek when I arrive, and I shift left to hug my brother, too. His face breaks into the mischievous smile he's been wearing since picking me up from the airport, when he told me all my future weekends are booked with hiking excursions and other fun activities. His joy at my move is clear and endearing, even if Lina organised this evening just for us girls. We couldn't object to his self-invite. "Do I need to lean on someone in particular to correct their behaviour?" She says, as I take a seat across from them in the lively restaurant.

They came earlier to buy me a gift they think I know nothing about. But Cristi spoke with Astrid today, who is in Bucharest and can't keep secrets to save her life. My brother stands with his phone glued to his ear and signals his immediate return. He works around the clock for a small but successful business consultancy company, developing projects for established organisations such as Fosters & Co, who even offered him a permanent position he refused. One Nicolescu per company is enough. His networking skills are enviable despite his cutthroat professional attitude. Hence why he is paid the big bucks and gets along with Astrid so well. Many moons ago, when he was at university, my parents and I were concerned with his choice of entourage and gambling penchant, but he dropped that lifestyle without a second thought as soon as he realised how damaging it was to his success trajectory.

"You were at my desk every two hours. Everyone was great. The reason for my slight anxiety, my tense attitude as we spoke, is related to the amount of pressure and expectations they place on my new role." I say to Lina studying the menu.

"Your manager didn't give you time to accommodate. I don't want you to regret moving from Warsaw because this guy buries you in work from day one. Youssef said he didn't like the man."

"Stop it. You know I always wanted to move here, and he gave me the opportunity. I'll find my rhythm."

"Let me know if I can help you with anything." She pats my hand to interlace our fingers on the white tablecloth. A few weeks before, I packed everything I had in the little Polish apartment where I felt safe and comfortable for years, I expressed my concerns about starting fresh in a different country at our age. When it's more difficult to make friends and integrate into already established groups. Since then, she's been nothing but supportive and has helped me unpack the never-ending row of boxes lining the walls of my Wimbledon house. Between her and Cristi, I don't

think I spent an evening alone since I arrived on the British shores with my hopeful desire to be delighted by the unexpected.

"I have meetings with every department head next week. Maybe you could share your insights about them."

"Should we spend Sunday together watching The Voice, strategising, and gossiping about every pompous executive in the office?"

"Yes!"

"Okay. I'll come to your place for a sleepover if you cook your tasty lasagne." She suggests knowing her place is closer to the office, but she's willing to spend Monday morning on the train with me because, as a friend, Lina wins all the awards.

"Deal." I pull on our connected palms to steal a side hug from her.

"What are you being all emotional about without me? Did you show her the surprise?" Cristi asks upon his return.

"No! I was waiting for you. My gift giving etiquette is better than you assume." Lina says with a pointed look.

"How lovely! Be still my heart. I have gifts for you two as well." I reply, searching in my backpack for the items I bought hours ago in my lunch break, after I chatted with Astrid.

"What? No! We were supposed to be the generous people tonight." Cristi cries, his face so much like our mothers when she's outraged.

"We wanted to surprise you for once!" Lina admits with a headshake, showing me her tongue and her middle finger as a gesture of maturity.

"Ha! Better luck next time, youngling. Nobody can surprise me."

Sixteen

From a biological perspective, how much adrenaline can a body produce before the overuse of those untrained glands shuts down production? Mine are getting the workout of a lifetime judging by the increased heart rate beating against the palm I press to my chest and the enlarged pupils I spy in the car's windows as I watch the scenery change.

"They'll release him once we are at a safe distance, or he spends some time in a holding cell. Your call." Aleš drives the silent vehicle with confidence, discreetly glancing over at me every few seconds. He's dressed in a dark green wool jacket and navy jeans. Honey-blonde hair slicked back. Longer on top, shorter on the sides. Silver watch. No wedding band.

"I can't believe you're here! That I'm here, in a car with you," I say when I find his eyes on me again.

"Vera, what should I do with the man my team is currently holding? Who is he to you? Same goes for his buddy waiting in a getaway car a couple of streets to the south."

"Oh! Assuming they can no longer catch up with us, let them go, unharmed." Mostly unharmed.

“They will not.” He sends a text and returns the phone to his jacket.

“He is very resourceful.” Finding me in a sea of dancing people.

“So am I. Now, I’ll drive you to my house and you can tell me all about it. Don’t worry, it’s a hideaway really, rather than just my current lodging. You caused quite the stir when you spoke with my business partner on Saturday. The individuals that have been arriving in Prague over the weekend searching for a woman with different names are hard to miss. All this alludes to an intriguing story to say the least. Do you agree with this plan?”

“Yes. Thank you. I’m sorry for causing trouble and honestly, you might not want to deal with this complication. With me.” I’m putting people in danger every day I am on the run and I’m completely at their mercy – I have no money, no connections. I hate being so defenceless when I am used to fixing my problems without external interference. Realising I’m too self-sufficient and independent in my ways saved me a lot of therapy money when I wanted an answer to why my relationships don’t work.

“Thanks for the warning, but that’s for me to decide. I came, didn’t I?”

“You did, but . . . I’m up against a powerful corporation that kidnapped me and most likely wants me dead. Dangerous doesn’t begin to describe this entire clusterfuck.” He deserves to know.

“I don’t shy away from danger in my line of business, and I am not starting now. I understood something was wrong when the facial recognition software found you running around London, Brussels, and Prague under a fake identity. Especially since I know your day-to-day activities are never that exciting.”

“Yes, I’ve been busy. Wait . . . how would you know how my days are?”

"Ah, that's just an expression." He shifts innocent eyes from me to the road.

"No, that's not what you meant. Have you been spying on me again? You promised you'd stop doing that. Back then." I am not really mad, I wanted him to find me. I knew of his proclivities since we were barely adults. Spying on me and invading my privacy was why we broke up many years ago. I'm just surprised he's still doing it, and a tad annoyed.

"No, I'm not spying, not in the real sense of the word. I kept tabs on you, but not personally. And just once every few years. Really! You forget I was taught at an early age how fucked up this world is. I deal with it constantly." His parents were killed at the hand of the organised crime syndicates calling Prague their home. His father, a detective that wouldn't bend at the pressure of the Balkan mafia, and his mother, a schoolteacher with a beautiful smile she passed on to her son.

Long into our internet courtship I found out about the pain the carefree Aleš was trying to bury deep within an arrogant attitude, silly puns, and illegal hacking. Before our communication stopped, I realised I couldn't help someone refusing to work through his issues, no matter how much I tried, but it still took me months not to feel like I have abandoned him.

"So, you had a stranger do it and that makes it okay? I guess that's an improvement," I say sarcastically. Did I trade a conceited jerk for a psychopath? "Are you still a hacker?"

"I work in national security. Among other things." He smiles brilliantly.

"Of course, you do." I shake my head at him.

"Come on, don't get upset. There is chocolate in the glove compartment if you find it in your heart to forgive me," he bribes.

There's a grin he can't wipe out of his face when I dive into the candy.

"This chocolate is the anchor keeping me from lashing out at the ridiculous men in my life, but spying is not permitted." He keeps beaming those straight teeth at me. He grew into his body, muscular without looking like a gym addict. Sharp cheekbones, masculine, freshly shaved jaw, and those gem brown eyes, still hypnotic a decade later. Does he have to resemble the guy in a perfume ad when I'm such a sweaty mess?

"Do you like it? Did I remember the right chocolate for you?"

"It's so good, thank you. You remembered. White chocolate with roasted coffee beans is phenomenal. Although I'm impartial to most sweets these days. And yes, I still don't share."

"I wouldn't come between you and your addiction, darling," he says, content to see me enjoy his family's recipe.

"The shop looks amazing, by the way. I was sad to hear about your grandfather. I'm sorry for your loss."

"Yeah, he's missed. But he was sick towards the end, and you know . . ." Aleš clears his throat but swallows the remaining words. Leaning in, I caress the open palm closer to me, squeezing it for support. Losing people is never easy.

"Not in a million years did I imagine our first encounter happening in this context," I say to his profile. The content face slowly taking form at our interlaced fingers disappears, and he takes a moment to reply, focusing on the drive towards a tree-filled area. Both hands on the steering wheel now.

"Right after you had another guy attached to your lips."

"Are you serious?" I choke on the chocolate.

"Not a pretty visual for me, despite the lovely dress you wear."

"You were inside?"

"We had surveillance operating since you left the villa for your spa appointment yesterday, but I only arrived in Prague an hour ago and I did not want to scare you by sending a stranger to approach you instead of me. Or maybe I should have asked them to break the public display of . . ." He looks at me all serious before releasing a loud laugh. "Relax Vera, I'm joking. About the kissing part. It's good to see you, regardless. When I got the call about the frightened woman looking for me, matching your description, I wanted you safe and my people find you quick enough. I got on a plane as fast as I could."

"I appreciate your help very much. I didn't realise I sounded scared to your friend. You came having no prior obligation towards me, making terrible jokes like you always did, but you are here, and it means a lot."

"What's the point in knowing how to hack a satellite and having special ops at your disposal if you can't help the woman who broke your heart, right?" he says, smile renewed.

"Thank you. You're still not funny but thank you." Staring out the window at the forest passing by, I add, "And you broke my heart too."

"I know." He offers after a beat, driving in silence the rest of the way.

Three wooden cabins appear close to each other, part of a complex outside Prague which he mentions the team uses occasionally. Only a few trusted people know the location, and it's currently guarded by four armed professionals.

Showered and dressed in men's clothes yet again, over a cup of tea I tell my secret agent, spy, ex-boyfriend everything that happened to me over the course of a week. He offers to break a few fingers when he hears about my unnecessary interrogation.

"I'm a paranoid bastard, and I would have suspected you and everyone else had I been in Worthington's and Neville's situation. But knowing young Nicolescu, the idea of her involvement in a corporate cover-up of this magnitude, is ridiculous." He snorts a laugh into his coffee mug.

"Your tone and choice of words should insult me, but it's refreshing to know someone believes me. As for who stole my identity to cast me in the mole's role, I have no clue."

"They used key details from your professional life, your employee number, and they knew you lived and worked in Poland, so it could easily be just a Fosters & Co employee with access to HR files picking your name out of a hat. My guess, we are looking for someone close to you, it's usually the case in these scenarios. Once I gain access to your company's network, I'll discover who has tampered with your account."

Did I obliviously ignore someone despising me to this extent? Surely not. Astrid once confessed she both envied and pitied my ability to only perceive the positive traits in my friends, family, and the individuals I fell in love with and that sometimes I build them up in my head. We argued that my naïvety was just her perception of me and maybe her penchant for fighting or contradicting *every* person she interacted with, friend or foe, was clouding her relationships. Evidently, we got nowhere fast with that discussion, but I foresee a big *I told you so* when she learns of my predicament. Right after she hugs me in her pixie arms with a strength rarely found in women her size.

"Do you need to be on Fosters & Co's server to connect to the network? Or how does that work?" I ask.

"Multiple ways to infiltrate a network and making someone click on a link to invite me in is still easier than blinking." He grabs a laptop out of a brown leather bag and returns to the small couch we've been using by the robust fireplace. The wood cabin has a living room with an incorporated kitchen, a tiny bedroom dwarfed by a king-size bed, and a bathroom with a walk-in shower.

"Finding the imposter will clarify why I'm in this position in the first place, but as I'm already privy to their criminal activities, Fosters & Co will not let me walk away like nothing happened." I move towards the cold window in the long sleeve thermal I borrowed from Aleš. His white socks cover my feet and I'm back in large boxers, no pants. A new day lights the wet ground and the mostly naked trees. It started raining a while back.

"One step at a time, Vera. We'll persuade them."

"I can't stay in Prague for too long, right? Now that they know I'm here. Was the arena really compromised?"

"We spotted several suspicious individuals mingling with the regular crowd, but we had eyes on you, and for some reason, they kept their distance. We might have been too concentrated on them, and they identified us as well. Until we lost you and Worthington for a second. You are safe for now, but we're moving you soon. A different passport is already processing for the appropriate moment. Why don't you try to sleep for a bit? Get some rest while I set some things in motion. Leaving my current job in a hurry demands I smooth some feathers and take a couple of days off to navigate your situation."

"Are my friends from Belgium safe? Should I warn them?"

"We have people watching over them. We alerted the Prague police force about the mercenaries without bringing attention to you. Don't worry." His arms open to accept my hug. He thought of everything.

"Aleš and Alexandra together at last," he murmurs into my hair, and I squeeze his middle with a tired chuckle.

"I can't really sleep, but I'll lie down for a while. Where will you be staying?" I look around the room.

"The free cabin next to yours when I'm done. Or the couch here if it helps you rest better."

"The couch is perfect for me, and you can have the bed."

"Nonsense. Go. Sleep. Now."

"Bossy," I say, opening the bedroom door and before it shuts with me on the other side, I hear a quiet, "You used to like me bossy" to which I offer no reply. I used to like him a lot, all the ways I could have him. But that was ages ago, when everything was simple and vivid images of Hector's lips touching mine weren't invading my thoughts every waking moment.

He must be furious. And what was he thinking? That I'll just go with him because he kissed me? Because he thinks he's my one and true saviour? As it seems, I have options for knights in shining armour. One more deranged than the other.

Manipulative as they were, I bite my bottom lip to the memory of those kisses. I see him when I lay in bed with my eyes closed, feel my cheeks heat from where my mind is heading, to the unchecked passion his hands and teeth bruised my eager skin. Can I blame my behaviour on the drugs they gave me last Monday or the tequila I had earlier?

Ah, wisdom, you have eluded me for years.

I roll on the mattress towards the wall leading to Aleš, the boy, the man I dreamed of for years after our falling out. I used to imagine his face next to mine, his open mouth on me, his voice memorised from all the phone calls we had when he asked me about my life in Romania. He would end every conversation with a laugh and a demand I think of him if I'm lonely. Even from a distance, he was the one who made me realise I liked confident men, dominant personalities that make bending to their commands attractive, yet playful enough to never feel like I am without control.

And now here I am. Trying to stay alive and sane, not overcomplicate matters with overbearing romantic interests. Maybe Astrid is right in saying I fill my head with fantasy delusions if I associate what Hector did as romantic.

To avoid endless thoughts regarding the kissing thief, I allow a barrage of question to invade my fragile peace. And once they enter, shaking all the mental doors I kept locked, to hide my hope in secret pathways, the damage they leave behind scars my insides.

Is my family worried about me not reaching out? What if Fosters & Co captured them thinking I'll eventually show up there? What if they lock them away and use torture?

What if word got out about Margaret's involvement in my escape from London? And despite Aleš' reassurance, is my Belgian crew in danger?

Exhaustion wins before I lose my mind. It offers no respite as I dream of tight spaces again, of running on bare feet until my lungs can't take it anymore. But what's new?

The sound of rain mixed with multiple voices arguing in the other room wakes me up. I reach for the phone I bought at the airport in Brussels. Aleš deemed it safe after five minutes in his wizard hands. New messages from Farah and Marc, and I cringe at their assumptions that I left with my ex-boyfriend without a word. The seductive, dark-haired mountain, according to her description. Farah tells me to have fun and be safe. That she packed my things and left them at the shop opposite the villa they vacated mid-morning for their departure flight. I can't reply. The condition of keeping the phone was to not send texts or call unsecured lines.

The teddy cam notifications catch my attention. I fortify my composure before opening the thread of videos that might illuminate my mission, but the chances of obtaining relevant information are slim. The camera reveals the maintenance crew arriving before everyone, a long video showing nothing interesting.

The second video has my manager's back in the left side corner. Relaxed voice and attitude as he speaks with a woman out of view. Her speech is soft, difficult to hear at first, but then she snaps at what the man says regarding my disappearance. The woman is Astrid! They vanish and the video ends, but not before I hear his voice assuring her that I'm fine and only in need of a break.

A break? What? How would he know? Is he the mole?

The third feed puts a smile on my baffled face and then shatters my heart. A phantom blow to the stomach that chokes me. It starts with one of my best friends taking a seat in my chair, reaching for a coconut-filled candy bar before opening my laptop, which I left locked on my workstation the last time I was in the office building. She stays there for seven minutes, looking ahead a few times to make sure nobody sees her using my laptop, my passwords, my account, to ruin my life some more.

This is a mistake. Surely.

Stepping out of bed on shaky legs, I hold my throat when I cannot swallow what I've learned. *No, no, not her.* But it makes sense how I've been framed so perfectly; she knows everything about me and used it to get me locked in a coffin.

Perhaps she did not understand what they would do to me.

Did she start this knowing I would get in trouble? Lina Haas is my friend, the sweetest soul of us all. Her no makeup face in the video was confident, if a bit impatient, natural blonde hair almost white, pulled back by the pink satin headband I bought her. Slow blinking blue eyes under her beautiful yellowy eyelashes, normal in the laptop's light. Her only sign of discomfort was her skin turning red around her throat and chest area. Over what she did to me or because she was afraid to get caught at my workstation? My vision blurs as my hands pull on the hair at my nape.

She wanted to cover her bases and not use her credentials when stealing valuable information. As a Risk Officer at Fosters & Co, her desk sees thousands of data files on everything under the sun. And maybe I know why Lina did it. Why she needed the money from Hector and Lawrence. What I don't understand is how my friend could throw me to the wolves so easily. But I guess saving her father, sick for years with cancer, penniless and lonely back in Germany, took precedence over thinking about me twice. About our friendship.

I'm such a naïve idiot. When Hector mentioned the mole and I combed for reasons for why anyone would harm me, I completely ignored my best friend taking time off to care for her parent after a costly operation. Costs that she could practically afford overnight when her salary is not that different from mine and mostly spent on living life to the fullest. I overlooked this because Lina's my person. I couldn't or wouldn't think badly of her.

How could she do this to me? For a second, even though I know he wouldn't put me at risk, she made me doubt my own brother, thinking that if he was a consultant on the W&N merger, he might be the informer.

With a sense of lost and rising loathing, I stand next to the bed, looking outside the window at the heavy downpour. *Make haste and shut down,* whispers the heart, as invisible poison pumps into my veins.

Goosebumps form on my skin, despite the radiator emanating heat underneath the windowsill. There's a draft coming from the other room. Where people are probably discussing my fate. How

I've been betrayed, kidnapped, forced to run, hide, and disconnect from the life I know.

No recovery after this. She hates you. Look what she did.

Why do I care if Lina hates me? I'm not the one in the wrong. I'll piece myself together.

You can try.

Shut up!

Crossing the room, I open the door to Aleš working at his computer, talking to a tall man standing next to him. I freeze when both turn, noticing my arrival, moving just my gaze from the brown in Aleš' eyes to the hard blue in the other man's glare.

"I thought you said he couldn't find me." I stare Hector down. His new haircut made recognition difficult, but he is the same devil I renounced twice already.

"He didn't, but once I realised the safest option for your future and well-being is for us to join forces with Worthington, the team brought him here," the handsome blonde hacker turned secret agent tries to placate me with a moderate tone, palms up, as if to say let's be reasonable.

Let's not! The bloody nerve on them.

"I don't like it either, but it's for the best," Hector dares to add from his spot, arms crossed, the picture of calm. Say that to your eyes, buddy, they look murderous. God, I hope mine look the same.

"Unbelievable!" I shake my head, walking to the bathroom and closing the door after me with the force to shake all the windows of this presumably secure cabin.

When I find my bag on the bathroom's floor, with all my things, the one Farah left at the shop, I become vicious. Either they followed my friends, or my phone is not as safe as I've been told. Clearly, I don't need to be consulted on anything before they decide. This is bloody ridiculous; they planned my life while I slept.

Irritating, arrogant, psychotic men. And a treacherous best friend who started this falling domino chain from hell.

The hot shower does me no good and I walk out half an hour later dressed to leave. They decided it was *for the best.* They can ride into the sunset together, for all I care. Yes, I know we should join forces to hit Fosters & Co more efficiently. I don't have the skills to take down corporate empires by myself. But I am also a functioning adult, not a nitwit to disregard so blithely. I don't need this headache on top of everything, and when I find them waiting for me on the couch, I roll my eyes to beg for heavenly patience. Should I have used the tiny shower window to break free?

"Vera, listen, I know how this looks. We caught you off guard, but as you know, we need to act fast. I uncovered news you will hate, but it clears your name of any wrongdoing, for those who needed convincing." Aleš comes toward me to place an arm around my shoulder, giving Hector a quick glance. The Englishman remains silent and seated, eyes glued to my face, then to Aleš' hand on my neck.

"You should have woken me up before taking decisions affecting *my* well-being," I snap, staring into Aleš' autumn eyes. I lift my chin to see him properly. Everyone is taller than me. A sigh releases the venom on my tongue. He is trying to help me. "I appreciate you came to my rescue. Without your support, my chances are grim, and I will be forever in your debt. But don't manage me, I need to be consulted and listened to. If you can't do that, I will make other arrangements." Thunder picks that moment to shake the skies, as if to mock my conviction that I would leave on this punishing rain.

"I hear you and I apologise."

"I mean it, Aleš. Our history together already makes me wary of believing what you say and what you do." The knot in my throat is hard to push down and biting my cheek keeps me from saying harsher words, or maybe from bursting into tears over Lina's actions.

"Earlier was not fitting to confess, but believe me, I regret the extreme and insane things I put you through ten years ago. Abusing your trust like that. I was a jealous, reckless, stupid kid with too much free time and anger in spades," he says for my ears only, holding my neck in his hands. "I wanted to wake you before Worthington got here, but you looked so peaceful resting in my bed. I intended to give you that safety and some efficient plans to solve this for you. But I fucked up and I'm sorry." He licks his lips, stopping his speech for a second. "Years passed, and we moved on from the feelings we had, but I promised myself if we meet, I will make amends. You can't imagine how much it meant having you in my life right after my parents died. How much you meant to me. The mad things I would have done if you weren't such a positive influence in my darkest times. I would jump at any chance to help you. To take away your worries."

"I don't expect you to fix it for me as much as I appreciate you being here. And I forgave you years ago, but it's good to hear these words." Pulling him into a hug, I bury my face in his chest, squeezing him as hard as he holds me. The ache I feel at our past is still there, but joyful tenderness pushes through, at the same time as bittersweet tears fall into my cheeks, soaking his t-shirt. He smells of forest and aftershave.

"I made you breakfast, too. Pancakes!" He smiles those pearly whites upon releasing me. Hector is by the window, with his back to the emotional scene happening mere feet from him. I all but forgot about the other man in the room and why I got mad. Embarrassment colours my skin when I think that I ended the night in his arms, then ran and woke up in another's embrace. An awkward start to another week as a fugitive.

"You said you had some news?" I use my hand to cover a mouth full of pancakes with jam and chocolate. Aleš joins me at the table with his laptop and a mug of coffee.

"You officially took a leave of absence from Fosters & Co," he says as his fingers move on the keyboard. "An email was sent from your account to your manager who then arranged with HR to approve your sabbatical. They left no trace for me to check who actually emailed, and unfortunately, I still need a few hours to know who used your account to sell stolen information to Worthington and Neville. It couldn't have been you since there's proof of the mole using your details when you were nowhere near a computer. Even these past few days."

"So, you are here not because you trust me, but because evidence proves I'm innocent. Makes sense," I address Hector's back. He remains silent but turns to us, crossing his arms. "And thanks for doing your best, Aleš, but I already know who framed me. Friend and confidant, Lina Haas. I win at picking people for my inner circle." Covering for her crossed my mind but they would find out, eventually. I wipe melted chocolate from my upper lip with the tip of my tongue. An action followed by both men.

"How do you know that? Were you suspecting her?" Aleš inquires.

"Nope." I sound more relaxed than I am, and I don't know how I'm managing it. What Lina did to me hurts. It crushes my spirit, but I also get it in a way.

No, you don't.

"Care to share how, then?" a closed off Hector asks, taking the chair next to me and a bite of pancake goodness he steals from my plate, and I watch his closed mouth chew for a beat too long.

"As a gift yet to send, I bought and forgot a teddy camera on my desk at work, and I activated it recently. This morning, the camera sent three video notifications. Two were irrelevant, more or less, and one was showing Lina accessing my computer, looking mighty suspicious. Maybe she wants to play a prank on me for when I return to the office. We do silly things in good humour. Maybe she doesn't know Fosters & Co kidnapped me and the mole's jig is up. But what are the chances someone else is the spy? Especially since she shouldn't know my passwords and her motive is now solid in my mind. Her father is sick. Very sick." I finish my breakfast, but it feels like I ate ash. The thought of Lina, what she did, ruining the sweet taste of chocolate.

"I'm sorry, pretty hobbit." Aleš uses the old endearment he coined during our internet courtship. He holds my hand. "That sucks. Also, I'm kind of proud, weirdly. You are a little surveillance fiend yourself. I must have rubbed on you a touch, as much as it pains you to admit," he says smirking.

"You would be proud, jerk." I punch his arm. "I got more than I bargained for with the hidden camera. I'm relieved I know who did it." The last part is a lie. "We can wait for you to confirm it, Aleš, but I'm pretty sure who took a sledgehammer to my peace."

"Making Fosters & Co aware they are after the wrong person and giving them the actual name of the informer to get them off your back wouldn't help," Hector cares to comment with his two cents. I interlace my fingers below my chin and glower into his cold, blue eyes. Such a significant difference from the way he gazed at me hours ago.

"It's not what I'm thinking, and to save you the trouble in the future, it will never be what I'm thinking. Don't assume you know me. I would never sell her out. Especially knowing what they will do to her. Not even because she fucked up my life like the foolish bitch she is." I raise my voice on that last phrase.

"Easy tiger. We are all friends here." Aleš tries to keep the peace.

"I'm not so keen on friends right now." My blood is boiling, I'm so furious at the dark-haired condescending prick in front of me. The door to my back opens and a freezing wind hits me before I turn to face a smiling Lawrence Neville. Exactly what this conversation was missing, the last variable of a disaster.

"I've got news!"

Seventeen

"Sleeping Beauty is finally up! Did you wake her with another kiss?" Lawrence says as he removes his jacket, and my face turns red at the suggestion. "Oh, don't look at him like that. He didn't kiss and tell; he just didn't turn his mic off when he shoved his tongue down your throat. Even with the music, I could hear the adolescent panting."

"Mate! Unnecessary!"

"Neville!"

The guys speak simultaneously, Hector directing a murderous gaze at his friend, and I study the ceiling for black holes to swallow me whole and spare me the embarrassment.

"Touchy, are we?" The new arrival swings smirking eyes between the three of us and stops at me. "Anyway, it's good to see you again, Miss Nicolescu. And all in one piece. I admit, I didn't believe you could make it this far on your own, but here you are. Full of surprises, connections, and men falling over you. Bravo!"

"Your praise means everything to me," I deadpan.

"Anytime. Uplifting people is a hobby of mine." He joins us at the table. "In all seriousness, I need to offer you my sincere apologies for my treatment at The Hyde. And not only because your other boyfriend threatened castration if I cause you any future distress." He nods his chin towards Aleš who clears his throat to say something, but chatty Larry continues, "My father died, my mate got kidnapped, and my frustrations got the better of me, not realising you are another victim of this disastrous predicament. It's making us all mad, and it's hard to trust strangers anymore. Truce?"

"I can't say it's all in the past now, but I'll stop hoping a giant piano falls on your head," I offer.

"That's magnanimous of you."

"I'm an inspiration, I know. And it's nice to see that some can actually offer apologies. Teach that to the more clueless." I refuse to look at Hector, but he knows I mean him.

"Oh, Worthington needs to calm down first, before he issues an apology. He worried himself sick when you ran away. Both times. He wouldn't tell you that, Hector's the strong silent type if you didn't realise by now."

"Don't hold it against me if I doubt your statement. And not only because it's coming from you."

"I'm a credible source."

"Sure, you are."

"If you are both quite finished, more important discussions are ahead of us. New findings to share," Hector says to our banter.

"Transparency would be wise," Aleš adds.

"Agreed. One question first. Is this location still safe with Fosters & Co henchmen hunting the city for me?"

"We are fine for a couple of days. The situation hasn't changed. Nobody will touch you under my watch." He stares at Hector and gives me a reassuring nod.

"Great. Thank you." I squeeze his hand. "Then I'll start with my short story. As I told you earlier, I found this morning via the teddy cam notifications that Lina Haas was using, is using, my work accounts to steal information from the company we both work for. That's the extent of my involvement. Besides being drugged, kidnapped, and forced to run around Europe. Little else I know from Hector, about his sister's company and the unfortunate event that took her, and Neville senior's lives. And that Fosters & Co is corrupt and to blame for our near deaths. I mean, probably not the entire company, but a selected bunch spoiled the assembly."

"You are right. One man, and presumably his team, is involved in the cover-up of my father's death and the takeover of the family business." Lawrence confirms my assumptions.

"The extent of his role and how corruption spreads in Fosters & Co are unclear, but it started with one board director. Elias Bodmer," Hector reveals, and I'm baffled once again. I saw Elias recently, and while I don't know him personally, he's one of the most popular faces in the company.

"Really? The industry knows him for his strong work ethic and for empowering employees to reach for their goals. We haven't been introduced, but I attended corporate town halls where he was presenting. One just last week in Canary Wharf. Maybe he's also being framed." The last comment is an afterthought. He was in London the day of my kidnapping, why am I surprised anymore when my own friend screwed me over?

"Not likely," Hector interjects in a harsh tone directed at me.

"Yeah, because you are the expert in knowing who is being framed or not." Why is he hostile towards me? I'm not too welcoming, but I have legitimate reasons for being mad.

"The small evidence we have is enough reason to accuse him. You just discovered even close individuals are untrustworthy and not what they seem. There is no limit to what one is capable behind closed doors. We can't prove it, link him to the deaths, but he was involved in the deal's negotiation, having a lot to gain and to lose."

Must not slap that tone out of his mouth. Out of those plump, not too wet, nor too dry lips. Okay, clearly his presence is causing my brain to malfunction. My delirium can't decide what to do to him. Luckily, Lawrence interrupts my train of thought.

"He's a Swiss national working for Fosters & Co since he interned there during university. Climbing the corporate ladder over twenty years to be the youngest board member in the organisation. The rumour is they are grooming him to be chair and the next CEO." He tells Aleš, who is already clicking away at his laptop.

The tapping sound of the keyboard continues in the otherwise silent room. Neville checks his phone as I lean my head against the back of the chair, moving my eyes towards Hector when I catch his stare. He blinks away, hand fussing with his short hair. His smoothly shaven face is different with the new hairstyle, younger but harsher at the same time. Crossing my arms under my chest, I gaze at the table and then at Aleš when he stands.

"I can't access his computer files on shared drives or calendar. Not remotely. The guy has a tight cyber security team. He is not in London anymore."

"We came to that conclusion as well. We planned to infiltrate his office, his house, or to get as close as possible to his work devices to hack them. But then the kidnapping happened." Hector steals another look at my face. His cold blue eyes and rigid posture that seemed to relax a bit, minutes ago, are furious again.

"Are you still logged into Fosters & Co network? Can I borrow your laptop for a second? I think I have an idea how to find out where he is. Or where he is going to be." At his nod, I drag Aleš' device in front of me. "While I'm not the computer wizard some of you thought, I know how to check what was printed at a certain location and by whom. According to gossip straight from our office assistant, our finance director will accompany the shareholders making the rounds globally with the summit I attended in London. I wasn't all that interested before in dates or locations, but where Mariusz Jurkowski is going, Bodmer is close. The assistant always prints itineraries in advance with flights, hotels, restaurants." I click to magnify the documents I discover in her name on the printer's server. "They will be in China next week. And a further confirmation, Mariusz is booked to have dinner in Shanghai with Bodmer, other visitors and directors from the Chinese office." I show the screen to the three open mouthed men next to me.

"Good job, Vera! So, we go to China and intercept him there," Aleš proposes.

"Yes!" I say enthusiastically.

"Not you, Vera! You are not skilled to—" Hector.

"It's much too risky to get you involved." Aleš.

"Well—" Lawrence says at the same time.

"Doesn't my track record of not conforming to the metaphorical or real boxes people wanted to force me in for the last week clue you to the fact that I'm ready to fight? We are not having this conversation. If you go, I go, because I'm not sitting on my ass while others put their lives in peril. I'm going to take a guess and say that I understand the risks, although I've already experienced a handful of deadly situations by now, so what's there to guess? This man, if he is indeed culpable of my kidnapping, deserves my wrath, unskilled as it is. End of discussion!" I narrow my eyes at them.

"There is time until next week to analyse risks, options and resources," Aleš says looking towards me.

"Plenty of days for actual trained individuals to track Bodmer closer to home," Hector adds as I ignore them both, swiping through the files printed at the London office in the last week. Invoices from the company employing my brother, and from my fast perusal, he was nowhere near the W&N merger. I relax in my seat, thinking he will not be dragged now, or in the future, in any perilous affairs. Perhaps I can ask Aleš to double check.

"As I mentioned when I interrupted your amorous reunion, I have news. Following his activities from previous years, Elias Bodmer might attend a yoga and meditation seminar in Bali, before flying to his next location. He goes every year. We can use this opportunity to spy on him. The yoga retreat has security, but not as intense as a business conference. Particularly in China," Neville shares with us, knocking the table next to me. "Your sleuth efforts were in vain, Miss Nicolescu, but thanks for playing." His nasal laugh complements his gloating. Just when I thought he was growing on me.

We spend the next few hours ironing out our plan. A private plane will be on standby, provided by Hector, the four of us and five members of Aleš' team will fly out to Bali on Wednesday. If we don't get word of Elias checking in at the hotel on the island, we change course towards Shanghai and prepare for the conference.

At dinner, I'm introduced to some of our guards who join us in the cabin. The rest are still patrolling outside. Petr, who's been friends with Aleš since their military days, juggles plates with roasted veggies and red meat. Since we shook hands, he started teasing my ex-internet crush about the last phone call we had on his birthday.

"Trust me, he mopped around for days after that failed attempt. Once he finished being mad and causing fist fights left and right."

"I did not. Shut up!" Aleš smacks Petr over the head, and I snort at the gesture.

"*You* were mad? I was furious! Your first words, after you said my name about ten times, were: *Are you with a man, Vera?* Who does that?"

"No. I asked, *how are you, how you've been,* I kept it smooth." He blushes but laughs with me. Lawrence observes our exchange with a grin while Hector focuses on his food. He's been quiet for the last half hour.

"Right, tell yourself that. You're lucky I ended the call and spared you further embarrassment."

"That put a damper on my mood."

"Well, against my better judgement, I called next day to check on you after the multiple drinks you probably had, but I got the voicemail. I didn't leave a message."

"That's because he crushed his Nokia that evening," Petr informs us with a hysterical cackle.

The talks continue late into the night, moving from our teen romance to the army, the guns we need for our future trips, gadgets to hack Bodmer's laptop.

I thank Aleš' team for their help with the mission and Petr alludes they get paid handsomely for their participation, so I shouldn't worry about it. Who pays them, he didn't share. The number of favours they owe Aleš is enough to have them agree without the money, but they are not stupid to refuse the already transferred funds.

Aleš takes me aside to inform me my parents, Cristi, and several friends have been trying to contact my British phone number over the weekend and that he will think of something to let my family know I'm okay. He's already monitoring their calls. The authorities are not aware of my disappearance.

The guys bring twin mattresses into the living room for Hector and Lawrence because the Czech agents taking turns at sleep and surveillance occupy the other cabins. As I search the bedroom for extra pillows and blankets, Hector interrupts me, shutting the door behind him. He ignored me all throughout dinner and the banter with the guys. We stare for a moment, neither wanting to break the silence.

"Do you need something? Do you want the bedroom?" I lose the battle. We haven't been alone since the arena and look where that took us. Does he want a repeat? Do I want one?

"No. Yes."

"Which is it?"

"The mattress is fine. What I need is for you to reconsider coming to Asia."

"And where should I go? What should I do in the meantime? Isn't it safer to be with Aleš and his team? With you and Lawrence?"

"I can keep you safe, hidden, and not in the hot zone Bali and Shanghai will be. In a secure house where we were planning to reconvene after Prague. That way, you will not encumber the hacking mission. In some capacity, we all have fighting experience apart from you. You'll be an inconvenience."

"First, thank you for the vote of confidence. It astonishes me you went through life without learning how to speak to women. That being said, I'll stick with Aleš and the initial plan if you don't mind."

"Do you trust him?" He barely opens his mouth to ask, his jaw clenched tight. He's by the door while I hug the spare pillow a few steps from him.

"More than you, that's for sure."

"I didn't mean to insult you."

"Yeah, well, you did. You keep doing it. Don't worry, I'll not hold my breath for an apology."

"The morning before the car chase and after I made you breakfast," he stresses the last two words, "I expressed my regrets about the necessity of our actions. Instead of being patient and understanding of the perils we were in, you fled."

"Riveting. Tell me more about how I should have behaved." I can't believe we are having this conversation. He continues as if I said nothing.

"Despite that, when I learned they chased you around in airports and had a fucking gang of armed men after you in Prague, I dropped everything to make sure you are safe. And what was my reward? The second I turned my back, you fled again, making me think they captured you. Where is my apology?"

"But they did not capture me, did they?"

"Can you see it from my perspective? Where I was standing, restrained by four men, it looked like he pushed you into that car and I couldn't bloody reach you. Call me a cave dweller all you want, you knew you were safe, but I didn't. And you *still* left!" He raises his voice and I flinch, my reaction making him cover his face with a palm. "I'm sorry."

Who says cave dweller?

As much as it pains me to admit, he has a point. It looked bad. I don't mention feeling manipulated by what we did inside the arena. That he only kissed me to make me compliant. That it hurt he still believed I was the mole and a little intimacy with the attractive, rich hero could persuade me.

"Perhaps I shouldn't have left, the second time, without explaining who Aleš was, but it was all in a hurry, you were trying to manipulate me. Your intentions were—"

"How was I manipulating you?" he asks bewildered, reducing the distance between us, forcing me to take a step back, bumping into a side table.

"Come on, Hector, what you did at the music event? That served a purpose for you." I try to keep my composure with a raised chin.

"You mean the kissing, Vera? What purpose besides acting on the misguided urge to kiss you? I lost control."

"That's hard to believe."

"You think I'm a block of ice? Did it look like I was faking my attraction to you?" We are a breath away. My rapid blinks capture the golden specs in his blue eyes. "The way we treated you at The Hyde, I shouldn't have allowed that. It was a mistake, even if we believed you were the mole. And because of my behaviour, I thought sparing you of the dangers we might encounter in Asia would comfort you." My palm on his chest tries to push him or to pull him in, when a knock on the wooden door decides for me.

"Vera, you okay?" Aleš inquires in a hard voice. He tries to enter the room, but it's locked.

"Not that it matters now. It's for the best," Hector says quietly, his face closing off again. Hard, unimpassioned eyes regard me a second longer before he turns for the door, unlocking it. He stalks Aleš, both refusing to back away and let the other pass, the tension keeping me from breathing properly.

"Aleš . . ." He looks up at the sound of my voice and turns slightly to let a grunting Hector leave. Moments later, the front door shuts with a bang. After dropping the extra bedding on the small couch, I brush my teeth and return to my room.

I don't hear Hector's return before I fall asleep.

Eighteen

Although wicked men are turning rocks in Prague to find me – and I'm still on the run, no closer to contact my family, stabbed in the back by my best friend – I wake up refreshed on Tuesday. Taking a minute to breathe in the day, eyes closed, I feel excited for Bali. No matter the circumstances, the trip moves me one step further to freedom. Aside from fighting with Hector, things look promising for the impromptu alliance against Bodmer.

Turning my head on the flat pillow, I discover Aleš sleeping next to me, under the thick covers. I snort softy before a headshake and a grin take my face. Now, I know the couch he was supposed to rest on is miniscule, but I reckon a posturing contest with a certain someone led him to my bed. His bed, technically, but I claimed it. He's on his side, facing me, one arm under his pillow, wearing a white t-shirt. At least he kept his clothes on.

"I feel you watching me sleep, Miss Creepy." He startles me with a husky mumble.

"Please! You dare invade my sleep and my temporary room and I'm the creep?" I say, amused.

"I figured I could beg for forgiveness in the morning and not spend another minute on that sofa."

"You can start your begging now. Make it good." I settle back on my pillow.

"Can I have a coffee first? My charm kicks in better after a cup." He opens one eye and grins out the corner of his mouth. I would say his charm is doing just fine without a coffee. Good grief, I forget I'm supposed to be mad.

"Make me pancakes again and I forgive you." I poke a muscled shoulder as he laughs at my suggestion, stretching his tall body next to me.

"They say you win a man's heart through his stomach, but you'll do anything for a jar of Nutella, some flour and eggs." He leans in to kiss my forehead, interrupting my sarcastic giggles, and I pinch his chest. He's not ticklish, but I am, and he takes advantage of that until I convulse with laughter. My heavy breathing sounds echo throughout the cabin.

"I give up! I give up!"

Released from my restraints, I tiptoe from the bedroom in search of water. Hector and Lawrence are already up in the living room, working on their laptops.

"Morning."

Hector doesn't look up, but I feel his eyes on me when I reach the kitchen sink. I lean on the fridge with my glass just as Aleš leaves the bedroom for the bathroom, giving the guys a nod and me a full-on smile. Teeth and all. He was wearing a t-shirt not two seconds ago, but he's only in tight white boxers now. The dastardly move makes me choke on my water.

"Swallow first, babe," the nearly naked idiot has the nerve to comment before closing the bathroom door behind him. Painting the lewd picture completely. Lawrence tries to mask a snort and I catch Hector looking between me and where the shower is running, before returning his gaze to the screen in front of him.

He goes running shortly after.

I want to say the communication between the two of us improves during the day, but apart from brief answers about the upcoming trip, we ignore each other, him spending time on various calls while I research Bodmer, Bali and Shanghai.

Taking advantage of the decent weather, I walk around the forest in the afternoon, accompanied by Petr and a burly guy named Radek. Petr is muscly too, but shorter with chestnut brown hair. Aleš has a flawless American accent he perfected years ago, but his friends speak English with various degrees of Eastern European intonations. They are not too sold on the leisure stroll, the temperature low, but apparently, I cannot waltz about alone. Lawrence joins us when we meet him near a creek, finishing a conversation with Hector. The latter departs for the cabin.

By nightfall, we are a go for Wednesday's flight to Bali. The plane is already in a hangar at a private terminal. They bring a new passport for me, yoga, beach, and business attires for everyone taking part in the stint. Aleš is leaving for the night with two of his guys, to collect all the computer gadgets we need, meeting us tomorrow prior to departure.

"Petr knows how to contact me. I'll see you on the jet. Don't be sad I'm not the first person you gaze upon in the morning." He smirks and tries to pat my head, and I punch his stomach.

"Ha! I'll try to contain my disappointment. Be careful, will you?"

"Where's the fun in that?" He leaves with a wave and a throaty laugh.

Excitement about what tomorrow holds keeps me in motion, and I won't seek sleep yet. Reluctantly, I accept Larry's challenge at a chess match. Knowing only the basic rules brings me at a disadvantage when he's highly advanced at the game, it's not even funny. For me. His maniac grin when he puts me in checkmate within a few moves reminds me of a cartoon villain.

"You won't expect it, but at some point in the future, I'm knocking you on your ass." I wiggle my finger at him after five games.

"Sore loser, Miss Nicolescu? You? Why, I never!" His eyes open widely to emphasise his sarcasm.

"You bring out the worst in me, Neville. Was it difficult to keep your friends growing up?" My jab makes him smirk.

"It's a lonely existence for those at the top. You're lucky to never be subjected to that," he hits back, and I throw my pawn at him half-heartedly.

"He's not being fair, and he knows it. He was a chess champion at Cambridge. Winning and rubbing it in his opponent's face is his joy in life," Hector comments from his spot on the couch. It's the first time he acknowledges me in hours.

"Hey, that's not right!" I say with indignation.

"Now, now, kids. I teach others by allowing them to play with me."

"Right! Well, can't say it was a pleasure, Larry, but you drained my energy and now I can sleep. Good night!"

Leaving them to their whiskey and a match of their own, Hector takes my place and whispers a 'sleep well' as I pass him. How I see it, he's got his feelings hurt because I let him press me against a wall with an intoxicating kiss and now, I'm comfortable with Aleš. Who, to be fair, is acting mighty friendly, touching me whenever he's nearby. A shoulder squeeze, a side hug when we were eating sandwiches by the window. When did I switch from being invisible on the tube commute, partly because of the illusion of options London places single people in, to the level of male attention I attract since I've been on the run? It's exhausting, if not confusing, especially since part of it is male ego at its finest.

We wake up to news of Lina's latest activities, who my favourite hacker has been monitoring online since we discovered she is the informant. As it became apparent that I wasn't picking up her calls, which I always do, coupled with my absence at work, she must have thought something happened to me. Connected to her corporate espionage done under my employee number. Her spend pattern shows she's gone into hiding, fearing a fate similar to mine.

The group decides to send Lawrence after Lina's whereabouts in the UK while we soldier on to Bali. A member of Aleš' crew will go along with him to provide cover, much to his refusal. We need to convince Lina to show us the full information she has on Bodmer. If she commits any more online mistakes, the people orchestrating my kidnapping will go after her and we lose the evidence, and her life. No matter what she did, I don't wish her physical harm. Or any harm.

The world outside transitions from forest to city as I sit between Radek and Hector in the back of an SUV, feeling sick to my stomach from nerves and lack of sleep. Luckily, we skipped breakfast. The upcoming flight is around fourteen hours, no stops to refuel when you have the money Hector paid to rent the best private plane.

"Are you alright?" He nudges me with his shoulder, and I offer a nod.

We should form a camaraderie if we play spies together until the end of this debacle, but I don't know how to act around him. What he displayed towards me since we met is complicated. He doesn't insist and turns to the window and the clear morning sky when I don't show signs of engagement. I haven't been chased in a few days and I'm paranoid it will happen any minute now. Horrible people are just around the corner waiting to ambush us. An unpleasant habit I fear is here to stay.

Alas, it doesn't take long to arrive safely at the terminal where Aleš uses his credentials for us to board the amazing plane with incredible speed. At the beginning of March, my horoscope did not predict the change from the crammed London transport choices to luxury aircraft. Everyone has a coffee in hand, and I join in the ritual. Earl Grey won't cut through this fatigue if I want to be sharp for the first half of the trip and sleep the rest to avoid jet lag upon arrival. I'm by the window, Aleš next to me, at the front of the plane facing the pilot's cabin, with Hector and Petr sitting opposite in this ultra-long-range heavy jet that accommodates up to sixteen people. The rest of the guys are chatting the two flight attendants about breakfast options.

The end of the rain season will greet us in the island of Bali, Indonesia's main touristic spot, with humidity and hot temperatures. The flight crew will remain close to the airport in the city of Denpasar, while our destination is the jungle of Ubud. Availabilities at the retreat Bodmer should check in tomorrow are scarce, so close to the yoga seminar, but we got a four-bedroom villa for the eight of us. One of the most exclusivist yoga resorts in the world, located amongst rice paddies and steep ravines with prices in sync to its reputation, awaits me and I can't take full advantage of it.

Aleš seems on edge next to me and when I inquire into his behaviour, he confesses he's waiting on news about his last job, but I shouldn't worry about it. The lack of sleep is clear on his face and while he brought the two large cases of surveillance spy equipment that he picked up last night, the sweet smell of women's perfume on his clothes reveals how some of his night was spent. I'm not mad or judging. It's annoying he flirted with me throughout Monday and Tuesday, putting on a show of light touches and innuendoes for all to see, probably aimed at Hector. I didn't mind the affection, and it switched my brain from the heavy kissing Hector administrated on Sunday night, but he should cut the petting in half if he is romantically involved.

"I'm crashing on a chair bed at the back. Come join me for some rest." He slides next to me at the refreshments table in the middle of the plane. Grinning, he tries to push the hair covering my face behind my ear, but I pull away.

"Yeah, no, I'm good."

"Is something wrong? It didn't bother you before, but that's the second time you flinch at my touch." I didn't realise I did. Concern builds on his face, handsome when drowsy, parted lips waiting for my reply.

"It might bother someone." The reply slips past the tiny filter I am trying to apply.

"Who?"

The woman he left this morning to go on a dangerous quest throughout Asia with me comes to mind. Not looking at him, I make my fruit plate, faking nonchalance. "It's not my business, and you know I'm grateful for your support in this mission, but maybe, I don't know, you keep the promises you made to other people too."

"What are you trying to say, Vera? Spill it out. My brain is fried at the moment." He crosses his arms and I see him frown with the corner of my eye.

"You reek of cheap perfume."

"So?"

"So, you spent the night with a woman. No further investigation required to know that. Which is fine, but let's not?" The bastard laughs next to me and attracts curious looks from our crew.

"I like your jealous hand gesturing."

"I am not jealous and keep it down."

"You are, and it's cute. There is no girlfriend. If that's what you are implying. We spent half the night at a loud gentlemen's club convincing the asshole we work for to release the weapons, the ammunition, and the rest of the equipment we need, without giving him all the answers he expected. Then I had a terrible three hours sleep on Josef's crappy couch."

"If you say so. Don't justify yourself to me." I pass him to go back to my seat.

"It's okay, I want to. If it gets me back in your good graces," he says quietly from close behind me.

"Go to sleep. You are delusional." He laughs all the way to the rear lavatories.

Hours pass watching a couple of in-flight movies while the others do similar activities, read, or play poker. The overly put together flight attendants are stepping on their toes to satisfy Hector's every need, faster and better. I can't contain my eye roll at the flirt show they juggle, and he catches me a few times, an enigmatic head tilt the only sign he gives before returning to his laptop. Meanwhile, the commotion in the cabin dies down and I turn my chair into a bed, select a long, relaxing music track list on my screen, headphones on with the complementary sleeping eye mask, and doze off almost instantly.

The display mounted on the wall in front of me shows we are ten hours into our flight when I'm jolted awake, all blinds closed. Rising to use the restroom, I notice Hector sleeping in his chair, covered with a cashmere blanket identical to mine. It's only us at the front of the plane. After I take care of business and drink some water next to my seat, confirming everyone is resting, the plane hits a rough patch of air and my belly drops. The metal box we are flying in shakes violently, and though I've been up for a few minutes, I still feel out of it, losing my balance and landing on top of Hector's legs, waking him up.

"Cabin crew, please be seated," the pilot announces as the chaotic tremble continues, and I shake my head at Hector when he tries to help me to my seat. I am terrified to sit alone, and I can't express the magnitude of my fear. Reacting fast, Hector pulls me up in his embrace, putting the seatbelt over us and lifting the bed back to a chair position as I cling to his neck. "Ladies and gentlemen, the captain has turned on the fasten seatbelt sign. We are now crossing a zone of turbulence. Please remain seated and keep your seatbelts fastened. Thank you."

"Shit. I'm sorry."

"You're okay. It will be over soon," he whispers in my hair, fingers cupping my head to him, and I breathe erratically in his ear. I've been braver in the past, during atmospheric irregularities, but it was never as bad. My nervous system took a dive two Mondays ago, and the smallest hint of peril shuts it down. I want to stop shivering and I encourage myself to do so because I don't like the scared woman I've become. Not that falling from the sky at incredible speed can be influenced by courage. The caress Hector applies to my back is helping.

"Are we lucky enough to survive a plane crash? We did good so far."

"We are not crashing. Don't be overdramatic." Another air pocket that has me screaming marks his statement.

Someone calls my name repetitively. When I remain silent, he answers for me.

"She's fine. I have her."

And internally, I recognise that I am fine with him. I feel safer in his arms, and that makes me drop my head to his shoulder. This is so messed up. Earlier, I made an embarrassing case of getting annoyed at Aleš' presumed dalliances, and now I'm glad I have Hector to hug in an emergency. His smell of mahogany and mandarin brings flashbacks of our heated touches. When we were as close as now. Involuntarily, my nails bite into his back and the sensitive skin of his nape. His approving grunt is barely audible. My lips tingle when I lift them to his unshaven jaw. A different type of tremor goes through my body when his nose and mouth brush my temple once, twice. We are just two people sharing comfort during a stressful situation. Nothing more.

The plane is cruising smoothly in minutes, but leaving his lap does not cross my mind. I realise someone is standing by our chair when Hector stops his movements and turns to stone underneath me. I don't move. If I pretend I'm still affected by what just happened, maybe nobody will bother me.

"Do you need help, sir?" The raspy voice of the flight attendant addresses him. "Madame?" Well, I'm not her main concern, clearly. She added madame as an afterthought.

Untangling my arms from around him, I put a few inches between my lips and any part of Hector's skin. He angles his head to make eye contact and asks me if I'm okay. He's still holding me tight. I couldn't leave even if I want to.

"Can I have a bottle of water and a shot of whiskey? Please?" I request kindly, not breaking contact with Hector's penetrating gaze.

"Make that two. Thank you," he says, laughing.

One by one, the guys check if everyone is alive and intact, joking about who was petrified and who slept during the ordeal. I'm sipping my drink in my chair, after expressing my gratitude to Hector with a murmured apology for imposing on him and giving him a kiss on the cheek as a thanks. Aleš reports on his well-being only after I turn around in my seat to look for him. He saw me in Hector's lap without a doubt, and he's keeping his distance.

Our destination is still a few hours away and everyone returns to their places to continue their interrupted rest. The details of what will happen after we land were discussed back in Prague. Diplomatic delegation privileges will get us out of the airport fast. A car ride to the hotel where we set in motion our surveillance. Last we checked, Elias Bodmer will arrive later in the day at the same five-star resort.

"Out with it," I say to Hector when I notice he's staring at me.

"Rather not. That hardly ever goes well. You get annoyed when I speak." Serious voice with a hint of mischief.

"You have that uncanny ability, yes. But I owe you one."

"I don't see it that way. And it's complicated."

"I'm sure I can keep up."

"I'll confess before the whiskey buzz wears off."

"Yours or mine?"

"Exactly." He smiles and signals for a refill of our drinks. "After my sister died, I've lost touch with everything else that wasn't revenge. You expect nothing to affect you so greatly until it does. She was my person, you know?"

"Yes." I nod because I understand completely. If something happens to my brother, I . . .

"I'll spare you the details of my childhood because it was privileged indeed, but let's just say warmth or stability weren't present most times. But with Helena, it was me and her." He clears his voice, moving his gaze from the glass in my hand to my face, touching every inch with an icy look. "I've tested my personal moral boundaries with the things I've done to expose Bodmer, and I know I'll probably do more. But I regret you got dragged into this fight. You've experienced appalling acts and if I've known someone was using your identity, I would have done everything in my power to spare you the trouble. Too many have suffered."

"Trouble is a watered-down word for what we've been served. You did what you could, and I understand family ties, how powerful they are. My reactions or the decisions made as a response are not flattering either. But as the player added to this game with no helpful knowledge, I'll cut myself some slack. And I won't apologise for running."

"Fair enough. You should be proud of your fast thinking. We are dealing with dangerous people, and you have shown incredible strength and resourcefulness." He sips his drink. "If life was normal, where would you be now?"

"Are you trying to get to know me, Mister Worthington?"

"What if I am? Will you suspect me of manipulation yet again? I am not as cunning as you think."

"Acting in a persuading way, to win favour, is done involuntary too."

"You mean like you drawing attention to your lips every time you lick them?" He hides the curve of a grin in his glass.

"No, but duly noted," I say self-consciously. The drink peels away at my layers until it reaches my centre, overexposing it to his heat.

"Don't stop on my account." He enjoys my shyness with a pleased face.

"Anyway, to answer your question, I would probably work too much and explore London in my spare hours. Day trips to the English countryside. Nothing explosive. The city was still very new before my forced departure."

"We will get you back safely to continue your discovery. I will even take time out of my busy schedule to show you the hidden paths." He runs his fingers through his short hair.

"As long as they don't lead to graveyards."

"Cabin crew, prepare for descent. Landing shortly," the captain announces as I leave the rear bathroom. Aleš stops me with a hand on my shoulder.

"Have a sit here while we land. There's been recent developments needing your awareness before we arrive at the hotel." His face is grave, and he doesn't leave me much choice on the matter, pushing me to the window seat he previously occupied and taking one for himself.

"Is Elias not coming? Did he find Lina? Don't we need everyone for this news?"

"It's not about Bodmer. Or your friend. What I am about to say will unnerve you, but please remain calm."

Seriously? Like anyone can be calm hearing that tone of voice. Show me a person reacting with a smile when someone says, ominously, 'I need to tell you something, but be cool.' To keep my anxiety levels from spiking, I need nerves of steel, and I'm working with limited tools right this instant.

"Is it my brother? You found out something about his involvement with the merger?" I don't breathe in the seconds he takes to reply.

"No. Like you hoped, he is clean. Cristian was working on other projects at the time."

"God, that's the mystery I most wished to uncover. Thank you for the confirmation, but then what is it?"

"I told you I was waiting on intel when we first boarded. Suspicions details shared at the cabin led me to conduct some inquires on Worthington."

"Why?" I lean back from him but maintain eye contact.

"Vera . . . he's behind your kidnapping."

"Ladies and gentlemen, we are landing shortly at Ngurah Rai International Airport. Please make sure one last time your seat belt is fastened. Local time is 05:03 AM, and the temperature outside is 22.5 degrees Celsius."

"What? How can you say that?" My head shakes in denial.

"He was never in Qatar. Not this March, anyway. He found out that you were the leak, just as Bodmer's team did, but Worthington captured you first. To make you talk, to scare you into revealing everything, he drugged you, kidnapped you, and for maximum terror, he placed you in a coffin."

Nineteen

I'm choking. There is a ghost hand at my throat, keeping me from inhaling precious air. The invisible grip has more power than one of flesh and bone. The pain is not idle, it moves down my frame and the only way to describe the anguish is to associate it to the chest ache one feels when mad, sad, and desperate.

Was Hector easing his guilt over the conversation we had earlier? My body froze in a mind-imposed paralysis, sitting between him and Aleš on the van ride to the town of Ubud. I try keeping it in, not reacting to the news my friend gave me, but I want to retch on the side of the road.

The hotel is a few miles outside the traffic jam of the artistic centre of Bali, and I'm a ticking bomb with the shortest fuse. I cannot accept that the kidnapping was Hector's doing. Him capable of a nightmare that will traumatise my life forever. A deranged behaviour unjustifiable, not even by the death of his sister. All to confuse me into giving myself up as the supposed mole.

Processing the events leading up to the Bali flight, chasing a man not connected with me being on the run, is difficult when everything feels fabricated. Bodmer might have used torture, killed me on the spot, or just fired me from the company. I will never know.

From whom am I on the run exactly? Can I simply go back home to my ordinary life? Not now, no. My mind jumps from that to Hector, not moving in the coffin. I had to carry him to the apartment in Nevern Square. He faked that? Has it all been a demented ploy? The Hyde, the car chase? But the men after us, I saw the cars, didn't I? And the airport stalkers in Brussels? His men?

To think I kissed him willingly, at the music event, after what he did. And a few hours ago on the plane, I was back in his arms.

Stop, stop, stop before you burst into tears. Or stab him to death with the pen in your purse.

Ten thousand thoughts go through my head, and I move from one emotion to another, ensuring a spell of dizziness. My ears started ringing on the plane and haven't stopped since. This cannot be true, and yet I know the taste of betrayal by now. Can it be called betrayal when he did not know me? It hurts like one.

We arrive at the resort, seeing little outside the car window from the fug clogging my sanity, and I push for normality. Shove everything in a mental box until I am alone and able to unleash my meltdown. *Focus.*

We are nestled in a clearing above the jungle covered gorge beside a river. The Como Andana Estate lives up to its high praises. If I wasn't so numb and lost, I would have been very impressed, and not register everything like I'm watching a video.

At the open walled reception, they greet us with complementary house tea, ginger sweetened with honey while nutritional plans, yogic stretching and Asian-based treatments are presented. Visiting the nearby rice paddies has always been a dream of mine, but my disoriented body has no reaction to their closeness. Our guests smile widely and encourage us to enjoy their facilities. I nod and move along with the rest of our group, staying close to Aleš. Smoky tension taints the air, a hostility coming from all the Czech guys towards the new threat that Hector represents.

Resort employees carry our bags to the villa, and our muscled men stick close to the ones hiding guns. The holiday home looks like a mirage in the dense green tropical forest, each separately rented abode given privacy and a private pool. Two floors of hard wood sustaining glass walls to give the impression of sleeping in nature, white cloth drapes used for seclusion.

"Vera, can we speak privately? You have a lost stare I can't bear seeing." Hector corners me on the living room patio and when his fingers touch mine, I flinch, taking a step back into an ornament. Aleš, tipping the staff to depart without explaining every commodity they equipped the house with, comes to my side instantly.

"Leave her alone." He pushes the Englishman away from me with the harshest voice.

"What did he tell you, Vera?" I feel Hector's eyes on me when I'm still looking at my fingers. Finding the strength to look up, my teeth grind together when he realises the trained soldiers have formed a wide circle around him.

"What is this?" He stares them down before returning to me. "Vera, what lies did he tell you?" When I don't reply, his legs move to cover the distance between us but stop when the circle tightens him in. "Did you think I didn't notice a change in your behaviour? Do you think I can sit next to you and not know your body is trembling with fear?"

At that, I burst into furious screams because it's not fear I'm feeling, but rage. My tear ducts can't hold my despair anymore, wetting my face. I use my blouse to wipe at them; he doesn't deserve my tears. I move to pass Aleš to get to this lying bastard's face and give him a piece of my mind, except muscular arms keep me in place.

"Let go of me!"

"Don't touch her!" Hector roars, pointing behind me. I turn to my rescuer. He dropped everything to help me, yet I can't stand anyone's touch right now.

"Aleš, please. He can't hurt me more than he already did. I need to talk with him."

"What more is there to say? I'm staying."

"How do you propose we move forward from this, then?" I lay a hand on his chest to pacify him and to convey how much I appreciate his presence, then turn back to Hector. I take a big breath to fortify my voice. He looks so prideful with his unreadable face. "You've been controlling me from the beginning. You ruined my life to get what you wanted. You knew who I was when I woke up in that coffin next to you." I've stunned him. "You can't deny it, can you?"

"Vera, it's not what you think." He takes a step forward and Aleš flicks his wrist to signify that's enough. "I can't deny that, yet it's more complicated than that. I'm not the bad guy, I just need a fucking minute."

"Bullshit! You had all the time to confess." An ironic laugh escapes me. "But simplify it for us, please! Go on! I already know you are behind the kidnapping, so drop the act." At this, he looks horrified.

"What? No! Absolutely not! Never that! Trust me on this! I never meant to hurt you."

"How can I trust you when you admitted you knew who I was, when I had no clue why I woke up in a bloody coffin? You pretended to be paralysed! Who does that?"

"I was paralysed!" he shouts. "How can you think I wasn't? They kidnapped me too. Like I said, I'm not a complete monster."

"From Qatar, right? How is Qatar in March, Hector? Another fantastic lie I have to take your word for."

He looks at Aleš with menace in his eyes. "It eats you alive that you've lost your chance with her once and now you fill her head with rubbish, afraid she prefers me, and you don't get a second go. And if I thought I had no right at her before, that she wants you, seeing her melt and feeling her heat in my lap makes this a fair fight. And I don't lose, asshole."

In an instant, I'm pushed aside and their powerful bodies clash with furious grunts. Fists fly everywhere. Pulling at each other like wild animals, a panther and a leopard, agile and bloodthirsty, I barely see the kicks to the ribs, both equally equipped to injure. I hear clothes tearing, the slight rasp of material ripping away, almost lost in the sound of continuous blows to the face, to the stomach. The rest of the guys give them space to go at it, ignoring my pleas to separate them.

Why would Hector say that? How could he think I would even look at him after all this? They are rolling in the grass now, after trashing the patio. We follow them with angst. The villa is so secluded, nobody hears their roars and insults. Aleš has a river of red coming from his nose and Hector looks insane, lacerations all over his face, neck, arms. They get to their feet and circle each other with murderous intent.

"You convinced Vera that I kidnapped her, which I didn't. I just knew who she was. Who I thought she was. How everything connected her to the titbits the mole was selling to me. But did you tell her about Lina Haas? Did you tell her you knew her best friend because she was your fucking rebound?"

Come again?

Shock goes through me in Petr's hold. I stop moving altogether at Hector's declaration, and Aleš' face conveys the trueness behind it. Not wanting to risk their fall into the ravine below, I unfreeze and scream like a banshee, distracting Hector, who looks for me. He loses his footing and drops to his back. Aleš doesn't waste time kicking him in the stomach, raising his leg repeatedly, blow after blow. I bite Petr's arm and run towards them before I'm caught again. I pull at Aleš' arm, and the force of his swinging body knocks me on my ass.

"Stop, please stop. Aleš, stop!" I say from my position on my hands and knees. He's so lost in his mind, my plea doesn't reach him. "You'll push him down the steep. You need to stop now. Enough."

He finally hears me and ceases his kicking, panting, hands on his head. Hector is on his front, not moving. What have they done? I crawl to him and try to turn him to his back. He's catching his breath, eyes closed, cracked lip, blood mixing with dirt and grass. Grunting, he takes a second to focus that intense blue gaze on me.

"I had no hand in kidnapping you." He fills his lungs with difficulty and continues, "They took me from London, not Qatar, that's true. I was meeting you that day. Not you, but Lina Haas, pretending to be Vera Nicolescu. At Waterloo. I thought you were pretending to not know me. I can show you the messages I have before and after the kidnapping."

He gets up, holding his side, and helps me off the grass. Aleš, lost in thought, stares into the horizon.

"She knew I connected her actions to this name, and I told her I would come find her and make things difficult. Like expose her, not kidnap her. She agreed to meet, to give me the rest of the files I needed to take Bodmer down. For a handsome reward. But she never came. I think she planned it for Bodmer to know we were meeting. I got a syringe to the neck instead. Later, they brought you in too. She's a fucking psychopath and he can confirm it." He nods his chin at Aleš.

Hell!

"I'm sorry I made you lose your balance. Are you hurt?" Aleš asks after a long pause. He's staring at me with guilt, the remorseful look mars his face.

We form a weird, pathetic triangle on the grass, overlooking one of the most amazing views I've ever seen. Miles of green rice paddies in our sunken backyard. The guys appear like they've battled an entire army, waiting for someone to tell them who won. And I'm . . . I know nothing, clearly. Completely clueless to the machinations happening behind me, probably for years.

"I'm okay . . ."

Are you?

"No, I'm not actually. None of this is okay. You could have killed each other. You should be ashamed for hitting a man while he's down." I shake my head at them.

"I provoked him on purpose. I wanted this fight since Prague," Hector says. Was everything he said only a provocation?

"He deserves the beating. I thought he kidnapped you. I really thought that."

"Shut up, both of you! Unbelievable!" I hug myself against a soft breeze. It's still early morning and despite the wind blowing the sticky hair from my face, the heat is coming down on the Indonesian island. "I do not understand my own feelings anymore. I'm locking myself into a mental institution after this." Right, I guess I'll have that breakdown for one served later. Their fight rubbed the pleasure of a good cry out of me. "Do you still want to kill each other? No? Great! I'm going to take a shower and order some breakfast. You sort things out for when Bodmer arrives and meanwhile, you two tell me everything. And I mean every fact, assumption, suspicion, far-fetched thought you have. And make it good." Looking at them any longer is a feat overwhelming my composure. I walk towards the house. The Czech crew disperses to different corners of the property, Petr sunbathing on a pool lounger, sunglasses, hands behind his head. The picture of a covert operation we are not.

"I'm sorry I bit you."

"I'm lucky you didn't kick me in the balls." He smirks.

"There's always next time."

"Ouch."

"Vera, do you still believe I kidnapped you?" Hector asks as I'm about to enter the house.

"You would kiss the bottom of that ravine if I did."

Twenty

After a quick shower in the luxurious bathroom, I brew myself a tea and admire the estate from the large balcony as it looks down over a hallowed valley. We are in a wilderness habitat. The Como Andana Estate design is every tourist's wet dream, especially when the best I can afford are old four-star hotels. My room has high-quality furnishing with expensive touches. White walls, large windows, and an extra-large bed.

In a moment, I will go downstairs to discover how Aleš is involved with Lina, my best friend since I started my corporate life. How everything I thought was painted in warm colours is actually a surrealist house of illusions. I need to pace myself when receiving the twists life throws at me, or I'll have a heart attack before my next birthday. Hence the break for tea. Or I'm stalling and who can blame me? Ironic how imagining Hector betrayed me nearly crippled me and finding out there is a connection between my teenage crush turned knight in shining armour and my best friend leaves me aggravated but still standing.

Do you believe Hector's story? Have you learned nothing? Shouldn't you pay him forward in the same coin? He didn't give you the benefit of the doubt.

Enough, I'm tired.

Downstairs, over breakfast, Aleš breaks into the resort's system and by elimination, we find the villa Bodmer reserved. We can't hide listening devices in his rooms, his team will surely do a swipe before he enters, so we need to be creative and not arouse suspicion. Our goal is to gain access to his laptop and copy its content, leaving a nice undetected gift to peek at his future screen activities.

We know Bodmer and his lackeys will recognise Hector and me, so we plan to wear disguises and not parade freely in plain sight, but we are still key elements to the whole operation. Aleš summarises everybody's previously discussed job demands and after he dismisses the team, I nudge him to go on with what I want to hear. Hector remains seated next to us at the dining room table. A fan blasts refreshing air above us. They've showered and cleaned their wounds, though surprisingly, after the blood was washed away, the damage they inflicted is not that severe. It still hurts to look at them, but I expected much worse.

"The story starts with the mention that I was unaware your friend Lina Haas, was someone I should know. I tracked your life as you moved from Romania to Poland and England, but I didn't want to invade your privacy by looking into your friends, boyfriends, girlfriends, work colleagues," he confesses and waits for my reaction.

"Clearly someone will give you a medal for that kind of restraint," I say.

"You know I am boundaries challenged. Anyway, a respectable period after I mourned the termination of our relationship, I started talking with a few women. In real life, online was a still a sore spot." He clears his voice at the end.

"Define respectable," I inquire with a serious face, but then smirk.

"Petr was dating this girl from Germany, studying in Prague. We went out a few times with her group of friends." He ignores my comment. "I didn't pay too much attention to anyone in particular, but long story short, I had fun. This one girl, Berdine, somehow became obsessed with me, after we spent a couple of nights together. Although I explained to her, and others, that I was not seeking a serious commitment. She came to my house unannounced at night, visiting my grandfather at the chocolate shop, calling me at all hours."

"Berdine is my Lina?"

"She was using Berdine back then and her mother's maiden name. Petr had a tremendous fight with his girlfriend about me ignoring her friend, and he told her I was still suffering after my last relationship and that I was broken-hearted. He obviously shared more than he relayed to me because she must have found you online afterwards and stalked you to the point of getting a job at the same company. The rest, I assume, is how you know it."

"No, nothing is how I know it."

"When I first saw Lina Haas on your teddy cam video application, I sincerely did not recognise her. We met too long ago and as disturbing as she acted back then, I wanted to forget the experience. I was drinking too much, being an insufferable prick. And she looks quite different."

"You don't remember a woman you slept with. More than once. As crazy as you say she was," I recap sarcastically.

"Vera, she used to have long hair, tonnes of makeup, and dressed in a heavy metal vibe. Now she looks like . . ." He is straight-faced when he waves a hand at me. "She looks just like you, but taller and blonde."

"What? No!" I'm going to be sick.

"She does. Same hair length, clothes. By the looks of it, she started assimilating your style, before she even met you in person. You mentioned meeting her through work. This is her months before you started at Fosters & Co," Hector says and turns his laptop towards me, opened on Lina's social media pages from that time. She deleted the pictures before her transformation, but she has a few photo tags from her time in Prague, where her style is as Aleš described. A beautiful punk rocker young woman.

I fly out of my chair to the nearest bathroom, where I empty my stomach.

When did the world turn upside down?

Dry heaving and coughing above the toilet bowl, I wish the pain in my knees from scraping the rock floor would rob me of my other senses.

I've always been flattered when my friends found inspiration in what I was doing, and to be honest, she and I have personalities from different planets, and I rarely notice the imitations. But what she did sounds psychologically wrong. Lina befriended me because she was obsessed with a guy I cared for but have never actually seen in real life.

"Don't come in, please. I'm fine," I say when I hear a commotion outside the door.

"Peppermint tea waiting for you when you're ready," says Hector.

"I'm sorry, little hobbit. I don't know how to fix this." Aleš clears his throat after the anguished apology.

"Not entirely your fault. Let me brush my teeth and I'll be out in a minute." The person in the mirror never felt more alone. Trusting people's intentions will be a sore spot, I'm guessing. Admittedly, Lina betrayed me when she did unlawful deeds under my name, but this feels like a serial killer move. No wonder she sold me out without a glance back. She thought I was the reason her relationship with Aleš didn't have a happy end.

Her relationship with YOUR boyfriend!

Ex-boyfriend.

Whatever. My pride taps her imaginary big shoe at me.

"How did you realise it's her? When did you realise my friend Lina is the same girl you had a fling with?" I ask Aleš when I get back to the table. As promised, my tea is by my seat.

"I didn't," he admits.

"Lawrence and David found her in Cornwall," Hector clarifies. David is the Czech guy having his back. "When she got upset about what was going happen to her, Lawrence assured her she was safe and she had you to thank for, she just needed to cooperate."

"Haas then said that she was right, Worthington kidnapped Vera Nicolescu like she thought he would when he threatened her. Since they were supposed to meet at Waterloo and you were in his company, she assumed he had something to do with your disappearance. Why I thought he was behind the kidnapping."

"And you believed her? That doesn't answer the question of how you recognised her."

"Again, she was the one in a sharing mood. When she overheard David's conversation in Czech with us, she made the connection that you are in Prague. With me. She understood the language and asked to talk with me."

"Ha! She asked to talk with you? Not me? I mean sure, it makes perfect sense!" I say laughing like a madwoman. "Did she even ask if I'm okay? Don't answer that. When did you learn all this stuff? We were in the air."

"I assume Aleš received updates from David, as I did from Lawrence. The Wi-Fi was working on the plane."

"You just decided not to tell me. Because what Lina said made both of you look bad."

"I already had my suspicions he was lying about the Qatar stuff, and then I received solid intel that the trip was never made. Plus Lina's confessions," Aleš says sheepishly.

"And your jealousy made you see what you wanted," Hector pushes.

"Whatever. Seriously guys, I'm done with the macho stuff. What I don't understand and why it made sense for me to believe you were responsible for the kidnapping, the thing bugging me from the very beginning was why Bodmer put us in a coffin to begin with. Why not kill us directly?" I ask. "Earlier, in my mind, it made little sense they would leave us there. In a crypt. So easy to escape."

"A tactic that backfired. When they took me, they drugged me for easier transport and interrogation. When I didn't confess who else knew about the stolen Fosters & Co files, I implied a trigger will alert the authorities. They injected something stronger into me and brought you in. They said they'll bury us alive, which I knew they wouldn't. I'm guessing Bodmer wanted to scare us, for that night, come for us in the morning expecting us to be grateful enough that we would confess to everything. And give up Lawrence. I told you this in the car when we left The Hyde."

"Maybe it's difficult for her to rearrange through your lies."

"Perhaps you stick to your computer before I rearrange your face."

"I can go another round."

God!

"Can the fight over the girl be over if the girl says she's not interested?" My tone shuts them up quicker than the rushed words. A sense of foreshadowing clings to my senses about

Hector's theory. We are missing something that will either cause us severe damage or we'll solve by keeping a unified front.

Easier said than done, but time will tell.

Things progress really fast after Bodmer checks in. A team of four accompanies him, an assistant, and three bodyguards. The same men involved in our trip to the cemetery, according to Hector. We have discreet cameras installed all over the resort's property by now. The Czech team works fast. The reception, all communal areas, the massage rooms, on trees in front of every villa. The most discreet drones fly around the perimeter. They fit in one's palm, they are so small.

So far, Bodmer stays in his quarters, lunch comes and goes, and he remains locked indoors. A sunset yoga and meditation group session officially opens the seminar, and we hope he attends, bringing his team outside their rooms and us in for a thorough probing exercise. Aleš has the blueprints of the villa our villain occupies, and the drones offer us infrared vision, detecting all life forms.

When the time comes, I don a pair of green tight bike shorts, a large airy white t-shirt, take my yoga mat, and, accompanied by Aleš and Petr, make my way to where the festivities will begin. I'm also back to wearing a wig, a dirty blonde short one I hope won't fall when I'm in a downward dog position. The brown contact lenses are not comfortable yet, but what I'm hoping to settle most is my skyrocketing pulse. Hector and the rest of the guys will monitor everything from our villa, and if the coast is clear, break into Elias' accommodation. We are equipped with tiny microphones to communicate discreetly with our base if necessary.

My mission that I suggested, not only accepted, despite plenty of objections, is to get close to Elias during our session if he shows up, and place a phone smarter than most computers next to any devices he brings. Minimal chances for him to arrive with his laptop. The seminar's goal is to disconnect from stress and sync into fulfilment of ever-present awareness. Whatever that is. A phone is more likely to find its place next to a business executive's yoga mat. Involved corporate people never want to be disconnected from their inbox. I should know. He won't protest too much or suspecting wrongdoings if a woman crowds his space, as opposed to a guy. Hopefully.

Petr will guard the exit, running surveillance on the entire assembly, and Aleš will be by my side, my protector and source of calmness. Although when I look at him, I see Lina and the two of them together, then our friendship, mine and hers, now viewed with a disturbed lens, and I want to weep. Was everything about our bond fake?

The wooden pavilion prepared for tonight is big enough to host a wedding party. On a cliff overlooking the astonishing rice terraces, the colossal gazebo structure is round and separated from all other property buildings. The stone path leading us here was a jungle experience, and once we arrived in the clearing, the island spreads underneath us. The high ceiling, sustained by large wood columns and hip tall wood walls, lets the sounds of the forest mingle with the attendees' excitement. Over thirty people present of various ages, and Bodmer is one of them. We spot two of his bodyguards.

The sun is performing its last stretch before sunset when they call our attention for the yoga part of the programme. My heart threatens to break free of my chest when I stalk close to Bodmer. One of his guards situates himself on his right, so I take his left. On sight, Elias's phone is missing. He's dressed in comfortable grey clothes to match his salt and pepper hair. He's of medium build with a Roman nose and kind greyish blue eyes. It shouldn't surprise me; he always looks kindly upon people. That's the image I have of him from Fosters & Co video calls and functions, but knowing what he is truly capable of chills the sweat at my nape, wig and all.

"Negative on the villa break in. The coast is not clear." I hear the chatter in my ear mic, and it deflates me further. The missed opportunity means coming up with other ways to access the data hidden in the technologies he uses. I shift slightly to observe the instructor up front. I can't be the only person not executing the moves she wants us to try. Drawing attention to myself is not what I want, and I'll have enough difficulties if this yoga practice turns into advanced territory. Who am I kidding? Any territory. Next to me, Aleš is calmly flowing from plank to Chaturanga Dandasana and upward facing dog. By the second downward facing dog, I'm feeling out of breath, and I already know the following forty minutes will transform me into a sticky puddle. The humidity in the air is not helping, forcing my hands to grab the mat for support with every exhale, my frame's clumsiness, not the only burden leaning me off course.

For a second, I want to seek Lina's face in the crowd, share an eye roll and a laugh at the inability to keep my balance. She introduced me to yoga and dragged me to a few sessions in the past. I'll always think of her when I want to share life's small particularities and I don't know what it says about me that I have moments when I want to forgive her and other moments when I wish we never met.

As expected, the end of the session transforms my body into a bag of liquefied bones on the ground. It might be the absolute wonder that is this location, the unique orange and purple colours of a Bali twilight, but I sense a peace coming over me when my body links with the surrounding energy and as we move into meditation, I feel invincible. I expected the journey I've had so far to break me, and in many ways, it did. The horrors, the betrayals, the reconnections. The losses and the conflicting emotions. And sitting in a lotus pose next to Bodmer, who is the perpetrator of this hellish operation and has an astonishing serenity about him, I ask myself why I'm not trembling in fear anymore. Instead, I feel determination pumping in my veins. I have not suddenly transformed into Mata Hari, nor reached Nirvana. I just want to get it done and live. And from now on, I'm my own best friend and council, until we apprehend everyone responsible. For after, I still have Dorota, Youssef, Astrid, and my brother. I am not alone.

Rain comes down on the roof like an omen when we hear the final Namaste, and I am aware of Bodmer being pushed towards the exit by his men in the commotion it creates. I follow involuntarily, propelled by the people behind me. The collective agreement is enjoyment in the unexpected weather change, taking it as a soul cleansing, wanting to bathe in it.

I'm soaked in seconds once I'm outside and staying upright on the wet grass is a challenge. Bodmer is in front of me, and I run, not wanting to lose him in the wilderness ahead. Adrenaline mixed with the invigorating drops pouring down my face intensifies my focus, steadying my hasty steps. A discarded palm leaf is my downfall though, and I trip, grabbing at something on reflex.

Bodmer's shirt. Damn!

In my impulsive race, I lost track of Aleš, Petr, and why I was chasing after three dangerous men on my own. Bodmer turns and helps me up from my knees, moving us a step away from the pathway to let people pass. Can they recognise me through my disguise?

"Are you injured?" I hear through the rain. He's expecting a reply, and when I nod, he smiles with compassion. "The rain is washing away the blood, but you've got yourself quite the scrape there."

Before I can say anything, he's forcibly dragged away by his bodyguards. The downpour drowns their harsh commands.

My team is by my side a second later. Cross as bears, or how we say it in Romania, with a jaw in the sky and one on the ground. Never understood that one.

Everyone admonishes me when I arrive at the villa. What was I thinking, running off like that? Well, I wasn't, was I? It was unsafe, no matter how much levitating power I had after the yoga and meditation sessions. Angry Aleš pads my knees clean with antiseptic wipes while I'm perched on a wood table. Hector sends invisible daggers from his wicker chair to my left. To whom, I'm uncertain. The white t-shirt I'm wearing is wet and sticking to my body, attracting a few different gazes to my hardened nipples. The thin swimsuit bra is inefficient, and before I cross my arms over them, Hector hands me a blanket from the back of his chair. Okay, then.

"We can bribe the boy that brings them food or the cleaning crew to get the copier inside the villa," Petr suggests as a solution to our problems. We've been exchanging ideas on the covered patio as the rain continues. Day turned into night.

"And risk other people's lives if they get caught? I can infiltrate as a housekeeper when Bodmer is out. If it comes to that," I say with a wince when Aleš applies a band aid to my left knee.

"Woah there, cowboy! And when did you gain secret agent skills? Do you even know self-defence?" He packs the first aid supplies.

"There's always a beginning in this sort of jobs, an origin story. If my life in procurement is over, you can hire me as a mercenary, hence seizing this teachable moment."

"You don't say."

"Hard pass on that ever happening," Hector dictates, and I throw my abandoned wig at him.

"Neanderthals, the lot of you."

Later we go back and forth with potential schemes for tomorrow during a dinner of Nasi Goreng, fried rice with vegetables and pork. We share amongst us other traditional dishes such as Pepes Ikan, fish wrapped and cooked in banana leaves before calling it an early night, and retreat to our respective bedrooms. I offer to put my name down for guard duty, but they find me overqualified. Go figure.

I wake up at 4 a.m., scratching my knee, perfectly rested, and in need of a glass of water. Good luck falling asleep again. This is not ideal, but jet lag is real and wicked. When I come back from the bathroom, an artificial light outside catches my attention. I don't remember leaving any on, so I pull the curtain to see Hector sitting in a balcony lounge chair with a laptop on his lap. The image of his glowing profile, attractive in his seriousness, compels my fingers to open the door and my feet to take a step outside.

He's not facing the door leading to my bedroom, but I know he hears me, even throughout the morning bird calls. The air is heavy, the dawn temperature predicts a sweltering day ahead. I walk past the lounge set to the railing overlooking the darkness of the tropical forest surrounding our villa.

"Good morning."

"Is it though? I would be still hugging my pillow if it was." Head on my crossed arms, leaning on the handrail. Maybe I'm not as rested as I thought.

"From where I'm sitting, yes, it is good. Wonderful even." A hint of a flirty tone in his amused reply suggests I'm providing quite the show, only wearing a tight black tank top and the same colour high-waisted briefs. When I finally turn to him, his gaze is on my thighs and moving up. The screen in his lap illuminates his face and naked chest. My cheeks burn from his intense focus and I'm glad the night helps cover my blush, the moon offering but a diffuse guide of my body.

"Couldn't sleep? I didn't know you took the bedroom next to mine. Are you sharing with someone?" Not that I regret allocating the master to myself, but we are eight people to limited chambers with beds and sofas.

"I don't share." My gut feeling suggests he means more than the room, and I won't have this conversation so early in the morning. I cross the balcony again, barefoot on its cool surface. He captures my hand before I pass.

"Don't go." His confused gaze keeps me in place more than the hold of his fingers. "I keep breaking my promise to spare you of pain." Goosebumps form on my exposed skin from his gruff voice and the light touch encircling my wrist, moving up my arm.

"That's not in anyone's control," I say with a hefty exhale.

"It could be if you would allow me to fly you somewhere safe. And you wouldn't risk your skin at every corner." He caresses the band aid on my leg.

"Do you think I could live with myself if I don't participate in this mission?"

"You would live."

"Hector."

"You are stubborn, but I understand. Vera, I take responsibility for the actions that led us here. After we escaped the coffin, entirely thanks to your perseverance, you seemed scared, all normal reactions to that impossible situation. But yesterday morning, with all the news revealed, you looked . . ."

I sit in the spare space at his knees.

"Hector, listen. I am not broken. And if a few pieces got smashed along the way, flatlining me, I'm gluing them back together. I'm nobody's responsibility but my own."

"It's okay to ask for help." He moves the laptop to the nearby table with one hand, holding mine with the other.

"Help? You are providing all the capital, Aleš brought the men and his computer expertise. My job is to keep it together and be as useful as I can." He leans in to touch my face. To push the hair covering my eyes behind a sensitive ear. Are all my nerve endings gathered there, or is his touch this potent?

"I expected you to be more upset about me knowing who you were from the beginning. For not being straightforward and for accusing you wrongly." His eyes shift from the pulse in my neck until the blue gaze captures mine.

"Where would that lead me, exactly? Being upset for things outside my power is pointless. Nothing from the moment I got kidnapped gives me any pleasure."

"Nothing?" He grins, and I huff at his implied suggestion.

"Do I wish to scream-punch all of you for being idiots? Yes. If I were you, I might have done the same, if I thought you were scamming me. I don't know. I can't spare the energy of losing my mind every time something goes wrong. Terrible things keep happening. I don't have the luxury. I do that and I die."

"Nobody is dying anymore. I won't let them hurt you. Or let you out of my sight, and partially because you brought me back from a state of self-brought numbness when I met you in the graveyard. You revived me, but you deserve to be protected, even if my feelings were different. I have been numbing myself since Helena died and what I said to Aleš yesterday before the fight was—"

"To aggravate him."

"In part, but I spoke the truth. I want you, that much is clear. I didn't expect it. Not the best month for a romantic discovery, but . . ." He captures my jaw with both palms, until his nose touches mine. His breath on my lips makes me lick them on impulse.

"Not the best time for intimacy, no." Our lips connect when I speak, and his tongue invades my mouth. He only waits for one rushed moan to lift me into his lap to straddle him, hands beneath my ass, crushing our lower bodies together. No space remains between us, and my hands shake on his naked chest. He bites my bottom lip and sucks on my tongue, fingers bruising my hips.

"How did I revive you? In the coffin, I mean," I ask between kisses.

"With your screams, of course." He bites my neck, smiling, reminding me of the vampire misunderstanding we fought about at the beginning when I never imagined we'll give each tiny fangs marks. "About you and Aleš. Like I said, I don't share."

"You want to talk exclusivity now?" I laugh with my breath, and I go for a kiss he denies. He pins my arms to my lower back, holding them with one hand while he pulls on my hair with the other, to bend me, exposing my throat, forcing me to look up at him.

"Should I wait until I'm inside you to claim you?"

"Confident much? You presume we're having sex." I say this as my body tries to connect with his again.

"Where do you think this is heading? Not before I make myself clear that I'm the only one who touches you. What happened between you two at the cabin—"

"It's none of your business. But nothing happened." The confession rushes to the surface.

"He slept in your bed." A small tug of my curls punctuates his declaration.

“He did. He didn’t touch me.” Getting on my knees and arching my back, I bring my sensitive collarbone to his mouth. “Hector!” I say moaning when I feel his teeth and licks on the top of my breasts. He releases my wrists to grab the back of my trembling thighs.

“I’m incredibly turned on by your body’s language, how you move to get from me what you want, and it’s messing with my head.” He lifts his handsome face to bring his tongue closer to my lips, the tip licking them wet. His hips rise to meet mine, and I tremble, my core tight with want and need and every fucking emotion it can feel. “And I’m not talking only about now that I have you in my lap, at my mercy, so willing, despite the sarcasm. But how you walk with your back straight in every room, even if you are scared, looking ready to confront any challenge. How you can still bloody smile, after the days we’ve had, when someone puts a dessert plate in front of you.” The corner of his mouth moves left with a smirk and my moans intensify. “How you follow me with your eyes when you think I’m not looking.”

“Hector!” Exhaling his name on his hot skin, I kiss and bite below his ear, wishing the world could go on living without us for a second. So I can savour with leisure his accent, his touch, the control he wants to reclaim on himself by seducing me with powerful words, when I can’t even think properly. Desire seems so much like greed when I wish for another kiss and when that is finished, wanting another and another more. But the world is cruel, and Hector stops moving underneath me, arms holding me close, and my ears perceive more than his rushed breathing.

“Bodmer is on the move,” Aleš says from the balcony door of my bedroom, making me gasp at his unexpected appearance. When I raise my face from Hector’s neck, he has evaporated as fast as he appeared.

Twenty-One

Dressed in a sky-blue maxi slip and only mildly embarrassed for being caught in such an intimate position with a man I plainly crave by another for whom I have complicated feelings, I make my way into a rented car with Hector and Petr. We are on the road in minutes. Two of our guys drove the van to follow Bodmer when he left the resort a quarter of an hour ago. All three of his bodyguards accompany him, not his assistant, which has us believe he is not leaving the island. Because of that, Aleš remains at the villa with the rest of our team to manage the break-in into our enemy's camp.

Before crossing the patio, I debated my usefulness, at the resort or in the chase, but choosing wasn't an option when Hector interlaced his fingers with mine and asked me to come with him. In front of everyone. Apparently, he meant it when he said he's not letting me out of his sight. Judging his expression, the prospect of leaving me with Aleš did not sit well with him. And the coward in me sought to avoid, desperately, a discussion with Aleš about why I was moaning minutes ago. Okay, so I might be more than mildly uncomfortable.

The traffic is not so bad close to six in the morning, but it's getting busier once we pass Ubud and head towards Denpasar, the capital city of Bali. Sunrise is nearing, the sky turns pink and orange, swiping away the cover of night. People on scooters hurrying towards work or tourists riding in pairs on the compact vehicles, probably starting their day of beach hopping and other incredible activities the island must offer.

"They are passing by Sanur, continuing on the Mandara toll road." Petr reads the incoming texts to Hector, who is in the driver's seat.

"Is it possible they'll end up at the airport?" I ask, concerned from the back.

"They weren't carrying any major luggage. Plus, the assistant did not leave the premises since last night," Petr says as I pass him some water. No time to eat breakfast, but I grabbed several ice-cold bottles on my way out.

The cars next to us flash by, quickly left behind when our speed increases, and I crack a bottle open for Hector, who takes hold of it and my fingers, not letting go of my hand when he drinks. The movement brings me closer to him, pressing my chest to the side of his car seat, and I hear the silent 'thank you' he whispers into my wrist, the skin tingling lightly. I glue my spine to the backseat when he lets go, cooling off my burning cheeks with the condensation on the bottle of water. Turning my eyes from the window after two heartbeats, my lips part slightly and my breath quickens when I find him looking at me in the rear-view mirror with a wolfish grin. I don't know him for long, but I have the impression Hector doesn't smile often. So, when he turns that potent mouth up, he steals the surrounding air. Makes me forget Petr is in the car too until he speaks.

"Further southeast," Aleš' best friend mentions, texting back with Radek, who is in the van.

"He's going surfing," Hector says.

"What? Seriously? I thought he's meeting someone."

"They are heading for Nusa Dua, most probably. A well-known area amongst surfers in the wet season with high waves and wild strips of beach. Early in the morning, to catch a good set of waves. And he does surf, according to our research."

"I thought Uluwatu is for surfing in Bali."

"In the dry season. And it would have been unfortunate to follow him there. Trekking the jungle and hiking an uneven terrain is how you find the best Uluwatu spots for line up. We could have lost him." Hector develops his idea, and it sounds like he knows a thing or two about this sporting activity in Bali. He's been here before. I wonder how he looks in a wetsuit, balancing on a board, because hormones rule my brain this morning.

"You are right! The latest text says they pulled in front of a board rental shop. The guys are on standby," Petr confirms.

We arrive in a parking lot to one of our men waiting by the van. He and Petr stay behind to break into Bodmer's SUV while Hector and I continue on foot to the meetup point Radek is conducting the surveillance.

To hide my face, I'm wearing big sunglasses and a round straw hat. White Converse trainers and a small linen backpack complete my sky-blue dress. Hector's khaki ball cap covers half of his face. The linen shorts of same colour and the white shirt make him beach perfect. Unfortunately, we are not here for the magnificent long stretch of gold sand visibly extending for miles in both directions, keeping the high waves of the west monsoon in check. With the foaming sea on my left and perfectly planted palm trees on my right, we pass luxurious sunbed after sunbed, red umbrellas shading their morning occupants. It's hard to believe not too long ago I was freezing in London and now sunlight warms my naked arms and back just as the wind makes my flimsy shift dance.

Only one bodyguard is in the water with the Swiss. We spot the others waiting at the beach bar, where Radek is enjoying a fruity lemonade at a low table. We join him without drawing too much attention, and he confirms our suspicion. The place is packed with surfers having breakfast or getting ready for a round in the agitated waves of the Java Sea.

"Did we hear anything from the guys at the house?" I ask Radek.

"They are in. But in radio silence since confirming their entrance."

"We should head back to Ubud. We are not getting much value from watching Bodmer surf."

"And if he meets with someone afterwards?" I drink my Earl Grey. We ordered hot drinks to keep with our ruse, but my stomach is full of nerves to process any food. I'll regret that later.

"Radek and the guys will continue the surveillance. There's no point having all of us on their tail for his entertainment and risk exposure."

"Okay."

"Okay." He smiles at my attempt to hold the beach hat on my head when a gust of wind blows through the crowded booths, teeth visible behind the full lips I crave already. Be still my heart.

"Going to the restroom and I'm ready to leave." He doesn't let me pass immediately, holding my fingers and squeezing them as I stand next to him. Only after checking on the two bodyguards still at the front table enjoying their food, he lets go. I weave my way through the loud tables, men and women in synthetic rubber, following the signs for the bathroom.

Once I'm done washing my hands at the small sink in the ladies' cubical, I catch my face in the mirror, unobstructed by the sunglasses attached to my dress. A bite sign below my jaw, previously hidden by hair, flushed grinning cheeks. As if I need a reminder of the man occupying my thoughts. The door rattles violently and my heart jumps to my throat.

"Occupied! I'll be out in a second." Impatient, are we?

The universe has its way of slapping the tiny grin off your face if it deems you only deserve disappointment. Especially when it sees you making the best of a dangerous situation. Enjoying something precious and unexpected.

Waiting outside the plastic entrance is not an annoyed lady with a full bladder, but a gun pointed at my chest by the man I evaded at the airport in Brussels.

Shit!

The brute lifts me up, his hands squeezing the air out of me, and drops me with force and malice into a speedboat after he held a gun to my back and dragged me through sand and icy water. I couldn't scream for fear of being shot, and it happened so fast I didn't know how to process a gun barrel pressed into my body. One moment we were in the open corridor of the restrooms, in the next he pushed us for the rear exit. Then in a run, drag, run movement, we were in the sea. He joins me in the swaying boat and signals his partner, who drives the vessel towards a group of tiny figures on boards deeper offshore.

Searching the beach with watery eyes, I spot people fighting at the terrace's entrance. Hector runs for the water until a gun goes off and he hits the ground. My scream rips from within and I try to jump, surprising my captor. Ultimately, he's faster than me, taking advantage of my crippling fear, he locks his arms around my waist and shoves me to the ground. Using a zip tie handcuff, he locks my hands together, knowing I couldn't jump now and swim. They shot him when his back was turned, running to save me. Because I was afraid of a gun and didn't fight harder. Like I said I would when I argued my case of coming to Asia with everyone.

You don't deserve people sacrificing their lives for you because you are weak!

The boat stops to pick up Bodmer and his bodyguard floating in the sea. I don't hear the turbulent water or the men talking. The piercing ring of gunfire is the only thing my ears transmit to my brain. What happened to Hector? No visible wound from this distance, but the shot pierced him down. Did they kill him?

Elias and his armed security ignore me and my useless cries at the back of the boat, and I wonder if the whole surfing excursion was a setup to separate us. If not, did someone tip them off after we departed the resort?

In a haze, we move from the boat to a car. I've lost notion of time, space, and emotions, we could have been at sea for hours and I couldn't differentiate the change. The car switches into a plane, private tarmac, when my whimpering head clears, aware of what is happening around me.

Before I voice my scream for help, a hand covers my mouth, urging me to walk towards the aircraft, his foul skin pressing into my nostrils. I trash and bite and kick the animal holding me. No signs of concern about passports or security checks and a woman being abducted. Nothing but the sudden torrential rain dropping from the angry sky when they dump me in a leather chair at the back of the plane. A cloth gag to silence me comes next. Then a slap that knocks my body into the small oval window.

"That's enough!" Elias Bodmer says to the man who hit me. I raise my head to see their silent confrontation. The man many times my size moves to the front and Bodmer remains a second longer to catch my eyes. I hope he reads the hatred I convey, the certainty that I'll destroy him and everyone on this plane first chance I have. He shakes his head and leaves.

The weather change doesn't delay the departure, and we are airborne all too soon. The slap received grounds me. It enrages me to where thinking of Hector, Aleš, and the fate of our group doesn't crush me from the inside. But gives me force to keep my wits and hope I'll see them soon.

How can you see him if he died?

Tears I can't wipe coat the material around my mouth despite my fury, and when I blink, he appears in the back of my eyelids, gunned down on the beach. No matter how hard I beg the vision to change, I can't make him stand up.

He won't rise because I want him alive with all my heart. He can't. That's not how bullets work.

Similar to how I arrived, I leave the island of Bali shocked to the core, surrounded by doubts and nowhere close to tilting my life on track. The wet trainers, the men's calibre, and the conviction I won't die gently as they please are where the resemblances disappear. I will rage against anyone keeping me from seeing my family again. It's time to go back to the drawing board and plot. Even if the only thought I have is murder.

Hours pass before an unknown man takes me to the restroom, freeing my hands and mouth. I've counted six people in the employ of the Fosters & Co director. The new guy places a food tray on my table, and the generic airplane meal is the first I eat since yesterday. He gives me a bottle of water and a blanket as well. I've turned purple from the AC, wearing only a summer dress and soggy shoes.

"Thank you," I say because I'm not savage, and you catch more flies with honey than with vinegar. I loathe their entire group of mercenaries, and I won't be the meek and fearful victim in front of them. I've had it up to my ears with fear, but I don't want a repeat of the slap, or worse. Also, maybe they will answer my questions about Hector's condition, if I behave.

Finished with dinner, Bodmer returns and sits softly in the opposite seat. He exchanged his wetsuit for business attire, most likely before we boarded the plane, and it shows how deranged I was after seeing Hector shot, if I didn't realise this until now. Refusing to break eye contact first, I analyse all the expressions taking over his face through my vengeful gaze.

Earlier, when the man hit me, remorse was what I saw. Maybe he's reluctant to be violent towards women but has no problem with burying them alive. He still emanates a peaceful vibe, like he faults himself for nothing. That or I'm sitting in front of a psychopath.

"You've been working for Fosters & Co your entire professional career, Miss Nicolescu, is that correct? And doing an outstanding job at that." Of all the things to say, he begins with the CV question? Okay, I'll bite.

"I thought so too. Until I woke up in a cemetery. Should I consider that your performance review approach? Seems more of an immediate dismissal, in my opinion."

"Things are rarely as they seem."

"Tell me about it."

"Yes, let's take your case, for instance. You have a surprising character. Very resilient and resourceful. Not what I was expecting."

"Sorry for ruining your plans."

"I'm curious as to what your friend Lina Haas would do if she used her own credentials from the start and she was dealing with these trials." At my stunned expression, he adds, "Yes, I know she framed you. Did you have any intention of mentioning her name as the culprit in your predicament, or did you want to remain a loyal friend and spare her the suffering after everything she did?"

"You are the culprit in my predicament, and more to come, I'm sure. Let's not kid ourselves. What she did was wrong. Your actions are criminally worse. But it's not a competition, is it? You've won it when you murdered Helena Worthington and Neville's father. Throw in a kidnapping or two." My temper simmers and this guy is cool as a spring morning.

"Yes. You would see it like that."

"The world will see it like that, Mister Bodmer, if evidence is brought forward."

"There is no evidence of me committing the crimes you accuse me of."

"Covering your tracks doesn't excuse you. I wouldn't be too proud about it."

"That's one way to interpret my words. I thought you'd see things differently. I guess the ask is too great." Is he delusional? Before I can make sense of what he's saying, a bodyguard is by his side, requesting his presence elsewhere, helping Bodmer up.

"What happened to Hector? What's our destination and your plans for me there?" I ask hurriedly.

"Shanghai. That's all I know," he says as he's escorted as far away from me as possible.

What does he mean by that's all he knows? All he will share, more likely. I thought only in movies deranged criminals talk in riddles. Nothing beats real life lately, I conclude, as I'm gagged and shackled a second time today.

Twenty-Two

Officials at Pudong International Airport in China see my real passport when we land, magically produced by one guard, with a diplomatic visa on it no less, to introduce me into the country. As if they want formal records of me being here. In the backpack they appropriated upon capture, lays the fake document Aleš created for me with enough visas to get to the moon and back. They could have used that one, I know they inspected my stuff. My protests go unnoticed by back door immigration officers.

Bodmer kept clear of me since interacting on the plane, and they drive him from the airport in a different car. My questions about Hector and where we are going remain ignored by the men guarding me. From the busy highway, the great Chinese city appears covered in a blanket of smog at first glance. Outside the car window, the hazy sunset transforms the buildings into dark silhouettes on an apocalyptic burnt canvas. A study in shades by a merciful God who washed his hands of me.

When we enter the lobby at The Peninsula, I'm wearing a man's suit jacket and my crinkled dress. A grand hotel with Art Deco flourishes in what must be the heart of the city if I use the view outside of Shanghai's famous Bund as a guide. My energy is waning from being up since 4 a.m. Our new location shares time zones with Bali, an airport discovery that compelled me to imagine the fate of my friends as I stared unblinking at a huge clock in a different country. I won't suffer from another bout of jet lag after the first one, but time zones are the least of my problems.

A short delay later, after check-in and a greeting from the General Manager welcoming him back to the hotel, Bodmer leads the way to the tenth floor. In the elevator up, I try to get some information on what he plans to do with me, but my personal pain and bodyguard, the slapper, forces my body into the corner. Mean eyes promising misery and most likely more violence, if I don't stop talking. Arriving at the end of a corridor, in front of two parallel doors, I push for answers before I go mad.

"Tell me at least if Hector is okay," I demand with an exaggerated, hard tone. If I can hear the slight desperation in my voice, they can too.

"Worthington signed his death certificate when he flew to Bali," he says coldly before the door to his room shuts in my face and I'm shoved into the other suite.

No!

He can't be dead!

The sharp ache in the middle of my caved-in chest and the lock sound activated with me on the inside, at the mercy of men without scruples, forces me to my knees, freeing a long, wet sigh. I can't stop shaking my head *no*, although a widespread numbness takes hold of the rest of my body. Sitting on the plush carpeted floor I wish closing my eyes will trigger an automatic day rewind and I would be magically placed in my bed in Bali with its cool, welcoming sheets.

Shaky legs lead me to the bathroom, and I hold my tears until the hot water washes over my naked, curved spine. Hopelessness like I never felt before gives room to anger, and I pound my fists on the shower's wall. The running water swallows my screams, but I don't care if the entire hotel hears my grief.

From the moment I woke up next to him weeks ago, even paralysed by the drugs they injected in his system, Hector seemed indestructible. Foolishly obnoxious, but so committed in finding answers for his sister's death. I felt the strength of his vitality just last night. The beating of his heart under my searching palm. The quick pulse in his demanding tongue.

And now he's dead. Gone.

He'll never smile again, never receive a hug, or feel the warmth of someone's caress on his face.

Is that what will happen to me? Will my family suffocate at the news as I do now? Will they know their daughter loved them? Did Hector die knowing how much influence he had over my fragile heart, or did he feel abandoned? I wish he could know that I cry for him and wish I met him differently, in an alternative month of March. Or not at all, if it means he would still be alive.

When my skin turns red and I don't feel the bitter taste of tears anymore, I return to the bedroom dressed in the white bathrobe the hotel offers. I don't have other clothes. As an afterthought, I bolt the door with the chain lock, draw the curtains shut and collapse under the covers. Tomorrow I need to get myself together. Hector wouldn't want me to give up and let them crush me. But tonight, I allow free rein to the depression scratching the surface of my mind. Unwillingly, the feeling of guilt for being alive when he died trying to save me worms itself into my subconscious. And like a sick joke, listening to my own pulse thud in my veins is how I fall asleep. Heartbroken and alone.

Heavy knocking on the entrance door rouses me – glad the lock works. Too bad I cannot stay in this room forever.

"Get dressed." He throws a paper bag in the suite's hallway when the door opens to the angry mammoth. "Bolt the door again, little bitch, and I'll invite every man under my employ to come and say hello. In their own special way. You won't like it. There won't be much left of you when they finish." I freeze before I address his threat, because how do I respond with anything that is not a bloody knife to his eye socket? And I don't have the knife or the training to complete such a task. "You have ten minutes." He leaves when his words reach their desired effect. Horror written all over my face.

A complete attire from Chanel's newest collection awaits when I snap out of my stupor and check the bag. Bodmer clearly wants me presentable for whatever he has planned. Maybe immediate death is not it. I'm ready with minutes to spare, fresh breath and brushed hair. Two-tone ballet flats, the emblematic black and nude. A black form fitting dress, long-sleeved and over my knees, made from a wool cashmere blend. Black tweed jacket. A small purse I have nothing to put in but my grief. Undergarments provided in my size again, and I block out who shopped for them and throw away that key. I can't do anything about my puffy eyes. Crying does that to a face.

An elevator ride to the thirteen floor and I'm escorted to Elias Bodmer's table at the hotel's restaurant. He rises when I approach and has a few tense words I don't understand with the chief bodyguard. The man that outright threatened me with rape on command, slapped me, put a gun to my face in Bali to kidnap me. You are the people you associate with, and in Bodmer's case, I can't say I've seen two more despicable individuals in all my years.

Left alone, the bodyguard wanting anything but, we sit in silence. The guard doesn't go far. I spy him near the exit sign when I glance around the modern restaurant. Our table is by the window over-viewing the Oriental Pearl Tower and the many skyscrapers located across the river in the Pudong district. The weather has improved significantly today, no cloud or smog on the horizon.

"I trust you had a restful sleep, Miss Nicolescu." Imagine the calmness he possesses after the horrible acts he ordered his goons to do. Thinking of something to add that won't get me in trouble, I say nothing. "I'm not unsympathetic to your mental state this morning. I've been told you formed a connection with Worthington in the brief time you spent together. I understand grief. But if you let it run your life, if you let it become your motivating factor, you'll inevitably face dead ends without a liable solution in sight," he preaches, eating his eggs with a normality that bewilders me. I refuse to talk about Hector with him. About the sorrow he permitted happening.

"Why am I here?" In this restaurant, at this table, in Shanghai? Why didn't he kill me already?

"What does it look like? We are having breakfast. You should eat. The food at The Peninsula is flawless and you need to build your strength. One never knows how a day progresses." He points at my plate.

"You are sick." He can't misinterpret the venom in my rasp.

"In more ways than one. Eat!" And I do because as much as everything tastes like dust and it pains me to follow his directives, I gather that this is not negotiable for him. I don't want the slapper's return. Silence stretches around our breakfast table. The sound of cutlery and other patrons enjoying their morning is all I hear as I finish my orange juice and sample my European meal.

"If you are not willing to engage in conversation, perhaps you'll indulge me in hearing a story with a subject dear to my heart." He breaks the quiet and doesn't wait to see if I'm interested or not. "This month, as fate would have it, is the anniversary of my great-great-grandfather establishing our family's business. In 1896, he opened a little hotel in Basel, Switzerland. He started small, with his own money, barely keeping his family clothed and fed; he was pouring every saving and profit into this business. In time, he didn't ration his food, or wear the same suit patched in too many places to look dignified anymore. Being a smart man, he knew how to attract and keep his customers. Everyone across the continent knew about the services offered at his establishment, their quality rarely matched. Soon he opened another hotel, this time in Zurich. His family's struggles paid off when he gained three hotels to his name by the time he was of old age and only acting as advisor to his sons on how those hotels should prosper. His sons and grandsons carried the tradition over the years, growing the business, feeding entire families of employees depending on the success of our hotels."

"Why are you telling me this?"

"Perhaps you'll better understand my actions."

"Do you think you'll share anything to justify killing people?" Unbelievably, I say that quietly, opposed to screaming it to the entire brunch hall.

"No. And that's not the point of my story. Can I continue now?" he levels me with a sombre look.

"Do I have a say in this?" I fake my incredulity. He breaks eye contact a second, glances towards the exit, at the bodyguard, at the table, and then back at me.

"No. But maybe you will. Once I finish my story." What a strange thing to say. He's speaking in code again.

"Soon after they enrolled me in school, my father started having serious difficulties paying off our business's debts. The bills had accumulated as a result of large and mostly unnecessary expansions, all of which had begun long before he took the reins of the company." He goes back to his tale, eyes on the view outside. "It wasn't until after my father was forced out of the business that I discovered the deals made with a silent partner who all but ruined his own livelihood, kept afloat by defrauding other people's life work. Such as my family's hotels. After we were forced out, and left with nothing, the hotel chain was sold to the highest bidder. Dozens of faithful employees lost their jobs overnight. Our extended family blamed my father for his poor management skills. By the end of it all, pressure took its toll, and we found him dead in his study."

He pauses for long minutes, lost in his thoughts, arms crossed over his chest, empty eyes staring outside the window.

"Life has shown me I have much in common with my father. Trusting the wrong people." What does he mean by that? "Care to guess who was the silent partner?" he says as an afterthought. Like maybe it doesn't matter anymore.

"I don't have the faintest idea." I'm sorry for his family's sufferings, but I don't see how this relates to anything.

"Wilhelm Satie. Worthington's Swiss grandfather."

"Severe Trust," I say, dumbstruck.

"The very same."

"So out of revenge you went for Helena's business and when she changed her mind, you had her killed? And now her brother? What a twisted way to honour your family's name."

"I went for her business, yes. And I wasn't honest about it. But I did not kill her." Someone coming towards us gets his attention for a split second before he focuses on me again and whispers, "Nor did I kill her brother."

"We need to leave now. The meeting's over." The brute pulls me out of the chair by my biceps and drags me towards the elevators. "There's been a change of plans." He addresses Bodmer, who is by his side. "We don't need her anymore. She's done. We fly back tonight. He said your job is complete. He'll be sending you the deeds as agreed."

What is happening? Am I to be murdered now?

Like an out-of-body experience, I look at myself in the elevator's mirror surface and I don't recognise the setting. My eyes blink when I see Elias Bodmer raise his breakfast knife behind the bodyguard's back and bring it down on his thick neck, shoving him in the process. The mountain falls to his hands and knees just as the elevators open in front of us. One occupied by crew mercenaries, and another by an elderly couple coming for breakfast.

"Run! I won't have more innocent blood on my hands. Run!" Bodmer pushes me into the now empty elevator on the right as he throws himself at the new arrivals, blocking their way to me. I press the ground floor button and hit repeatedly to close the doors, a second too late. A sharp pain explodes in my arm when a bullet pierces both clothing and skin. Through my scream and before the elevator makes its way down, I hear two more shots being fired.

Leaning on the steel wall in agony and shock, unsure how to react, I curse in all the languages I know. They shot me and Bodmer stabbed the big guy. And who is the 'he' they were referring to? Isn't Bodmer in charge? The elevator stops, picking up more people on the descent, and my hand goes to the injured arm, applying pressure. They always show this in movies. But it stings to even dab the area.

Downstairs, navigating through various hotel employees and tourists carrying their luggage, I arrive at the exit door at the same time as one of my captors, who lunges forward. He leaves me breathless with a squeeze meant to immobilise me, but my leg reacts, hitting his thigh until I manage a satisfying blow to his privates. Yelling and trashing in his hold, despite the pain radiating from my arm, proves effective when he drops me and draws the attention of building security.

"He has a gun! Help! He has a gun!" I stumble back a few steps when people in hotel uniforms surround him, speaking in both Chinese and English.

Taking advantage of the commotion, I run outside. The air is crisp, even with the powerful sun blinding my eyes whenever I look up. As I mingle among a group of teens, I spot The Bund, Shanghai's famed waterfront area, reachable with a short walk from the hotel. If anyone is coming after me, I hope to lose them in this weekend crowd. Turning right, trying not to raise suspicion, I walk fast and with purpose along the riverside. Locals and tourists are taking pictures of the panorama. And I'm bleeding through my clothes.

Think, Vera, think!

Where to go? My breathing is not where I want it to be. I can't shake the agitation; the entire morning is screening in my head like a movie. A private toilet would give me a respite to verify the damage after the bullet encounter. I pass a restaurant, but I can't go in the closest one to The Peninsula, afraid they'll check it. No friends in this country, no money, and my passport seized by Bodmer's men. Or maybe not his men? My interactions with the guy were strange, and his report with the men guarding us even weirder. Harsh, even. He said he trusted the wrong people, and he didn't kill Helena. Or Hector . . .

Don't think of him now!

Fifteen minutes of power walking and turning my head to see if I'm being followed, I cross over to my right, entering a wide street with a Chinese name. Just when I think communication is impossible in a country I don't speak the language of, I see a plaque with Lost Heaven written on it. A sign sent from above. I enter the establishment, a restaurant not open to customers yet, where a lady wipes tables as she takes me in. Others are busy with various activities but stop to stare.

"Hi! Can I use your bathroom, please? I fell and my hand is bleeding. My knees too, I think." I show them the red hand I pressed to my ruined jacket, hiding my wound, and mimic a clumsy fall.

"Certainly. Let me get you the first aid kit. The restroom is this way," one lady offers with a concerned face and perfect English. Thank you, Jesus!

In the bathroom, I wait for her to bring in the medical supplies, and once she leaves, I lock the door, remove the jacket, unbutton, and drag the dress down with my good hand. Manoeuvring my arm and head carefully to check the injury, a sigh escapes when the wound appears to be only a flesh one. The bullet went through my clothes and arm, grazing a coin size of skin. It hurts, but it's reassuring to know I'll not bleed to death. I feared worse, my brain working against me, thinking of destroyed arteries and other medical shows dramas. I wash the blood away from body and clothes, dress the wound and wheeze. What now? I need to contact Aleš.

"Thank you so much for your help," I say to the ladies at the hostess desk a few minutes later. "Can I ask another favour and use the phone?" They smile, handing me a cordless landline phone and I dial numbers I know by heart, a small distance away from the young women.

Surprise almost knocks me off my feet when an automatic voice asks to wait for two incoming identification questions. By mistake, instead of dialling Aleš' number, I phoned the conference machine Hector gave me that morning at The Hyde. Before I end the call, the ache in my chest demands I listen to the questions only he and I would know. Wanting to see what they are. That's what he promised, if I answer them, he will come for me no matter where I am. Though he can't reach me anymore.

"First question," the machine says before another voice comes over the line.

"How did you call me the first time we met?" A timid smile takes my mouth. For a second, I think it's really him, in real life, and not a pre-recorded message. His no nonsense, deep speech. Tears flood my eyes without realising, before hearing his voice it seems, and now they fall to my cheeks. I thought I had no more left. The machine demands my answer.

"Ed the Dead," I say, wiping my face. I didn't realise I said it out loud.

"Second question." The robot again.

"What did I say when I found you dancing?" I'm uncertain when he recorded the first message, but the second is definitely after the arena encounter in Prague. It might be only in my head, but he sounds amused in this one.

"You said I looked better without the wig, but you were glad I kept the smoky eyes and red lips."

"Thank you. Location found. Stay on the line if you wish your call to be answered by the owner of this mailbox." I close the call before an unanswerable ring pings in my ear. He can't help me anymore and as much as I want the chance to bring him back, like he joked I did in the coffin, that feat is impossible. Clever people realise when to stop deluding themselves, and while I never dreamed of being the most sensible woman in existence, I know to cut illusions before they catch me in their mirage. Regrouping, I dial Aleš' number, his voicemail picking up straight away.

"Aleš! I hope nothing happened to you too, or to any of the other guys. I'm okay and in Shanghai. I escaped, but it's been a mess and they are still after me. I can't stay in this spot, it's close to where they held me. And if you are coming to China, as was our plan initially, I need to think of a location to meet you guys." Where should I tell him? The hotel booked for our stay, in case Bali failed, is next to the Fosters & Co office. Where Bodmer intended to have his town hall meeting, the reason he was coming here. In a different part of the city. The bad guys, whoever they are, might go there looking for me.

The answer is on the restaurant's tourist board showing close attractions and upcoming events, and I tell Aleš to search for my old nickname. That's where I'll be today, tomorrow, or until he finds me, surrounded by hundreds of people, as the perfect cover. If I can arrive there before I'm found and murdered, countries away from my family. If entering the building without detection is possible. If tickets are not sold out and if I can convince strangers to sponsor my voyage through Shanghai. Just another Saturday with a *killer* 'to do' list. Finishing the call, I turn to Lost Heaven's wonderful ladies.

"Last favour, I promise." I offer a confident smile. I don't work in sales, but these are desperate times and after all, procurement taught me how to negotiate. "Who wants to buy a brand new £5,000 Chanel bag, certificate, and all, for a minor portion of that price?"

Twenty-Three

Bargaining skills, a soft but concise voice and a bit of blood mistakenly forgotten on my arm, seal the deal in Lost Heaven. And women everywhere love a discounted, authentic Chanel. With the money I obtain from the exchange, a free map of Shanghai and the bittersweet knowledge I can always call a number to hear Hector's voice, I leave the restaurant to face the foreign city again. I have my own rescue mission to plan on top of revenge. On the cursed Monday, a thousand years ago, when I escaped the cushioned four walls of imprisonment, I wanted answers, safety, and normality, now getting even is a driving force.

Keeping my head down and sticking to highly populated streets, I find a bazaar and buy a cheap baseball hat, a large sweatshirt, and leggings to change into once I get the chance. What two weeks on the run have taught me, and all the action movies I've seen over the years with my brother and father, is to change my appearance often to blend in.

My own mother wouldn't recognise me in the state I am today, after the time spent on trains, buses, planes, chasing my slippery fate. Hiding and rushing from country to country, my appearance in the passing shop windows is of a woman losing weight involuntarily and with a sickly complexion of impending fever. The flight hours spent in a cold airplane wearing wet clothes and the fatigue accumulated have finally caught up with me. I've been delirious since last night. It would explain Bodmer's confusing actions. I'll have to waste precious money on medicine if my condition worsens.

A screen image from the hi-tech newsstand I leave behind catches my eyes and I go back the few steps. I shouldn't stop, except I'm compelled to watch what unrolls on the television glass. He was wearing a suit when they took the video, and his hair was still long, but it's him. I don't need to read Chinese characters to know the major story of this news report is Hector. I want to understand what it says, even if my mind cries that I already know the answer. The fist size knot in my throat is difficult to swallow when I try.

"Hello, sorry to bother you. Do you mind telling me what it says on the screen? Please?" I ask the older vendor with a cracked voice. A headshake is his answer and a few words in the local language.

"It says mister Hector Worthington died yesterday." I turn to a man in a grey suit holding a paper. "I can translate the rest. Let me pay for the newspaper first," he says with a slight accent, pushing his glasses with a finger.

"Thank you. I'll buy you the copy. It's the least I can do. He was . . ." The polite stranger sees my shaking hand when I want to pay, refusing my money.

"It's a sad day. He was a good man. I work for his bank, across the street." He points to the building's façade behind us. Severe Trust. "We heard some unofficial news this morning." He looks at the TV running the same narrative in a loop.

"They mention a man killed him in an altercation in Indonesia. Died on the way to the hospital from gunshot wound complications." He reads about Hector's life, but a buzzing in my ears prevents me from hearing more.

This makes it official. A part of me, a molecule-sized one, dared to believe otherwise. I met Hector less than a month ago, we argued the entire time, but he shouldn't have died.

"Are you okay?" the kind bank employee asks. I hate this question and what people see on my face to ask it. Can't blame him because, look at that, more tears. No matter how much I try to harden my composure, tear ducts are so fickle, ruled by emotions, not by one's will. Expressing my gratitude for his support, I leave quickly.

He died.

Hector died.

Hard to control hiccups shake my frame. I already felt his death, I knew it, and this is the absolute worst time to indulge in another meltdown that will not revive him. A second of carelessness, and I'm back in my abductor's clutches. Doubt filters the mind to the point of panic, crossing another street and reasoning the improbability of a quick rescue.

Ultimately, I'll return to Europe by myself, if the guys have encountered more devastating situations. I have the Romanian consulate to consider, no matter the risk, if in a few days I'm no closer to finding my team. Or when the money runs out.

Why did they bring me to Shanghai in the first place? What was their purpose in getting me here under my real identity? Bodmer parading us for all to notice at breakfast and then wanting to kill me. No different way to interpret the brute's plan if the man I thought put everything in motion read the same intent in his words and helped me escape. My mind flies in circles over the latest occurrences, and it's a wonder I don't walk into upcoming traffic from the confusion alone.

I walk and swipe at my face.

Walk. Swipe. Blow my nose. Exhale pain.

Scoping the location I gave Aleš is a necessary step for today. And finding a hostel close to the Shanghai Comic Con site will present its own challenges. I was vague in providing Aleš the direct address of the convention centre because paranoia is running high, and I know he will figure out where I'll be only with the nickname clue. My limited funds don't allow for a new phone and getting a SIM card in China might require an ID. Will need to check on that if the accommodation I end up in doesn't have a landline. And if I don't find one bloody payphone in this entire city to check in with him.

A quick change in a fast-food bathroom and a subway ride later, the Shanghai Exhibition Centre looms over the Jing'An District like the soviet neoclassical buildings in Bucharest and Warsaw. The convention started on Friday, and it ends tomorrow. Seeing so many people queuing outside, excited faces and high energy, is like a déjà vu from a week ago when I was in Prague with the Belgian crew, visiting a new city, attending a music festival. Without a care in the world, as if Fosters & Co wasn't after me. And Hector safe in London. Or so I thought.

There are so many unexpected similarities in my weekends as a fugitive. But this time, I'm alone, too far away from my family, and someone shot me. The real pain, though, the one I'm trying to hide desperately so I can function, is not from the physical wound in my arm. The one squeezing my chest whenever a thought of Hector pushes through the mental barrier I try to impose is worse. Try being the underlined word.

Though pricey, a weekend pass to the convention is a necessary expense, as I'm not able to get inside otherwise. Luckily, the awesome women at Lost Heaven shared different discount vouchers I apply to my ticket. I use crowd protection against prying eyes as I move from room to room in the enormous centre. People are wearing costumes depicting movies and books characters, and when I find the corner with the gate to Middle Earth, I breathe a little easier. Destination reached and I hope he gets the reference. The *Lord of the Rings* posters advertising the convention are all over Shanghai, and I'm the hobbit in desperate need of my fellowship.

It's too soon to see a familiar face near the successful trilogy booth, but I cannot control my eyes and my expectation of finding my friends.

For hours, I form an invisible path on the floors of the convention, wandering the many corridors, not staying long in one area and every so often navigating back to the meeting point. Maybe I should have suggested a different rendezvous spot, but I thought I was smart with this evasive manoeuvre. And it's not like I've been to Shanghai before.

Countless foreigners are in attendance today and more than once I believe I see the Czech guys. Thanks to his height, Aleš' blonde hair should be easy to recognise when he comes, but I get more anxious with every passing minute, realising I'll finish Saturday on my own. I keep thinking my abductors hide behind every presentation stall. Whenever someone bumps into me, the hair on my neck urges me to run. The pain radiating through my arm from the gun wound acts as a reminder of what will happen if I'm caught.

Later in the evening, organisers encourage participants to leave and come back the next day, and I slip outside to do a couple of laps around the entire property. It's a lengthy process and I'm exhausted from standing all day long, however, I can't give up yet. They will come.

In the end, the pressure of finding a place to sleep forces me to abandon the centre's premises and explore the streets of Jing'An district, shivering and hungry.

Saturday night restaurants and high-end boutiques make way to luxurious hotels. A grand temple with golden lights strategically placed on the walls and the pagoda style roofs offer a splendid view of the ancient Buddhist construction. The glass skyscrapers behind it, with their commercial lights and newness, illustrate the blend between the old and the present Shanghai.

In other circumstances, I would have loved to explore the city and take a million pictures, Lina by my side, experiencing the new culture, eating the amazing food. But she decided to be an exceptionally bad friend, and at this moment, I don't appreciate the events leading me to this amazing part of Asia. Which is getting colder by the minute as the night progresses, reminding my feverish body it's still spring and I'm without a proper coat.

Three visits to cheap hostels later I find an available bed in a four persons female dormitory, minutes from the Jing'An temple and walking distance to the Exhibition Centre. My relief at not spending the night outside in the cold is short-lived, when I use the hostel's payphone to try Aleš' number again. Disconnected. I am truly and utterly alone and ironically that's not what makes me take a seat on the dirty hallway floor, but the reality that something horrible happened to Aleš too. What have I done by asking for his help?

Is this you being vengeful and courageous? They expect more from you.

No energy left in my body to plead a respite from my doubts.

I tried to be practical, and rather selfish today and think about my life and finding solutions to my problems, concentrate on moving forward and not on the harsh reality of what happened so far since mid-March. And I felt terrible, but I owe it to Hector, Aleš and the people who helped me at their own risk, to not lose my sanity, to take all the worry and thoughts I have of them to heart but reach the finish line still breathing. Now the guilt crushes into me.

Robotic legs take me to the shared bathroom, holding the plastic bag with the products I bought earlier, and I powder a few tips of my black hair a temporary shade of cherry red as a test to prepare for tomorrow's disguise. It comes off when I shower, clean my wound, take some medicine, and get ready for bed, where I don't cry myself to sleep, because technically I make no sound. Why should I interrupt the sleep of my roommates, a grandmother with her daughter and her niece visiting from some other part of China, when my lumpy pillow catches the flow of tears without complaint?

Sunday finds me wearing the same non descriptive grey sweatshirt, boasting clammy skin, and powdered red locks, walking the same exhibition corridors as yesterday, with little hope. I've slept some, but I've been up since dawn, shivering. Tonight, the centre closes its doors to this event and prepares for the next, and I need to switch to a different strategy. Perhaps a visit to the consulate.

By midday, I'm impatient and ready to abandon my post. The idea of waiting around when maybe nobody knows I'm here, and my plan failed, doesn't give me too much confidence. Still, I grant it a few more hours, not because I am a coward, but it's reckless to leave early when someone could show up. Choosing between the two raises my anxiety levels and keeps me in place until nightfall.

Ultimately, I should have listened to my poor instinct and left when I had the chance. But we know what they say about hindsight.

Twenty-Four

The air is crisp outside the Shanghai Exhibition Centre at the end of Comic Con. All around me, people walk with purpose towards their Sunday night schedules, cosy homes waiting for them, families expecting their presence at dinner.

It might have been this game of imagination that makes me ignore my surroundings, and an immediate alarm goes through my body when two men marching against the stream of pedestrian traffic take hold of my arms. A third one positions himself behind me, covering my mouth, making it look like a group embrace. A hard object pushes against my ribs, the bruising pressure of a gun.

"Go ahead, scream. I would fucking love to use this on you." The brute's voice takes me back to his threatening speech delivered just yesterday morning at the Peninsula. "The silencer makes it easier to put a bullet in your leg, right here. Nobody cares about you in this crowd." He drags my compliant body to a dark corner behind the building I just left. "You will be in a world of pain from now on and you have lost the privilege of a quick death."

Another memory is triggered at the tone of his speech. He's the one that put me in the coffin, the one that met me at Waterloo. The one in the police uniform.

I try to shout anyway, to avoid a fate harsher than death when the two guys take the lead, and the monster shoves me towards a parking lot. He hits my side with the gun when I try to bite his hand.

"Do that again and I can make it my mission to find your family in Romania and kill them if you play stupid. Do you want to play stupid, hm? Answer me!"

"Nnmh!" I shake my head behind his repulsive fingers. So much for my master plan to have the team come meet me in a place with lots of people. His words paralyse my moves.

"You had me run across this entire god damn city looking for you. You couldn't hold into that bag like a good bitch and spare me the hassle of finding you without a tracking chip?"

Once we are out of sight, a quick blow to my stomach brings pain and nausea to the surface. I double over between two cars, and I catch myself on palms and knees when his boot hits my back, but not before the asphalt scrapes my chin and hands, breaking skin.

"Even if your tricks made me appear like a fool throughout Europe, I would have given you a dignified end. The constant embarrassment in front of my team and employer needs addressing with a good show. You get me?" Earth's biggest scumbag has a tight grip on my hair as he breathes his poison on ringing ears.

"Go to hell, you pathetic excuse of a man!" I can't hold my tongue, and I regret it when he hits the side of a parked car with my head, smashing my face into the hard metal door. Over and over again until I collapse on the ground. Blood drips onto cracked lips, and I choke. He wants me to lash out so he can justify his brutality. His lecherous smile is wide when he puts me on my feet again with a grip on the wounded arm. I swallow a cry at the excruciating pain.

A driver is already waiting for us in their SUV, and I am placed in the middle seat between the scary individuals from before. I don't recognise the bleeding reflection on the car window. Is this how my life ends? Tortured and murdered at the hands of a meaty individual with no remorse for hitting women when they can't defend themselves? I refuse to believe I escaped from a bloody coffin in the middle of a London cemetery, travelled half across the world only to die now. Killed by anonymous, as I don't even know his name.

We leave behind the crowded city streets and exchange them for a highway travelling to my doom. I don't ask where we are going, the answer would probably give me nightmares. Will I get to wake up another morning? I had no courage to call home, and now I missed the opportunity. The prospect of torture is horrifying, but I would give anything to take my parents' suffering when the authorities find my body. If anyone ever will. Unfortunately, Cristi will see it as his personal failure at not protecting me. I ache thinking of his pain and the failure is mine alone as his big sister, for putting him through this.

Nobody mentions Bodmer, and by the nasty-looking bandage enveloping the brute's neck, he recovered quickly from the knife stab. Does this mean he patched things with Elias or is the Swiss' body at the bottom of the sea and I'm to join him soon? No doubt terrified, on the inside I'm also angered by this turn of events because *no*! Absolutely not! This is *not* the end for me!

Are you delusional?

Suddenly and with force, a metallic crash assaults our car, my body leans forward as a result, interrupting my disbelief at life. The car behinds us hits us repeatedly until our SUV is bumper to bumper with the car in front, who doesn't speed up. Blocked in the back and front when two other vans on our left and right box us in.

"I can't go around them! What the hell is happening?" says our pissed off driver. Did my friends find me, after all?

"Are these the Chinese?" asks the man to my left.

"Not sure, but they are here for this bitch! I guarantee it!" The brute spits in anger from the front seat.

If he calls me bitch one more time . . .

Masked men open the lateral doors on the vans besides us and aim machine guns at our car. Why is the Czech team wearing masks? They shoot the doors of the SUV with no immediate impact. Then sharp explosions make the car tremble and cable cords drag the back doors open.

A gun is at my temple courtesy of one of my companions. They know the masked men surround us, with bigger guns pointed at their faces. This ambush will end badly for someone in the car, and it would only take a slight mistake for that person to be me.

"Give us the girl and you live!" yells the man with the black mask. Not an inch of his skin is exposed, dark ski goggles covering his eyes. He has an American accent. "Give us the girl! NOW!" He must be Aleš, right?

"Fall back or I'll shoot her!" the brute yells.

"Do that and you all die! You have five seconds to think about it or say your prayers with a bullet in your skull!"

"Give them the whore! There's no way out of this!" The driver hits the wheel with anger. All the while I'm sitting there thinking they can't possibly mean to hand me over at high speed on a motorway. If I slip, I'm over. Guaranteed. The loudness of the road overpowers my sledgehammer heart.

"I already messaged him she's back in our custody," says the brute. Him who?

"We can't cash in if we are dead!" another comments.

"Move her!" the brute finally decides, evidently wanting to remain the group's leader and not inspire mutiny.

The guy to my right, the one gluing a gun to my forehead, lifts me for transfer and he doesn't give me time to approximate the distance, pushing me towards the open door. A hole in my stomach forms as I slip towards the asphalt that will rip my skin away before killing me. I nearly lose my balance and go underneath the car, if not for my fast hand on the vehicle's top frame. Self-preservation kicks in and saves my battered skin. My heart is in overdrive. I can't keep my body from shaking.

As I attempt a second try to position myself outside the SUV, the man wearing black like his mask holds himself with a hand on the top of his van, leans his body forward and grabs my waist. He pulls me in and drops me on the van's floor, then shoots the guy that pushed me. The van closes, and the last image I see outside is blood gushing on my captor's slack face. All hell breaks loose as gunshots pierce the static motorway noise and I'm pushed face down.

"Don't get up!"

The car now moves with incredible speed, making my stomach drop, and it's hard to ignore the thought of an unfortunate accident after I've just been rescued. They drive in silence for a time, and only when I sense someone taking a seat on the floor next to me, do I rise to my knees. The van is windowless, apart from the front, but even with reduced visibility I spot four masked heads. The negotiator, a female driver, and two others. I'm not sure if any of my guys are here. With four cars in the rescue formation, they could be in one of them.

"We have back up at our tail," the driver, Asian American from her accent, the only one without a mask but with sunglasses, says with ease in her voice. "The threat is driving reckless to catch up with us."

"Let them. Half of our team is with us, and the rest will deal with the threat. They have permission to terminate. Asset secured. Move to destination," the negotiator says while everyone ignores me.

"Thank you. I thought nobody received my message. They promised me torture and sure death. I'm glad to see you," I relay to the two in the back with me.

Silence.

"Not that I don't appreciate the rescue, but can we wait for the car to stop moving next time? I think I'm having a heart attack." When nobody replies for lengthy seconds and my chest is about to crack, I scan my surroundings. "And what's with the ski masks, Aleš? They all know how you guys look like."

Silence.

Clearly, I'm meant to experience every shock possible this weekend. Miss nothing. The leader removes his cover, and my gut shifts once again. I don't know him, and he doesn't appear friendly. A tall, muscled man, strong dark-skinned face with ragged scars on his neck and left cheek, serious black eyes that analyse my reaction. He sounds a lot like Aleš, I thought . . .

The rest of the men pull out their balaclavas. Not my Czech crew. What in the actual hell? Who are these people?

An explosion outside the van rocks our balance.

"Can someone tell me what is happening? Where is Aleš?" I yell. They ignore me and take positions by the slide door, guns at the ready for an impending attack. I stand on wobbly legs.

"No Aleš here, lady. Stay down!" the American snaps.

"Who are you?"

"You are worth a lot of money. And I presume you want to stay alive, yeah? We can chit chat or we can man the guns. Which do you prefer? Now put that vest on and get on the floor," he commands, but doesn't sound all that worried. His colleague hands me a bulletproof vest.

"Do I get a gun?"

"Are you trained to use one?"

"No."

"Then why ask?"

"Was that an explosion?"

"They drove themselves into the side of the road to pass Beta team. Probably no survivors," the bearded guy riding in front with the driver says and turns to their leader. Have my captors died?

"Remain alert until drop off. Final push guys."

"Copy."

"Where are we going? Did Aleš Hemský send you?"

"The airport. And no."

My new companions remain silent and vigilant all the way to a private terminal. Once out of the car, the guy in command leads me towards a small airplane. Déjà vu.

Wait a second! Back up! Back up!

What just happened? Who gave the orders to save me? I realise I don't know where I'm going. Again. Refusing further suspense and mystery, I stop a few metres away from the craft.

"You know what? No! Thank you for what you" – I turn and point at the car where the rest of his team wait – "did earlier, but no. I'm not boarding a plane without knowing the destination and who hired you. The other men were planning to break my body and mind in ten thousand ways and there's no chance in hell I'll move another inch without knowing where I'm flying off to."

"Listen." He guides himself in front of me, with his back to the plane. "I know you are scared. You shouldn't be. He can't touch you anymore. But others will come to Shanghai looking for you, so we can't linger. By now, the trouble we made on the highway got us on the Chinese intelligence radar, so they'll come knocking sooner rather than later. We need to get you in the air and make ourselves scarce. Someone paid a lot of money to get you out of China. Safely. We received our orders and full payment upfront. That's all I know. All the information came through our handler. Names were not shared apart from yours. You were to be saved. Are you saved or do you want to go back to those guys?"

"No, I don't. And I thought they are dead."

"You were not to be harmed. We failed to prevent that. It took us a while to find you."

"Yes." I touch my broken cheek, flinching before and after, coming back with blood on my fingers. Shaking the flashback of the brutal attack from earlier, I refocus my attention on the present discussion.

"We don't need to stretch our imagination too far to realise that if whoever paid for your rescue wanted you alive and unharmed, they will make sure you remain that way. You were to be placed on a plane leaving" – he checks his watch – "in five minutes. After that, job completed. Clear?"

I don't break eye contact as he waits for an answer and when I don't deliver one fast enough because he makes sense on one point but I am still unconvinced, he lifts me up on his shoulder, carefully, and climbs the stairs, like I weigh nothing. He seats me on a chair in the middle of the plane.

"That wasn't very nice. Didn't they pay you to be nice to me?"

"Empathy and cuddling costs extra. We are not an escort service," he says, removing his jacket and placing it around my shoulders. "Someone will look at those cuts for you." He nods his head and leaves.

"Thank you again, I guess!" They risked their lives to get me out of the brute's murderous hands, and for that they deserve a medal.

"Yeah, yeah." He stops to talk with the pilot.

"I still don't know where my destination is. How can I relax until I get there?"

"That sounds like a *you* problem," he says as he salutes me, and disappears from sight. Out the window, I see him climb into a slick two-door car and speed away. The rest of his team is nowhere to be seen.

When I woke up this morning in my hostel bed to the sound of snoring and outside traffic, I wouldn't have bet my limited money on ending the day seating in the third private plane of the month flying to, for all I know, Mozambique. A flight attendant startles me out of my thoughts and window gazing, appearing out of thin air.

"We are ready for take-off, Madame. Could you please fasten your seatbelt? I'll come back shortly to take your dinner request and anything else you might need."

"Do you know where we are going?"

"Certainly. We have a layover to refuel in Istanbul, with Warsaw being our final destination, where we arrive in fifteen hours from now. Anything else?"

What?

"Do you know who paid for this flight?" I remember to ask in my stupor.

"Unfortunately, I am not privy to that information." She makes sure I am buckled up and leaves to her seat. The pilot repeats the details the flight attendant shared, and we are airborne without delay.

Before she revealed the destination, I hoped Aleš and his team had paid for my rescue and removal from China. That he would appear from a car involved in the earlier chase and we'll leave together. Or maybe he couldn't come himself, but he contacted the soldier guy. But Poland? How does that make sense?

Could Bodmer be behind this? He helped me escape at the hotel, knowing that I'll die if I don't flee, only to go to this extent afterwards? I don't mean that much to him, and is he even alive?

Lawrence wouldn't know what happened and where to find me. Someone else at Fosters & Co, Margaret and her husband's old connections are a few of my guesses who has the money and interest to pay for this mission. And they all seem improbable.

Who is the man referred by both Bodmer and the brute? Elias implied he trusted the wrong people, so perhaps he had an associate to deal with the Worthington deaths and inheritance situation. Am I going to meet him at the end of this flight? However, that also makes little sense. The brute was in communication with this allusive character, and I was technically at his mercy already. No reason to fabricate this production of rescuing me.

The nice flight attendant brings by a new set of lounge clothes with fluffy long socks and, after wearing only ballet shoes, albeit Chanel, I embrace their warmth. She cleans my wounds with care, the light touch of a professional. Food is next and a decent whiskey glass to absorb what happened since leaving the convention.

I might be wrong, but what waits for me in Warsaw is not dangerous. Stupid, really, after all I've experienced this month of March, to have my instinct tell me to relax. That I'll deal with it either way, like I've done following every menacing moment on this horrendous adventure. Is there a syndrome folks develop after being kidnapped twice, threatened, shot, beaten, dragged all over the map – and do I have it?

You are all sorts of crazy, or you'll be soon enough.

My reference points for what could happen next, when I land, are not positive, but who wants to put a bullet in my forehead after flying me privately? Also, the difference between landing in China, where I've never been before this weekend, and Poland, is that I used to live in Warsaw. The Polish capital is familiar to me, my friends are there, and it's closer to Bucharest or London than Shanghai. And I mean to go home to hug my mum and dad after I deal with this disaster and probably sleep in my old room for an entire season. Like I plan to sleep until we disembark because there is nothing else I can imagine happening that hasn't already occurred.

Hours later, my only cabin companion shakes me awake minutes before the wheels of the craft touch European soil. I put on some tennis shoes, watching soft rain drip on the oval window. It's early morning, and the sun might win the fight with the few clouds gathered over my new destination. A place I called home for years. Adrenaline spikes through my system, and my knees bounce up and down. I stashed a butter knife in my sleeve from the jet's kitchen, and I'm prepared to use it on anyone with a devious agenda or looking even remotely funny in my direction. Either way, ready, set, go!

Twenty-Five

Nobody could have prepared me for the way my chest contracts as I plunge down the five steps of the airplane ladder. And then I'm running.

Running as fast as my legs allow on the short pathway and in seconds, I have no air left in my lungs. Silent tears wash down my cheeks, and I'm afraid to turn around, scared to blink. Nothing in my thirty years, Sunday night in Shanghai and these past weeks included, has terrified away my ability to blink before now.

I hear my name called from a distant space behind me, but I have no interest in returning. That's my old life, the one I'm done mourning, when I thought impactful, heart-wrenching moments like this are not possible.

Breathing heavily, I stop and as afraid as I am, my eyes close because when they inevitably open, I need to know the vision in front of me is real and not a figment of my imagination. That monster hit my head pretty hard last night, and I'm hallucinating, surely.

I take a step forward and then another in the dark shelter of my eyelids until my shaky feet bump into the sidewalk edge.

"What have you done to your hair, Vera?" the person in the wheelchair asks with a voice unused this dawn. The question brings a burst of laughter to my lips. Yeah, what did I think when powdering my hair red?

"It goes away after a wash."

He says nothing about my bruised face, and I don't mention his inability to stand. Smiling at Petr and Josef behind him, I then finally lay my eyes on his frame for more than a flash. White knuckles on veined hands indicative of undeniable life grab the chair arms with restraint.

After the one remark, all my words are stuck at diaphragm level, or at least that's where I feel them. He's not aware of it, but I'm hypnotised by his stare. Do I imagine he wants to speak a thousand words at once, or is that my own internal battle? The struggle in those pale blue eyes raises the hair on the back of my neck. After an infinity and a second, Hector speaks in a detached voice.

"Welcome to Poland. I trust the flight was restful." Well, maybe reading someone's eyes is not my thing after all. As far as greetings go, in a situation like ours, this registers below disappointing. The booming tick tock in my chest tries to regulate itself, but a spike of irritation amplifies its power.

"Bloody brilliant. Is that all you have to say?" I challenge. Greetings aside, for no apparent reason, anger and impatience bounce my body on the spot. I should rejoice that he's alive, words don't matter.

"I . . . no. We would have come to China when we found out that's where they took you, but—"

"He's supposed to be in the hospital now. The doctors forbade any travel, and he's here at his own risk because the poor bastard couldn't wait for us to pick you up. That's what he wants to say.

And that he was going mad with worry," Petr says with a hint of annoyance.

"Absolutely. Word for word, I'm sure. Considering until now I believed you were dead, showing up to give me a ride from the airport is the least you could do." My body moves on its own accord, and I embrace Hector Worthington, the most infuriating man. Feeling his warmth around me, being in the grasp of his arms, the beast inside me calms and retreats. I thought I lost that forever. I can't believe it, yet my fingers touch the skin of his neck, the softness of his hair, and confirm the absence of feverish illusions.

"My apologies, Vera. My arrogance allowed Bodmer to put his hands on you." His beard stubble grazes my jaw. My body electrifies at his gruff murmurs. He mentions Elias, reminding me I have a lot to tell them. But I don't want to analyse Bodmer's behaviour, the brute's fists, China, or this entire blasted month. The only desire I have is focused on his touch, his breath, his lips.

"I thought you died. It was all over the news in Shanghai. And I was told . . . How is this possible?" My face moves to steal a kiss, but he leans back, shifting in my embrace, and I let him go.

"That's also my fault. And a long story. There's something else I need to tell you first."

"I'm so happy you're alive. I have a lot to tell you too." I go around and hug the guys. Like I'm in a mirage and soon enough I'll wake up in the sand. Alone.

"Vera, Aleš is in a coma." Sharp nails on a school blackboard screech me to a halt. "He's stable. They operated twice on him already, and the surgeons are keeping him in an induced coma for recovery." I turn to him, staring at the ground. Of course, it had to be something.

"What? How?" Pins and needles penetrate my heart, visualising Aleš' bright laughs silenced by trauma. Because of me.

"They ambushed him and the team at the villa in Ubud. It was all part of an elaborated scheme. The whole Bali trip intended to lure us out of hiding." Hector looks up to see my reaction, guilt clear in his face.

"We need to leave. Let's continue the discussion on the way to the clinic," Josef offers, opening the door to a van, and we depart shortly.

Minutes pass in mute communication and I take in familiar streets, uprooting memories of flying between Bucharest and Warsaw every few months when I was working for Fosters & Co, Poland.

"Where did Aleš get injured? What happened exactly?" I ask Hector, who sits in the back with me.

"They hit his head right when he was breaking into Bodmer's rented villa. He recovered quickly, and he was fine for hours. Just a superficial wound he got checked at the hospital in Bali where they were treating my cuts."

"Cuts? Someone shot you!"

"Technically, he got shot and knifed," Josef clarifies.

"I was fine."

"Just a tad unconscious," Petr says.

"Irrelevant at this point. By nightfall we were told Bodmer took you to Europe, so we boarded the plane immediately and to come for you."

"With both of you injured! Is everyone else okay?"

"We counted a few bullet wounds between us, but no lost lives on our side. Radek is still in the hospital in Indonesia, in good condition," Josef answers.

"Glad to hear it. I will not lie. I wanted you guys to come after me so bad, but I was afraid something happened after I saw Hector shot. And who told the press about your death?"

"We realised that too late to change the narrative. The circumstances forced us to land in Warsaw when Aleš collapsed from his injury. He had post-traumatic seizures. It was touch and go for a while. And that's what the media in Bali assumed as well when they rushed to report my condition. The online press related videos posted from the beach after they took you and when a bullet grazed my spine. They ran with that story when the hospital refused to provide updates on my condition because I was not there anymore. They knew a body was in the morgue."

"Insane! How are you now? What did the doctors say about Aleš? Will he be alright?"

"The first reports are encouraging. The swelling in his head is going down. We'll know more later today."

"And you? The wheelchair?"

"I'm fine. Weak in the knee and back."

"That's what he'd like you to think. He had surgery last night too. Both of them waited to hear the hired team saved you before letting the doctors cut them open. Thank God you're back, Vera. These uncontrollable assholes got on my last nerve. Retirement after this mission," Petr confesses from the wheel.

"Wow! That is . . ."

"Moronic?" Petr.

"Romantic?" Josef.

"He's exaggerating." Hector.

"A bit of both? Why did you think I was being brought to Europe, and how did you find out about Shanghai? I tried Aleš' phone a few times but got no answer."

"We lost our equipment. Phones, laptops, everything destroyed in the fight in Ubud. They wanted to cut all our communications. Petr was the only one with a working phone, and Aleš used it to contact Lawrence and David. They found a flight number for Zurich, Bodmer and an unidentified woman on board. Much later, when we were close to arrive in Switzerland, I got a notification on my watch from the conference service I shared at The Hyde."

"So that's how you found me." I hold his gaze.

"Yes. I told you I would." He blinks and looks down. "We turned the plane around, and Aleš went into shock. As much as I wanted to come to China and put a hole in Bodmer and his men, I couldn't. I knew you would kill me yourself if Aleš died."

"He thought about it for a second, let me tell you." Petr with the facts.

"Will you shut up?"

"We also had to refuel if we were to take the plane to Shanghai. That slowed him down." Petr again.

"Should we tell her he trashed the plane as well?" Josef jabs.

"Oh, God!" Hector covers his face in annoyance.

"Why would you do that with your injury?"

"I led you to them and I was half across the planet doing nothing to help you. I mean, look at your face!"

"Thanks," I say with a hint of irritation.

"No, I don't mean that."

"Hey! I lived! I got kidnapped twice, and I escaped both times. *On my own.* With these little hands. Limited resources, unknown city, but I kept myself alive until the crew cut guy and his fantastic squad arrived. How did that happen, anyway? You sent them."

"Once we landed in Warsaw and drove Aleš to the hospital, I made a few calls. The team was fairly local and very effective in what they do. We knew you escaped, and we knew the world thought I was dead. We used that to our advantage to locate you as soon as possible. Evidently they were too late." He analyses every bruise and cut on my face, and I turn away to stare at the city I know and love.

The Palace of Culture and Science will be visible if we continue on this road. A few streets behind, hidden by the Old Town's pathways with its rainbow buildings taken out of a storybook, is The Royal Castle and Sigismund's Column, guarded by the Vistula River. When it wasn't raining, and the sun was warming our city, I had a tradition with Dorota and Youssef to walk those streets every few weeks with a soft serve vanilla and chocolate ice cream. And when Lina and Astrid were visiting, we would spend hours walking and debating life between bites of local food and refreshing beer. I sigh away the memory.

"No, they came when they should have. I won't sugar-coat it, getting beaten is no joy and I'm not sad that animal died a horrible death but I'm alive and I'll heal. I'm happy you sent them at all. Thank you," I say, not looking at him.

"Of course. How did you escape? You are fucking brilliant, you know that, right?" I bask in his crude compliment, knowing I'm moments away from crumbling from the fast change of events. "What did they do to you?" The second question is for my ears only. And another gentle comment at my silence. "If it's too soon to talk about it, I won't pry. I'll get you all the help you need to process everything." He takes my hand in his lap.

"Oh, when we finish and go home, you'll have to spoil me with half a dozen cakes." I sniffle and smile between tears. "The guy who did this to my face was waiting for me with a gun by the bathroom door of the surf bar. Got me to the boat from where I watched you die. They collected Bodmer, floating in the water, and we boarded a plane to Shanghai." I tell them about arriving in China and my captors using my real passport. About The Peninsula hotel. I skip the crying session ending that horrible night, to the open breakfast with Bodmer. I replicate word for word the story shared by Elias, about his family's history and the hidden relationship to Hector's ancestors.

"That is impossible and complete nonsense!"

"Why would he lie?"

"You don't understand. My grandfather was an ethical man, a fair and compassionate person. What Bodmer says is a fabrication. Killing us was not enough for him – he wants to drag our name in perpetuity for his enjoyment."

"What would he have to gain? There must be records showing some involvement between the families. But that's all in the past."

"Yes, my past. Wilhelm raised me. I won't take these accusations lightly and I can't believe you gave him credence."

"Hector, even if he lied about your grandfather, what concerns me is he implied working with a third party in this whole affair. That he has a partner, and he's the one that killed Helena and kidnapped us. Or a confusing mess of them both. Bodmer got caught up in his revenge against the Satie living heirs and his accomplice side railed him, blowing everything to the extreme."

"He would say that. Of course. To deny any blame."

"I thought so too, but then why did it look like he was as much of a prisoner as I was amongst the mercenary security that took me from Bali? Why did he stab the chief bodyguard to help me escape? To what purpose? And then have the brute beat the crap out of me outside the Shanghai Exhibition Centre? Why?"

"He helped you escape?"

"That's what I'm trying to explain. The big scary guy implied they don't need me anymore. They received a call that something was done. I think it was you dying, and it was decided I was to be eliminated. Someone else, not Bodmer, wanted me dead."

"Bodmer is behind everything, and we know it. You're confused and misinterpreting things. When I'll show you the evidence we have on him, you'll see how you've been manipulated," he says, refusing to believe my statements. The effects of the painkiller I took on the plane hours ago evaporated minutes before we touched down in Warsaw, my face injuries throb with slicing pain, yet Hector's attitude hurts me deeper. I was wrong. Words do matter, and the power they exercise over you when they are spoken by someone you care for is unlimited. Hard to forget and forgive.

He doubted you at every turn. Why would you assume differently now? The man you mourned doesn't exist.

"You can think that, but I know what I saw, and my gut tells me there's someone else involved. Someone pulling the strings, and I had enough running around scared to even breathe in the wrong direction. Afraid to put my head down and sleep. With or without your help, I'm bringing this out in the open."

"What do you mean?"

"I made a plan on the way over when I've learned of Warsaw. I have many friends here. Friends in the media. People who will believe me and get my story out. Then I'm going to the Romanian Embassy and ask for help. Guess what? I have a friend there too." A slow sigh escapes when I wet my cracked lips. "Aren't you tired of this? It didn't cross your mind to expose everything after you were gravely wounded? Don't you want this to be over?"

"Frankly, I thought little beyond having you return unharmed. But perhaps you're right. I promised to keep you out of harm's way, and Bodmer is always one step ahead."

"Bodmer might be dead by now, but a threat is still focusing on us. Will you help me tell the story to a news outlet? Who knows that you are alive?"

"Nobody. I haven't even told Lawrence. Or my mother."

"I want to see Aleš and later, I'll reach out to my friend."

"As you wish. I'll request international media too. We can involve both embassies. By nightfall, you could go home, if you wish."

"I'm not going anywhere when Aleš is in the hospital. His condition is all that matters now." My words ring true, but I say them to wound him, in bitter regret for his dismissal of my theory. "I would like to call my parents. Make sure they are safe."

"Right, of course. They are safe. I hired a team to watch over them after I sent the Americans after you."

"Thank you."

Arriving at the hospital to see my beautiful friend with a tube sticking out of his mouth, connected to machines, takes the breath out of me and my plans to expose the story. I'm to blame for his condition, dragging him into this mess. I shouldn't have returned to his life. Because of Lina, we've reconnected, but I'd rather remain in the dark and my friendship with her not beyond repair. I would know she used my credentials to get me kidnapped, but I would forgive her, probably, thinking she did it for her father's health and because she's a coward. Putting the pieces of this sinister puzzle together, it's unlikely for me to consider forgiveness soon, not when her actions have had such deep and severe consequences.

One missing piece remains unsolved. Bodmer's partner. No matter how much Hector denies it, that person exists. I sense it in my aching bones, he is out there searching for me. How big is his reach? I'm hoping he'll go into hiding once we release the news, but that's wishful thinking. Unfortunately, I have to watch my back until he is exposed. Keeping my eyes on Aleš' unconscious form, I make the call I wish I had made two Mondays ago.

"Alo, mama? Sunt eu, Vera." I exhale the exhaustion out of my body at the sound of her voice. "Yes, I'm fine. I'm okay, Mum. I know, I'm sorry, I couldn't call you. Listen, Mum, something bad happened but we are uncovering it and I'll be home soon." And that's how I spend the next hour, talking my mum out of killing me with her own hands because I didn't ask her for help. Ignoring the irony of her chosen words, I release a wet laugh as she continues, hugging myself in her absence. Eastern European mums for the win.

Noon comes and goes. The doctors declare Aleš could be out of the induced coma in a couple of days. We prepare for a press conference at the Romanian Embassy where Hector will reveal his resurrection and we'll present this entangled tale.

"Lawrence says hi." I turn to see him using a crutch to walk into Aleš' hospital room. "He congratulates us for not succumbing to our death and flying over to be part of the conference with the information he retrieved from Lina Haas. We have more data to connect Bodmer to my sister's death and the rest of the heinous acts he committed. They've found no evidence of a mysterious partner."

"How do you explain what happened in China and his behaviour there?"

"The actions of a madman? He clearly had these grand revenge illusions against my family that were justified in his head, and he still imagined himself a victim while orchestrating crimes on a global level. Perhaps he disagreed with his men and that's what you saw. Conflicts about money. Things getting out of hand when they weren't respecting his wishes. He might have indeed wanted to set you free, when he thought I was dead and his race was over, but the mercenaries knew you've seen all their faces and can identify everyone. You were a liability to them, so they couldn't let you live."

"On top of wanting me dead because I bested them. Especially their leader."

"Exactly. And now that guy is dead. The Americans confirmed it. All the men in the motorway car died in the explosion."

"You've connected the dots in your head and I'm glad you feel safer knowing you have everything figured it out. But I'm saddened I can't make you see my reasoning. We are still in the dark for a lot of what really happened. Give me the courtesy of trusting what I know in my heart to be true."

"Yes, because Bodmer is still free. He is finished once every agency worth their salt goes after him, starting tonight. Don't let paranoia take over your mind."

Paranoia? Freaking great!

"You do you and I'll do me. It kept me alive so far. I'd like to be alone with Aleš until we leave for the conference, please." I can't have this discussion if he refuses to acknowledge my concerns. I turn back to brushing Aleš' hair from his slumbering face.

"Vera."

The door closes softly behind him after long seconds, where I don't reply to his plea. A different door shuts on a could have been. If I ever wondered how fast or how profoundly lack of trust damages a relationship between two people, the answer is in the heavy sigh leaving my fevered body. This is not the reunion I imagined when I saw him hours earlier in a wheelchair, but alive.

◆

At ten minutes before 7 p.m. I'm in the embassy's antechamber in central Warsaw, talking to my friend Dorota, who has been a news producer since she left the PR department at Fosters & Co. The

English and Romanian ambassadors are next to us. Hector is conversing with his mother, Lawrence, and his solicitors. My parents wanted to fly over too, but I told them it's better if they wait for me at home. Cristi is already on a flight to Poland because you can't control brothers. I still feel radioactive, especially when I think of the damage I've inflicted on the Czech crew, but I'm so happy I'll see my brother in a few hours.

The noise and anticipation that's palpable through the door next to us, where the journalists await, spikes my anxiety levels. We are taking the stage in mere moments, and my fingers won't stop shaking as I hide them in my pockets. I'm wearing a slim pant suit with a silk shirt and high-heeled shoes, all black. Similar style and colour as I was wearing on the night when my life changed. To say that I'm hoping this evening finishes on a different tone is an understatement. I took a shower at the hotel Hector booked and Dorota's team did my make-up and hair. Not because I care how I look, but because the bruises will scare my mother if she sees me on the news.

My gaze finds him across the room at regular intervals. He's really here and not dead. Also dressed in a suit and using a cane for support. I keep marvelling at how everything changes, day after day. Yesterday he was dead. Today he is not. Hours ago, I was friendless. Now Dorota and Youssef can't stop hugging me. Almost as if everything is well. If Aleš wasn't in a coma and I didn't believe true evil waits for me when I walk out at night, which I do, I would bury my fears away. I almost hope Hector is correct, and I misheard or hallucinated over conversations in China, even if that means I can't trust my own instincts and sanity.

"Are you ready?" Hector comes over and asks. I nod and take a sip of water out of my bottle. "Let's get our lives back," he says with conviction and leads me towards my first press conference.

When they realise Hector Albert Worthington is alive and the reason for the impromptu gathering, they shout his name and take hundreds of pictures until embassy employees restore order. The solicitors read a statement detailing events spanning from Helena's death until our kidnapping. Not everything is shared publicly, but we are hoping to have official charges pressed against Elias Bodmer and his paid thugs based on the evidence we accumulated and released to the proper justice channels.

"Miss Nicolescu! You would want us to believe there is no relationship between you and mister Elias Bodmer? There are online pictures of the two of you enjoying a nice meal at a high-end hotel in Shanghai. You work for the same company," an English journalist asks.

"Fosters & Co employs both of us, yes. But I was there under duress. Not of my own volition."

"It doesn't look like it. The role of a guest comes to mind."

"Your—"

"If anyone tries to smear Vera's name in any capacity, they will deal with our legal counsel."

"Thank you, Hector. If I may?" I look into his angry eyes for a permission I don't need and then shift my gaze towards the camera's lenses. "I was there as his kidnapped guest. If that's what you mean. If not, don't hold your breath for a different story." I have my answer for why they wanted proof I was in China on Bodmer's arm, presumably of my own accord.

"Elias Bodmer single-handedly masterminded the suffering of two families when he took over Worthington & Neville. The lives of my sister and godfather did not register as important enough. To keep his dark secrets from becoming exposed, he dragged an innocent woman into his game of power and destruction, with countless other victims. The devastation stops now. The authorities have my collaboration and resources to apprehend him. We ask for privacy and understanding in the days to come for Miss Nicolescu, Neville and myself so that we can begin what I suspect to be a long recovery process."

The conference finishes in a blur of blinding lights and we retreat into the ambassador's office for another discussion with the legal counsel and the authorities involved in the newly opened case and ensuring our protection. Aleš' guys have my back and his, but I won't refuse the guards to be stationed at the hotel and hospital. A grip of fear settled around my stomach since I let it be known where I was, publicly. Was this the smartest way out? To be discovered. I embrace Dorota's goodbye and thank her for the role she played in bringing the events of the past weeks to an end. Youssef is with their kid, and I refuse the invitation to spend the night at their home. Maybe in the days to come, as for now I need to care for my wounds in solitude.

"I brought you that thing and I put it in your bag, just to have it. It will make me feel better. I know you have these big guys protecting you, but you never know."

"Thank you."

"As for Lina, we'll process that together. Okay? We are here for you, and we love you. Astrid called. She's beside herself with rage and indignation." Dorota's eyes go big to emphasise her point, her hand caressing my cheek with pity.

"I bet."

Outside the embassy, on the way to our cars, Hector's mother requests a private discussion with her son and as reluctant as I see him in wanting to grant her wish, I excuse myself and insist on having the guys drive me. She doesn't radiate outright hostility towards me, nor warmth either, so in my current state, I don't want to deal with her. I've been on the run since forever, and my patience slips through my fingers.

There is also the hurt caused by Hector not believing in me. Distancing myself now will help me, eventually. He's not pleased with my ride choice, but he doesn't want a scene in front of the journalists lingering around the embassy. While he still intends to keep a protective layer around me, I'm not the only one rationalising the separation and its necessity. I've felt his guarded look and the emotional miles between us since I've embraced him at the airport this morning. Who would think *we* would be a good idea?

"That's a discussion I'm happy to skip. The flight from London was my quota for the year with the Worthington-Satie matriarch," Larry whispers from my left as he makes the gun to head sign. "Josef tells me your brother is coming later. Who's picking him up from the airport? Let me know if you want me to head over. Everyone is exhausted."

"Petr will give me a ride. But thanks, Larry. You've come a long way in our relationship." I laugh and give him a side hug. We didn't have time to talk much since he arrived, and Lina-related questions, which I should probably keep to myself are on the tip of my tongue.

"I wouldn't go that far, Nicolescu. How's your other boyfriend?"

"And that's the Neville I know and tolerate." I shake my head at his smirking face. "I'm actually heading to the hospital now to check on him before picking up my brother. If I go to the hotel, I might crash and forget about the world."

"Understandable. Come on, I'll drive you and show him some support. He was there for Hector and it's the least I can do."

"Thank you. That would be great."

"My car is over here." He leads me to a rented two seats luxury car. Always the show-off. "Guys, follow us to the hospital?" he asks Josef and the rest of the gang.

"Have you been to Warsaw before?" I inquire once we are on the road.

"A few times with business, so I'm familiar with the city centre. Don't worry, I'll get you where you need to go."

"No, no, I wouldn't dare give a man directions. Even if I used to live here and walked these streets many, many times."

"Thanks for the vote of confidence." He laughs my comment off. "How are you really? Bali and China were exceptionally rough. An impressive feat to get yourself out of those circumstances."

"I don't want a repeat, that's for sure." We drive in silence across the next intersection.

"What makes you think Bodmer has a partner?"

"Can we do this tomorrow? My brain has turned to mush after answering the journalists' questions."

"Sure, sure. It makes little sense, you know?"

"That's Hector's opinion, too, and I am kind of done with this. I was there, I know what I saw. If I'm reading the situation wrong, so be it. It will come out eventually."

"Indeed. Only, we've been investigating him a long time and we've learned how he operates. Lina has scores of illegalities piled under his name."

"Funny how with zero investigations into him, I've withstood a lot. Regardless, Lawrence, what are you doing? This is not the way to the hospital! Josef's car went that way!" I point my finger to the left.

"Hold on. Someone is following us."

"What? Who?" He increases the speed as I spot two cars driving behind us. "Go back towards the hospital, Lawrence. We need backup."

"I need to lose them first. Hold on tight," he says with a determined face, moving away from the city centre with every passing second. This is wrong.

"Turn around! Turn around, Neville!" Dread grabs me by the throat. How did they find me so fast?

"*Shut up* and let me drive!" His tone enrages me, but I will deal with it later if he doesn't put us through a wall. If there is a later. The chasing cars position themselves closer, left and rear, pushing us every which way.

We enter a part of the Mokotow neighbourhood peppered with business parks and new construction sites. Coincidentally, we are close to Fosters & Co offices. Lawrence is forced to stop the car in the middle of an abandoned patch of land. The tall, dark trees ahead make it impossible for us to advance. No cameras in sight. No people either. Just the vehicle that pushed us off the road creeping up behind us. It has its lights turned off and I notice ours are too. Just the overshadowed moonlight to guide my eyes.

"Get out of the car, Vera."

"No way. Drive!" He's mad if he thinks we are good to stay here. Before I turn my head to yell at him, he presses the all too familiar cold metal of a gun against my temple.

I want to say I'm surprised by this, but somehow, my brain accepts the betrayal better than my heart, which is now at the bottom of my stomach. Damn it all to hell! I inhale loudly to mask the rummaging noise in the envelope bag by my thigh.

"Lawrence, don't do this. Please don't be the weasel beyond redemption I thought you were in London. He will never forgive you and they will all hunt you down."

"He'll see what I want him to see, darling. He always has. Thanks to you, I nearly killed him." He nudges my face towards the window and says with a gleeful tone. “Look outside, I have a present for you. A special friend is here to greet you.” The second car that followed us earlier parks a few metres ahead. “He made you some promises, and he’s going to keep them. Simon is good at that, especially if he wants to be paid.”

Time stops as a man gets out from the back of the car and my blood halts in my veins. When I blink, he’s still there, a more menacing presence than Lawrence Neville with his fucking gun. But I heard the explosion. He was supposed to be dead and on a different continent, Simon the brute.

“What have I ever done to you? I was just trying to get my life back,” I calmly say to Hector’s best friend.

“You wouldn’t give up the idea of Bodmer having a partner. You would have convinced him to continue the search. You made him go to the media, so it’s either you or him, and he’s lucky I even consider giving him a second chance.”

“And I thought my friend was shitty. I didn’t know the partner was you. I didn’t even suspect it. Elias didn’t say your name.”

“He said enough and he’ll pay, too. I can’t take the risk.”

“What do you think Hector will say when Josef reports our disappearance? When you will be the only one who shows up later?”

“When they find me tomorrow, heartbroken and bloodied from trying to fight off the animals who took you, they’ll know I did everything I could. But I am just a man.”

“No. You are the animal. You’ve always been the animal, haven’t you? You killed Helena and your father.”

“Not that it matters anymore, but I didn’t plan on that happening. All they had to do was complete the sale, and they needed a little push. It happened though, and as much as it pained me, I had to cover-up my involvement. That escalated and escalated until your insignificant presence entered the scene and nearly destroyed everything again."

"You did all this for money? Jesus! Such a pathetic reason. At least Bodmer sought revenge for the misfortune his family suffered at Satie's hands. Still madness, in my opinion, but I get it. You, you just wanted money and your father out of the way?"

"This is not the ending of a bad movie where, before I kill you, I ramble on about a bunch of reasons. I don't have those urges. You die tonight without the explanations you ridiculously think you deserve."

"You say that, but you can't even kill me yourself. You brought me to the middle of nowhere for others to finish your dirty work. Again."

Lawrence laughs and gets out, bringing his gun with him. The car door opens on my side too, and before his meaty hands try to grab me, I press the taser gun Dorota hid in my bag to Simon's groin. He curses and falls on his side. I jump over him, barefoot, and run on the frozen patch of earth towards the gathering of trees ahead.

Shots fly at me, not hitting their target but making me fall to my knees in blinding terror. *Get up! Get up!* The muddy soil hinders my movements and I hear them following behind with their guns and murder on their hands. This is it! If they catch me, this is where I die. They'll break my neck on the spot. I saw it in Simon's eyes.

I pass branchy tree trunks on bloody feet and hands from falling on unforgiving rocks. From memory, there's a short hill at the end of the forest with a bridge at the top. Usually, cars drive on that road at any giving time. But I only walked around here once, years ago, and I don't remember if this is the right direction.

Lights and city noise guide my steps, and when I think I have no breath left in me, I see the entrance of a clearing a sprint away. Just another push. Another step and I'll make it. I don't want to die!

The roots of my hair burn as a mysterious, cruel power pulls on them and stops my progress.

So close. You were so close.

In a blur, my shoulders hit the ground. Enough impact to lose consciousness. Regrettably, I don't, and I remain very much awake to feel the stomach kick, the blow that shatters my knee and the boot to the head that silences my wails.

Pain. So much pain.

Then darkness and the feeling of nothing. I used to consider myself lucky, and I guess the end of suffering is a special type of luck. The world as I know it disappears and I vanish.

I am no more.

Twenty-Six

A familiar detachment took over my body since they told me about Vera's disappearance on her way to the hospital. I should have never let her out of my sight, and I'm confident Lawrence will keep her safe, but him not answering my calls puts me on edge. Something unexpected must have happened to them. The unexpected has control over my days since meeting Vera and as much as I want to manage every aspect of this situation, by ways of money, willpower, or brute force, I am thrown back into darkness and despair at every corner. I won't lose her again.

"How many teams are looking for them? The airport area is mine," Petr says over the phone. My violent mood feeds from the tense atmosphere in the car, even if it's just me with two Polish private security men from the team I hired after it became clear we would be spending some time in the country.

"Local police is involved. Then there's you, my car, Josef's and two other vehicles with contracted men." And I still couldn't keep her safe. Bodmer is always one step ahead. Not giving credence to Vera's theory about a partner might be what gets her killed, along with my best friend.

"We'll find them, Hector! This girl has more lives than five cats combined. And luck in spades. She's a fighter, and Lawrence maintains his cool when needed. That much I know."

"They have to stay out of trouble until we find them. Regular updates, understood? And thank you, man. I know Aleš is your priority."

"Clear. We have someone guarding him. He would want me on the search team, no doubt. Over."

On top of not knowing their location, the injuries sustained in Indonesia hinder me from holding my own in a foot chase or a fight, if it comes to that. My knuckles bleed from taking my anger out on the car door.

"They reported a vehicle with the same descriptions speeding in Mokotow. I advise we follow this lead," the driver translates the rapid communication coming over radio.

"How far are we?"

"Ten minutes. Should I proceed?"

"Yes, and make it in five. It's the only lead we have so far." I'll glue myself to her hip when I find her, and she'll have to deal with it.

"Multiple shots fired in Mokotow! Police are on their way."

"Drive!" Lord, protect them.

When Bodmer's animals brought her in on the night of our kidnapping at Waterloo, unconscious from the chloroform and so fragile in her forced sleep, my annoyance towards Vera Nicolescu, the mole dangling cheap, tricky bits in my eyes for months, diminished. She seemed powerless at those savages' mercy while I couldn't lift a finger. Here was the woman extorting money for me, and probably at fault for our capture, and yet my own beast raged to protect her vulnerability.

Then she woke in the coffin, terrified out of her senses, and I thought she was pretending to not know me and why she was in that position, pretending to not understand the damage she'd done, I wanted to strangle her myself. I still wanted her nowhere near Bodmer and his men, but the beast screamed to break her ourselves. In the days that followed, my own self-importance, arrogance, and delusion failed to accept the innocence in her cries. I was convinced she was playing games, especially when her sarcasm, her long unflinching stares, and the times we touched were so effective on my weakening resolve.

At The Hyde, I let Neville convince me to push her limits, to make her come clean and pull the stolen information out of her lying lips. Because he suffered as much as me and she was the pawn trying to manipulate our goals. I lost myself in drink that night, my conscience, and my duty warring over a furious green-eyed seductress. The guilt I felt the next day was overwhelming, but I knew the fight inside me was far from over and the only escape I had was if she left.

Blinking the memory out of my eyes, I check the time on the car's dashboard. The longest minutes of my life end on the side of a frozen field illuminated by police vehicles. They've surrounded three cars in the middle of the land. One is Lawrence's rented German car. He's held at gunpoint, but there's no sight of Vera. Where is she? I make eye contact with my livid friend.

"Don't come closer or he's dead," the mercenary shouts and pushes Lawrence to his knees, execution style. They share tense words that don't reach our ears.

"Where is Vera Nicolescu? What have they done to her?" I ask the officer leading the negotiations.

"She was not present when the first responders arrived, and upon questioning, they have not disclosed her condition or location. We caught two men trying to escape with the hostage in a car and when they realised we surround them, they returned to the abandoned vehicles and brought him outside."

"Could she be in the back? What are their demands?"

"They'll release the captive once they know we are not following them."

Petr and Josef arrive and take their places behind me in the police barricade. The barking police dogs agitate the armed men holding Lawrence.

"The leader pointing a gun to Neville's head focuses on us, but the rest keep looking towards the forest," Petr notices, confirming my observations.

"The dogs are pulling to run for that area as well," I say.

"We are not sure what the suspects will do if we release the dogs. They are trained to find fresh blood."

"There is something in the forest."

"Hector, you need to have everyone back down or they'll shoot me where I kneel," Lawrence yells over the sound of growling dogs and looks from his captor to us with a slight tremor in his body. The police surround them and have the upper hand. Nobody is backing down or going anywhere. Not before I know where Vera is and if she is safe. Regardless, they won't kill Lawrence knowing there's no escape, and they would be complete idiots to murder someone in front of so many witnesses right before they are arrested.

The dogs jump and pull on their leashes, the handlers barely containing them as they bark at the outline of a dark figure emerging from the tree border.

"Stop right there!" The police officers direct their lights and guns at a person covered in mud, blood, and dead leaves from head to toe. A savage warrior with murder in their eyes and chest heaving.

The lone creature walks slowly and without shoes towards our heated stand down.

"Hands in the air!"

"There's a body on the other side of the woods," the raspy voice announces. "I'm not sure if they're dead or alive."

"We need to see your hands!"

"The only thing they hold is a rock to bash Neville's head in and I'm not dropping it," Vera says to the police officer, spitting dirtied blood with a cough. What?

"Stop pointing guns at her, she's one of the missing persons we were looking for," I address the armed officers.

"Don't move or we'll kill him and the girl too," the lead captor says when I advance towards Vera. She needs to leave the shooting area, instead of defying the criminals. A few feet separate me from her, the same distance she has between her fragile, abused body and the menacing guns.

"Lawrence Neville is the man responsible for all my misfortune. He brought me here to have his assassins eliminate me." Is she insane? That's not possible.

"Vera, you hit your head. You need medical attention. You're getting the both of us killed," Lawrence supplicates her.

"Stop pretending these thugs and the one I clubbed in the forest are not working for you! This ends now! You're holding yourself at gun point and I can prove all the horrible things you did!" she says with agitated gestures.

"There's nothing to prove! Vera, calm down. What's the matter with you? I'm in your corner. They've tried to kill me, too. They are still trying to kill me!" His eyes move from me to her.

"Shut up! Don't look at Hector! He can't help you now! Not when I can prove you murdered his sister." This can't be right.

She's accusing the man who suffered as much as me from Bodmer' s revenge on my family.

"She's delusional. How can you prove such a thing when it never occurred?"

"I still have the mic from the press conference, you huge prick!" She takes out a black wire attached to the back of her shirt. "It's been active and recording this whole time. Dorota forgot to retrieve it, and I'll be thanking her the rest of my life for this small gesture. You are done!"

"Impossible!" Lawrence yells.

"The unabridged discussion in the car. The shootings, your brute Simon chasing me in the woods, nearly smashing my brains in. Everything! You were right, you bastard, I *am* your worst nightmare! You should have pulled the trigger yourself, coward!"

Time stops as I look at Vera, fully assimilating her words, their implication, and catch Lawrence from the corner of my eye taking out a gun and pulling the trigger. She goes down as shots fly across the field. A vision of red obstructs my sight, and I don't take cover, but advance on my oldest friend with a strength I shouldn't possess in my current condition. A split second of indecision when he fails to use the gun on me, and I have him underneath my fists.

He shot her.

He killed Helena.

I lose track of how long ago he stopped fighting, and the only noise around me is the sound of his unconscious whimpers and the wet slush of bone hitting raw meat. Strong arms remove me from the target of my rage, and I turn to fight them. Still blinded by a heated mist.

"It's over, Hector. Let him be for now. He can't fight or hurt anyone tonight. Take a deep breath and think, for God's sake. Focus on me." Petr slaps the daze out of my crowded mind, and I stumble back a few steps. I search for Vera where Josef checks on her with someone in a uniform. Should have listened. Should have realised she spoke the truth about a second force behind Bodmer's actions. Never thought that force would be my honorary brother. She did not imagine misguided plots; I was the misguided fool.

Sirens announce the impending ambulance arrival just when she opens her swollen eyes. Staying at a short distance, I don't dare touch her. How much she must hate me? How much suffering and unnecessary pain have I brought into her life? I've destroyed her light. She looks so small and broken on the chilled ground. I did this to her, no matter if Lina Haas involved her and Bodmer with Lawrence starting the sick game of ruining people's life.

"He shot her side, but the bullet went through. Clean exit wound. I don't think it touched any major organs. Her knee looks bad," Josef says, and I release the breath I was holding. She doesn't speak, focusing her gaze on the starless sky. Her only movement, the heaving chest.

The police capture the remaining kidnappers, locking them up in a van. They locate the body Vera mentioned earlier in the forest, still breathing.

"Neville is alive and taken to the hospital," Petr announces from my right and I can only grunt. I don't care. Maybe it's better to have him face the justice he deserves. Him rotting in prison has to be my consolation. I'll have to learn to live with that. That my sister is dead, and he's alive. That Vera could have died a horrendous number of times since meeting us. That Aleš Hemský is still in a coma.

They transport us to a hospital as well, paramedics checking me for wounds I don't feel but apparently have. A bullet pierced my shoulder, and another one hit my left leg. I leave Petr to settle next to Vera in the ambulance. I can't take her avoiding my gaze for the whole ride. And who can blame her? Her smooth skin is marred by new cuts and bruises when the old ones never healed. Their presence awakens the beast I put to sleep after my attack on Neville. It wants to jump out of the car and pummel everyone that touched her. That hurt her. I should start with myself.

"She was bluffing. Earlier. When she said the recorder had Neville's confession. There is no recorder," Petr announces with a hushed tone, and I take a second to process this information.

"She got herself shot to convict him. To convince me." This brave, mad woman put herself in danger, recklessly, to expose the truth, no matter the consequences.

"She wanted his reaction to the possibility of evidence. To be sure we believe her, she played him. I'm sorry, man. He was your friend. That's a lot to take in," Petr says with pity in his voice.

"I should have seen it. He's been lying for years. Making me believe things, obscuring facts to his advantage."

"No sense in beating yourself up now. You'll find out why he did it. If it matters anymore." Like a true chess master, Lawrence moved me around his board, following his own sick rules. Does it matter why he did it? Will it bring people back?

By request, they take us to the same hospital they admitted us since arriving in Poland for a long night of treatment, police interviews and liaising with official authorities hunting for Bodmer. But what matters the most is knowing Vera is away from danger. That she gets the best medical attention possible, and her distress ended back on the field. I could not protect my sister and I failed the only woman since Helena's death who means something to me.

It happened fast and was clearly unexpected, but she's absorbed in my skin. Analysing or even describing the levels of infatuation and apprehension I have towards Vera Nicolescu would require a reboot to my nervous system and a lot of whiskey. Not that it will do me any good. Or her. I've consistently proven how unworthy I am of her joy and company.

Closing my eyes under the powerful artificial lights flickering above my head, the bed creaks as the doctors move my limbs to assess tonight's damage. The strobe effect settles, but not before they invite images of Vera dancing in a crowd of thousands in Prague. Her smile was so big, so carefree. I wanted to punish her for her recklessness and kiss her red lips at the same time. And when I had her pinned to the wall, blood pumping from the short chase, I lost it. Years of control, of calculated risks, meant nothing if I couldn't taste her and respond to her provocation. The second her tongue touched mine, the beast took over, and we both died a little in her arms. Thank God she still had her senses and pushed me away.

"Are you Hector? The guy they kidnapped with my sister?" a younger man with a familiar face asks as he enters the room they used to clean my wounds, bringing me back to the present. I'm glad somebody remembered to pick up her brother from the airport.

"Yes. How is she?"

"I've seen her for a few minutes between scans. Vera's . . . she'll get better."

"She's the bravest person I know."

"My sister's a fighter, even if she often forgets. She'll recover by stubbornness alone."

"I'm sure having you here will cheer her up. Let me know if you need anything." I move into a sitting position on the standard hospital mattress.

"Thank you, but if I understand this clearly, you are also responsible for the condition she is in. So, I would appreciate if you could involve her less in any future activities the cleaning of this mess requires. What my sister needs is to come home to her family and rest. I think you took enough from her." Speech finished, he keeps eye contact to intimidate me into submitting to his request.

"We all want what's best for Vera. I do not wish to complicate her life further." As much as I want to punch a hole in the wall hearing her own brother articulate the same concerns and demands I feel, I know them to be true. Do I want to hear them when desolation and rage I have yet to eliminate completely rule my judgement? No. Not from a guy I just met, no matter his chivalrous reason. Until he nods his way out of the room, I grind my teeth and glue my jaw shut to hold whatever comments my ego wants to release. Like his sister is old enough to speak for herself. I don't need reminding I've been poison to her from the beginning.

Later that night, the stairs prove too difficult to climb, so I take the elevator to Lawrence's room, finding him handcuffed to his bed, an officer standing by. From tomorrow, I'll let my team deal with him, his incarceration, and his madness. I thought it unnecessary, but human nature wants to know why someone would hurt his own family like this. Because that's what he was to me, family.

He is sedated and sleeping, face not beyond recognition, but my fists did a number on him. Every time I was close enough to discover information on Bodmer's involvement in my sister's death, he was working on the side-lines to stop my progress. He fed my hatred for the man while sending me chase false leads, always suggesting finding our own way into convicting Bodmer, getting our revenge outside the law. I had to see innocent people nearly lose their lives to realise what was in front of me all along.

"You came to finish the job, mate?" A weak voice halts my steps out the door.

"I won't lay another finger on you. Death would be too easy for your conscience if you still have one."

"The almighty Hector Worthington, always on a high horse. I expected better from you, not a beating without letting me explain myself."

"Like you were letting Vera explain before you shot her?"

"That was—" He coughs with difficulty around the stitches in his mouth. "Another unexpected development. Fancying the little Romanian corporate mouse. She's not part of our world, don't kid yourself." Arrogance and certainty in his tone.

"If I were you, I wouldn't dare bring her up. You didn't have your father killed because of her. A betting man would say money was your motivation. Greed and influence. I'll take my pick."

"I didn't want my father's death, nor Helena's. And the kidnapping, the first one. I didn't agree to it, but we wanted the mole. I had a plan to fix everything. Believe me."

"Those days have passed, brother."

"It wasn't greed. It was respect I was after."

"I hope whatever you found helps you sleep at night." I leave the room and my oldest friendship behind.

The phone chimes with a new message on my way to check Hemský's condition. I'm too much on edge to verify Vera's progress yet, and I prefer to wait until her brother and the Czech crew retire from her room.

A complementary gift for not securing your girl on time. Unknown sender, but I have a hunch it's from the American commando team. I'm sure Vera will take offence at being called a girl or mine. Even before I failed her so gravely today.

Later that night, CNN reports Chinese authorities located Elias Bodmer chained to a post in an abandoned warehouse on the outskirts of Shanghai, half beaten to death. His two captor guards were found tied upside down near him. An anonymous call helped the local forces arrive at the scene.

Twenty-Seven

It fucking hurts. How do action movies work when they fill the protagonist with bullets in one scene, and then he or she jumps off a building in pursuit of more bullets? I won't be moving soon if I have a say in how I spend the next few days. The practice wound from Shanghai did not prepare me for when a projectile visits with my organs before shifting to a more worthy environment.

The doctors patched me up and declared I'll live, but as the judge and jury, I'm unconvinced in my state of minced meat. I feel drained, physically, and emotionally spent. However, as much as I like to feel sorry for myself now, my body will recover. Despite the beating I got in the forest from Simon the brute. My knee will remember him with dread, but a certain feeling of catharsis took over me when I dragged my body out of that wood.

I would have loved to spare my nightmares from knowing his name and the depth of his violence. On the cusp of death, imagine his surprise, and mine, at my audacity to find a second wind of fury and a sharp rock, after he knocked me out. I felt like Uma in *Kill Bill*, without the cool sword, as I used all my power to lift that rock and hit him over the head as he inspected my breathing. The rock smashed into his temple, over and over again, its jagged surface pressing into my palm, so hard I was clutching it, channelling my wrath. It wasn't pretty, and I couldn't be prouder. Everything is a weapon with the right motivation. Laughing quietly now, I remember screaming in his face like a maniac, 'I keep my promises too!' as my spit landed on his closed lids.

A bit of that insanity remained with me when I confronted Lawrence and forced him to pull the trigger. The asshole should rejoice during his time in prison that at least he got to shoot me the once. The unexpected villain revelation screwed with my head, and I can only imagine how it affects Hector. Neville wasn't my favourite person, but I was starting to maybe one day understand him.

"How do you feel, Vera? Are you sure you don't want me to sleep in a chair for the night?" my brother asks for the fourteenth time, his hazel eyes cataloguing my every wince. I'm happy to see him, even if his face says I'm not stepping a foot in the real world again. He'll have a rude awakening when I remind him of my age.

"Cristi, there's no point in staying. I'll see you tomorrow. I'm fine now. Butchered, but I'll learn to love my disfigurement until it heals."

"I think it improves your face a bit. Dried blood suits you."

"Ha. Watch it! Oh, don't make me laugh, you dummy!" I flinch in pain.

"Are you pondering what I'm pondering?"

"Yes. Mum will have a fit."

"Oh man, you better pray for a fast recovery before we fly home. If she sees you like this, it's over. Okay, one more hug and I'm out."

"How about a weak handshake?" I fake not wanting his hug.

"Fool." He embraces me and heads for the door, where he meets Hector.

"She needs to rest," Cristi says to him.

The intriguing spark that made my pulse speed up whenever I saw him extinguished in his eyes after he took Lawrence to the ground. In its place lays now guilt, disappointment, anger. Some of it, I feel, directed towards me. Or maybe I'm projecting my own feelings.

"It's fine, Cristi. I'll see you tomorrow. Love you like the best brother you are. Go."

"The *only* brother," my sibling mumbles back but listens to my request, closing the door after him. Leaving Hector to breathe the same antiseptic air mixed with the taste of iron. Hands in his pockets, gaze taking notice of my state. He's been hurt tonight too, and what a pair we make. He wanted to bring his sister's memory the much-deserved justice, and focusing so much on the Swiss, he missed his friend's involvement.

"I apologise for not trusting your instincts. It seems mine were warped for a while. Because of me—"

"It's over now." I don't let him finish. "You couldn't have known. The best liars hide amongst us, and most times live within us. The truth would have revealed itself when you were ready to see."

"You don't have to spare my feelings. I welcome your blame."

"Not blame."

"Ah. Your face chooses to show pity." One after the other his words sound remote, colder, and colder still.

"Hector."

"It is indeed over. I trust you've heard the CNN news report." He mentions Bodmer's capture, and I nod. My brother showed me the video when I finished in radiology.

Whatever was building between us before Shanghai, I feel it disappear with every unspoken thought. It would be selfish of me to ask "Hey, I know you just discovered your best friend played a key role in your sister's death and I forced him to put a bullet in me to prove it, but do you still like me?" I can't, too afraid of what he'll say. Rejection on top of everything would leave a sour flavour in my mouth. And even if I dare ask, my own feelings are unclear. Because I had to take a bullet to my stomach to convince him.

"They are flying Neville back to London tomorrow." He breaks the silence.

"Okay."

"It would be best if I follow them there."

"Right."

"Other arrests are required, and David still has Lina Haas under surveillance. My legal team needs to know how to deal with that situation."

"Sure." Interlacing my fingers, I add what my heart pleads me to say without looking at him, "Go easy on her."

"I knew you'd say that and while I'm fresh out of compassion, vengeance got me nothing." He clears his throat. "You will be taken care of, everything you need, I made sure of it."

"Don't worry, I'll manage. You don't owe me anything."

"I'm not doing you any favours, Vera. It's what you deserve. I'm cleaning up my mess."

"I need nothing." My eyes rise to find his, defiantly. Everything he says makes sense, but it feels like a slap and because of that, I don't want to be indebted to him.

"You will, with half the European media already outside the hospital. It's done, being stubborn about it will not help you or your family. What sort of man do you think I am if I don't make it my responsibility to repair the harm done to you by my interference in your life? Especially considering the ill-advised attachment we were lucky was cut short."

See? Sour. I guess I had to be patient and rejection would manifest itself to finish the wrecking job March envisioned for me.

Despite his words and their meaning, my fingers twitch in my lap from the pain of not touching him when he's so near. My skin vibrates for his attention and because of that I curse my body's weakness when my brain dictates with logic. It was just lust and a convenient tension release for two people in an extraordinary circumstance. No wasted love.

"You give yourself too much credit. Your presence didn't make such a big impact, apart from the obvious, so trust I don't need to bounce back from anything but the physical injuries others inflicted."

"Then you fare better than me. You won't lack financial support that comes with no strings attached or expectations. My team will settle all matters in my absence."

"Are you finished?" I snap. He watches me for another long moment of silence. If I had no influence on the river when it left the mountain, what hope do I have to change its course before the welcoming sea? He is both the river and the mountain in his conviction.

"Yes. It's better this way."

"If you say so." Scanning the television mounted on the wall, I feel his stare linger on my face, but before I say anything else, the door opens and closes with his departure. Not a moment sooner salty tears sting the cracked skin around my cheeks. I don't take my eyes away from the television set for a long time.

The next day, after one weird and unexpected phone call with Fosters & Co board of directors and my manager, the first visitor I have is Aleš, rolled in a wheelchair by a nurse. He looks weakened, but still handsome, even with a bandage wrapped around his head.

"How are you up? You shouldn't be out of bed! You were in a coma last night." I walk slowly to give him a hug.

"Pretty hobbit. I woke up to see for myself that you are alive and kicking. They removed the tubes early this morning."

"Not that pretty anymore, but I'll be kicking again."

"Nonsense, you wear your battle wounds with grace. Petr told me how brave you were last night. And in China. I'm sorry I couldn't come get you. I promise I'll not let a head trauma stop me next time you need saving."

"Don't worry, I'll not hold your coma against you. And let the record show, I did fantastic in the end. This is me in all my glory. Next time I ping you for a favour, it will only be for internet connectivity problems. But I understand if you won't return my call. Coma is not a lovely present to receive for all your troubles. The chaos I involved you and the guys in cannot be repaid in a million years. I'm sorry."

"You didn't give me these injuries, and I would have fought until the end of my strength to keep you safe. I won't hear you feel sorry for me. Don't let the guys hear you believe this rubbish. They all care for you and none of us regret helping. And if this is the price I had to pay for having you in my life again, in whichever form, I pay it gladly. You won't get rid of me so easily."

"Don't joke. God, why are all men insane?"

"You mean courageous and strapping. So, what's the plan? Are you going to Bucharest or to London?"

"I'll spend some time in Romania for a while. I'm not due at work soon and Fosters & Co expressed their desire to have me back whenever I'm ready if I want to. London sounds too complicated for now. And I'm sure my mum will want to issue a permission slip before I'm allowed to be an adult again."

"Funny!" He gives me that brilliant smile. My heart is full at the thought of not missing him anymore. I didn't realise I could be friends with Aleš, after our history, but we deserve to be in each other's lives.

"Will you go back to London, eventually?"

"To be seen."

"Vera—"

"Oh. My. God! Cristi, her face looks worse than what you said." A throaty voice interrupts Aleš in Romanian.

"Jesus, Astrid. You forgot your tact at baggage claim?" My brother and Astrid fight next to my open door. Dorota and Youssef close behind them.

"She looks like a failed boxer," she continues in English, shocked face between her palms.

"I can hear you. And the other guy lost by knockout. Don't tempt me," I half snap and she laughs.

"Good. You still have fight in you. Vera Nicolescu is nobody's victim." Everyone grins at that while Astrid shoves Aleš' chair aside to hug me.

"You didn't have to fly here to verify."

"Shush. Astrid is here to hold your hand while you recover. Leave everything to me."

"Wonderful." I roll my eyes with fake annoyance.

Over the next few days, I receive visits from all my friends in Poland. The news of my adventures travelled the world and while recuperating, I contact Margaret and the Belgian group who are not mad at my lying about my name and mostly everything else. They call me 'The Spy Queen' and they invite me on future trips now that the murderous threats are over.

Bodmer's confession brings light to these past weeks, but also concludes years of corrupt associations. Plotting to ruin the

Worthington-Satie family, he bribed and joined forces with Lawrence Neville, who was working with crooked police officers and drowning in loan shark debt. To scare Helena and Neville senior into concluding the business deal, an avoidable accident occurred, bringing an end to their lives. And later on, a start to my kidnapping series. Fearing discovery of his role in the tragedy, Lawrence misguided Hector in his investigation. Then Lina entered the scene. I got snatched at Waterloo and the rest is history.

One thing remains unknown, and that is why Lawrence helped us escape The Hyde while Hector and I were hiding in the car boot. He was not informed or involved in the Brompton Cemetery coffin situation, but he was definitely scheming my demise afterwards.

I decide I don't care to know. I have my own friend's betrayal to deal with when the dust settles. Surprisingly, as if I had the spare time, I matured during these survival trials, if I can sleep without knowing every detail of every single action that happened. Wanting to control forces outside my own feelings and impulses is futile, and even that's extremely hard sometimes. Adulthood knocks us horizontally constantly, and all we can do is wake up every morning and try.

On the last day of March, a deceivingly sunny Friday, I'm ready to leave Warsaw for the second time in twelve months. Previously, my move to London excited me with hopes and idealistic plans. Now I'm heading in a different direction to heal, and process having lived through the most intense period of my life. And made it out alive.

During that fortnight I tried to be brave, or at least fake it, but hands to heart, I would not have bet on myself most days. And that's a fact. I did it though, more power to us, the average people with no upper body strength. Recovering slowly, I'm strong enough to travel to Romania. Aleš transfers to Prague next week and I want to stay until that happens, out of duty and worry, but he told me to fly home and relax.

Bittersweet smiles and tears, mostly mine, when I hug Petr, Josef and the rest of the Czech crew and I thank them for the millionth time for their help. For risking their lives and being overall exceptional guys.

"Helping damsels in distress is what we do best, Vera!" jokes Petr. "You were not particularly good at letting us save you, kicking ass by yourself! Work on that lady, be a team player."

"You did plenty! Love you forever and ever!"

My arms linger around Aleš' frame. His heartbeat synchronising with mine, joy flows within me thinking of his wellness and safety. At seeing him again soon. The teenage feelings of love, lust, and regret morphed into friendship and respect. People come and go in my life and he's here to stay. His smirking lips press into my forehead as I hear my brother's conversation besides the idling taxi.

"Text me when you land." His hands hold mine between us.

"I will, take care and be good," I say, and he bursts into laughter.

"Stay out of trouble, Vera dearest!" I try to turn and pull my fingers from his, but I'm met with resistance as he leans over and whispers in a deep, liquid voice, "You deserve the world, beautiful, and I'll wait if you want me to be part of it." He lets go after he scans my huge, surprised eyes and burning cheeks. I still can't take a compliment.

One more wave and we are off. Back to normal, no running around scared existence. I will leave dangerous excitement to others, getting my required dose from books and television, like most people do. Learning how to deal with the fresh nightmares I've been having since last Monday night takes practice. They are here to stay for a while and part of the reason I'm not going back to

London yet. Working on my mental health sounds less intense when I'll wake up to my parents' hushed morning voices. Life is good or it will be in a couple of days. But you know what they say about spending too much time with family.

Twenty-Eight

Warm sunrays filter through the cherry flowers above and play on my face, closing my eyes as I lie on the wool blanket. My sunglasses are off, they hurt my temples after too many hours in the smouldering daylight. Next to them is the fantasy book I've been reading since this morning in my grandparents' backyard garden. While March turned me green, yellow, and purple, April has put some warmth on my skin.

The novel I'm reading is wonderful, but my thoughts return to last night's dream. The one that woke me up and compelled me to sit on a bench outside, next to the old countryside house I spent half of my childhood in and listen to the roaster's wake up song. It wasn't a nightmare, not really. No one was chasing, stabbing, or locking me in tight spaces, but it had a dark vibe to it. Like someone was hiding in the shadows. Knowing this is PTSD linked to the events ending only weeks ago does not offer reassurance, and I still overthink matters. I do it in my dreams more often than not.

Authorities from several countries have arrested and are prosecuting all the shady characters with ties to my kidnapping. No, correction. Kidnappings, plural – it happened more than once. They deal with the past murders too, so theoretically, no one is hiding among shadows anymore. But the mind defies logic sometimes.

I have not pressed charges against Lina, but I know she's involved in some legal battles with Fosters & Co. Aleš keeps me informed. She wrote a lengthy story on one of my social media accounts, and maybe I'll read it someday. Maybe I'll even forgive her as a faulty human being. As a friend, the verdict is clear, and it's not in her favour.

Rising slowly to not disturb my healing wounds and collecting my phone from the blanket, I go in search of a homemade bread and cheese sandwich. We came to the tiny village my mum hails from days ago to take part in the Easter holidays with the rest of our extended clan. I'm grateful for the trip, being cooped up in our apartment in Bucharest was not helping my nerves. It is good to see everyone at the lunch table, paint eggs and drink a glass of wine with my cousins. They plan a church visit tonight, bringing back a candle lit with holy Easter light, as tradition dictates, then move to a friend's house across the road for a night of card games and too much alcohol as one does when young and dealing with multiple days off in a row.

I intend to be part of that celebration if I don't fall asleep early, which is a genuine threat these days. Going to sleep early and waking up at dawn. Thinking about March, my last night in Shanghai and the first one in Warsaw. About Hector, with whom I haven't spoken with since the Polish hospital. The visceral pain I felt when I thought I lost him as hours before my fingers were threading through his hair, still lingers. Some might call a hair memory stupid, but if they are not alone and miserable, they should shove it. Then having only a hug to process his very much alive status before we fought again over the mysterious second villain. In the end, the devastation, the physical and emotional hurt brought by the truth, sent us into separate parts of the continent. We are different people, and I can't imagine us agreeing on anything worth mentioning. Perhaps it would have been silly to think a bond forged in war times would survive during peace. I can't help but wonder what would have happened if that early morning in his arms on the balcony in Bali ended at our own pace.

"Finished your book, sweetheart?" Dad asks, half of his body inside his car's engine when he hears the garden's wood gate bang shut.

"Nearly there, Dad, just got hungry. Want a snack too?"

"I wouldn't say no to some of yesterday's barbecue meat with a slice of bread your aunt baked."

"Got it. Coming up."

"And a glass of cold beer will help me swallow it better," he yells after me when I enter the tiny summer kitchen.

"Of course, it will," I yell back.

"What does your father want?" Mum shouts from the door connected to the house. I swear to God, there's always a 'what did the other say' game in our house.

"Nothing. I'm making us sandwiches. How's the paint? Does it stick?" I ask about her experiment with an old purple egg paint we found in the cupboard. I don't inquire about making her something to eat. She's fasting and eating vegan until tomorrow, for Easter Sunday.

"Yes, I did the remaining eight duck eggs. We have twenty food plates to give."

"That many?" We share plates of different foods with our neighbours each year on this holiday to honour our dead, but that's a big number.

"I'm taking some to church and cemetery in the morning."

I leave my mum to organise the cookies and candles that go with the shared plates, and after giving my dad his food, I kiss his cheek and sit on the bench by the road. I've told them the pertinent details of what happened last month, and they cried as they held me, offering their support at the same time as chastising me for not running home to them first thing. As if endangering their lives was not something that could have occurred if I did that. Then we haven't spoken about it since, because oversharing your grief is not common in a Romanian household. But seeing their worried glances and reading hope in their eyes that I'll stay a little longer close to them, I feel supported all the same. Only with their presence, they help me smile and focus on the happier months ahead.

The big question is what to do with myself. I am excellent at my job, and I don't hate it, but I can't work in an office just yet. Surviving with my heart in my throat, like the poisoned apple, difficult to swallow, I thought every one of those days will be my last. Fear pushed me forward, kept me vigilant, and I realised my happiness links to expressing gratitude for the treasure already overflowing my metaphorical chest. My health, my family, my friends, the ones that love me, and they are quite a bunch. I can't wallow in a state of sadness and boredom when I'm the tailor of my fortune. I can make it worthwhile and not just for me.

Fosters & Co promised a settlement, their apology for one of their higher-ups taking liberties with my life and so on. And to be fair, a nice sum of money doesn't sound bad, but I don't feel any excitement towards it. Maybe I'll do some good and pay my parent's mortgage and take them on a holiday.

Cristi has to go to London in a week and I'll join him for a short administrative visit before returning to Romania for the summer holiday. Facing the city to make her understand I'm still on my feet should smooth my restless behaviour. My love affair with London town did not vanish because of some unfortunate events. I smile at the thought of dating my city. She'll give me the inspiration I need.

Considering how fragile life is and how it all can change with the next exhale, sweating the small stuff is of no consequence. Happiness is not determined by what's occurring around me, but by what is flourishing inside me. I sound like a broken record with the positive talk, but if I truly believe at least one percent of this daily, there will be benefits to reap in time. My phone vibrates next to me on the bench, and I flinch. So much for not being jumpy and easy to startle.

"Hi Aleš!"

"Vera! How's the egg painting?"

"All finished. What's up with you?" Last I heard his voice was a couple of days ago, but we text regularly. He's in Prague with the rest of the guys and he's supposed to be resting, but I think he's back at doing secret agent hacker stuff.

"Just wanted to hear your voice. To see where your head is after you had some time to deal with what happened. I'm here if you want to talk, or if you need me to slay some imaginary dragons."

"Should I change your name to Knight in Shining Armour on my phone? I'm making peace with my dragons, but thanks. Are you at the airport? Flying somewhere interesting?" I ask at the background noise.

"Depends on what you mean by interesting."

"Sharing is caring," I singsong. He's being evasive, meaning it's work related.

"Oh, I care a lot! I can show you how much I care when you're ready!" he says, smirk implied. I'm reminded of the promise he made before I left Poland. As if it's that easy to fall back into flirtatious mode with an old boyfriend. I'm smitten with him as a person and who he grew up to be, but my infatuation lays elsewhere. On a lost cause.

"Smooth! For shame, is that how you get all the girls?"

"That and a mention of their ruby lips," he jests, and we both laugh. "But I don't want all the girls. I only want one," he says with a serious tone that shuts me up.

"Aleš." I sigh after a long, awkward moment.

"That's okay, love. I'm just putting it out there. Listen, I have to go. Have a lovely Easter day with the family."

"Be safe."

"Always. Goodbye." Disappointment drips from his last words.

The crisp April night begins with a loud dinner and my acceptance of accompanying my cousins to church. Mostly because I'm fidgety and the walk will provide the break I need from my phone. The village community spirit and the guaranteed amusement at the old ladies fawning over the priest's attention, if they don't fall asleep during the sermon, is another benefit.

I've been reading news articles upon articles about Bodmer, Neville, Fosters & Co and more importantly, about Hector. They are chasing him around London, with little photographic success. The one picture I saw circulating, with him walking behind his mother and the blonde woman identified as his ex-girlfriend, threatened to force my meal out. I kept reading, surpassing the nausea at how those articles portrait me. A poor helpless victim in some, in others my role is unclear, but accusatory conclusions are drawn with journalistic indifference.

I had to deal with paparazzi harassment when I first arrived in Bucharest, but the men hired to protect my family intervened. Romanian media requested interviews I refused, and not only because of the open investigation. I looked like a smashed tomato from my encounters with the brute, and I felt too raw to answer more questions about the ordeal and share my opinion thereafter. Someone is keeping them in line because the pile outside my parents' apartment died down quickly. They haven't followed us to the countryside, located a couple of hundred miles southwest of Bucharest. That someone pays for my legal team as well, and I can't say a word about it.

Our group of eight neighbours, cousins and two of my departed grandma's old friends arrive at church in time to occupy the remaining standing spot at the front. Right by the gold framed altar with its antique and colourful icons.

"Did we have to be in spitting distance from the DJ?" Marcu, my teenage cousin, asks. I can barely contain my snort.

"Bite your tongue, you pagan," I admonish, hiding a smile behind my palm when I do the sign of the cross. Okay, this should be fun. If we don't turn into blocks of salt as punishment for our childish remarks.

The small orthodox church soon fills with followers of all ages, some of whom I've known all my life. Folks who have lived their years without leaving the county, others working abroad like myself, but unlike me, visiting more often.

The Saturday Night Easter service moves slowly with songs of resurrection, and odes of lamentation are recited. The off-key voices of parishioners complement the little choir, their high levels indeed rising even a reluctant Jesus. By midnight, I wager on tomorrow's breakfast, no one sleeps on the half-a-mile radius from the church. And on the ones inside it, the feeling of blessed excitement is clear amongst them. Including me, a mostly agnostic sinner.

"Hristos a Inviat!" Christ Resurrected.

"Adevarat a Inviat!" He truly Resurrected.

They pass around the two traditional sayings when people light their candles from one another and make their way outside, taking with them the smell of wax and smoke. The courtyard is nearly empty when I emerge with my two older companions. I wave to the rest of our group to go ahead. I'll stroll along with the grandmas' gentle pace for the twenty minutes' walk back home.

Tall electric streetlights illuminate the wide asphalt road with brick houses nestled on lower ground, left and right, but they don't disperse all the shadow pockets of the night.

"Your grandmother wanted you happy, no matter where you decided to live or your occupation of choice," one lady says, squeezing my hand as we take a left onto the dirt road, leaving the asphalt behind. They've been interrogating me about my life and setting me straight.

"You need to marry and start a family with a nice Romanian man."

"Getting married or even meeting someone is not as easy as snapping your fingers. And not everyone has that as a priority, Grandma." I call all of them Grandma.

"What's wrong with getting married?"

"Nothing."

"Then it's settled."

"Sure. I'll send the invites tomorrow."

"Don't jest. I'll find you someone if you are not too fussy."

"I'm afraid to give you that kind of power."

"Nonsense. In my day, the elder of the family arranged matters and everyone was content."

"Yeah, see, some things have changed since the sixties."

Distracted with our banter and trying to navigate the uneven stretch of side road on poor light, we don't see the car parked in the dark a short way ahead. The brief activation of its interior light startles us, and I don't notice who is in the driver's seat. But I know without a doubt they are here for me.

The sound of a car door closing.

A throat clearing.

I'm almost home. Four houses away. My cousins and the others have entered their yards and respective houses. A dog barks from some place in the distance. Who could it be? I feel the air still, elevating my pulse with the last breath I draw.

"Vera."

"God! You scared me to death." His features appear next to me as my eyes adjust. But I recognise his voice first. His accent.

"I'm sorry, it wasn't my intention. I tried calling you," he says with a nervous lilt.

"I don't have my phone with me." I forgot how tall he is, how consuming is his presence.

"Your brother mentioned as much." There's a story there I'll have to pry out of Cristi.

"How long have you been waiting?"

"A few hours. When finding you in the church seemed impossible, I came back here."

"Did something happen? I wasn't expecting you."

"No. I realise I should have waited for tomorrow." Hands in his jeans pockets, his eyes follow my companions' progression to their gates. Waving them a reassuring signal, my covered candle jar flickers between my fingers. There is no wind, but my entire body is shaking. The reaction is involuntary, although in no way surprising.

"I have to take this in." I show him what I'm holding, and his jaw clenches, misinterpreting my words.

"Of course. This was presumptuous of me. Have a good night."

"I am not letting you drive back at 2 a.m. Do you want some tea, Englishman?" I ask, already moving towards my grandparents' gate. I hear his following steps and the pulse in my veins at his closeness. Why is he here?

"For you. And I was told April is a perfect month to visit Romania. If you'll have me." The gruff voice sends shivers down my spine. Did I ask that out loud?

"You'll probably meet my entire family now because I doubt they are sleeping, knowing you drove by earlier. Prepare for weirdness."

"That's okay. You've met my mother. It couldn't be more awkward than that."

"I like your positivity. How much Romanian do you know?"

He passes in front of me to open the entrance to our courtyard.

"None, yet, but I'll put my charm to good use." He smiles down at me, leaning in when I offer a big grin of my own. His face comes closer, eyes hopeful in the candlelight. The corner of my mouth tingles from his barely there kiss, too quick for my liking. But his lips are still there, ready to touch mine as my chin lifts. His breath is warm and rushed as he bites into the bottom one, his fingers igniting the skin of my neck and jaw.

"Is this charm of yours a new acquisition? First time I hear of it."

"You wound me, Miss Nicolescu. But we'll have to rectify your limited knowledge of my dazzling personality. Address and fix my past mistakes. Do you have the time?"

"Hector, for that, I've got all the time in the world. If you can keep up, I am bound to live an adventurous life." I grasp his hand and pull him towards the open foyer. I guess London has another point in her favour. But Romania is a wonderful place to fall in love.

Acknowledgments

The entire process of writing this book has been an adventure I am truly grateful for, now that I finally published. Even the days when I felt unprepared, uninspired, and couldn't link two words together, have taught me patience and perseverance. I've learned to accept the necessity of a writing routine and the need to disregard it when the internal pressure was too overwhelming.

I have to give my thanks to my beta readers, Jailyn and Monica from Fiverr, with a special mention to my friend Andreea. Three lovely ladies with amazing feedback on how to improve The Trials Of March, how to polish my manuscript to create an immersive and thrilling read. Also from Fiverr, Katie shared her wisdom on line editing, proofreading and book description, and Spurga took my vision for a great cover and exceeded my expectations.

To the SPF Podcast and their community for helping me understand the publishing business, to all the generous authors on social media that share a piece of their process with their audience. Thank you!

All my gratitude to my personal motivators and amazing friends. Ania, Alina D, Alina N, Cosu', Iulia S, Iulia M, Marius, Olga, Oana, Petra, Raisa, Susan, Vlad, Yasser, over the years, you have enriched my life with laughs, encouraging words, hugs, and long talks into the night. To Ayodapo, the best free life coach a person can ask for, and to Michal, for starting a discussion in 2017 about passion and how it can be found at any age.

To my best friends, Anda and Laura. You helped me build my voice, my compassion, my knowledge about the world. The woman I am today wouldn't be complete without you. I aspire to have at least a quarter of your strength, your determination, and your sunny disposition.

To my sisters, Verginica and Nicoleta, always and forever, the keepers of my heart. Thanks to you, I will never know what it means to be truly alone. You are an inspiration, a source of unlimited happiness and sisterly pride. To my honorary brother, Gabriel, because life would be so boring, and tasteless, without you. Thanks for having my back and most importantly, thanks for Luna!

To my parents, Florina and Nicolae, for instilling in me, from a young age, the importance of learning. For your patience, your protection, and your undying love. For always being happy to see me.

To the rest of my family and friends in Romania, Poland and England, I love you all.

Lastly, a heartfelt thank-you to my readers for choosing to spend a few hours in my world.

About The Author

Liliana Drăgnescu is a London-based author of fiction books. She graduated from the University of Bucharest in 2009 with a Bachelor in Applied Modern Languages. She loves creating intriguing stories and she considers finding the courage to write them down for all to read one of her biggest achievements.

CONNECT ONLINE

Instagram: @lilianadragnescu

Facebook: @AuthorLilianaDragnescu

Don't forget to sign up for future books updates, special offers, bonus content, and other news.

www.lilianadragnescu.com

Please consider leaving a short review if you liked, loved, or only tolerated *The Trials of March*. Reviews help new authors more than you know. Thank you for taking the time to support me and my work. Sharing your review on social media with the hashtag #TheTrialsOfMarch is appreciated and encouraged.

Printed in Great Britain
by Amazon

71459248R00194